WITCH WAR IN WESTERHAM

Paranormal Investigation Bureau Book 14

DIONNE LISTER

Dionne Lister

 Created with Vellum

For those we love who were gone too soon. We will never forget you.

CHAPTER 1

"Argh! You're blinding me!" Imani threw her forearm up to protect her eyes. "Be careful where you angle that thing."

Liv laughed, and I grinned as we walked home after enjoying brunch at Costa. "Ha ha. Very funny." I splayed my hand and admired my dazzling engagement ring. "Anyway, I can hardly be proficient with managing it—I've only had it a week. Surely wearing bling like this should come with a grace period?" I see-sawed my hand side to side. Such pretty twinkles. Who knew light refraction could be so enthralling. "It could probably do some damage if I punched someone in the face."

Liv nodded. "It could definitely take out an eye."

Imani had removed her arm from her face, but she jokingly side-eyed the ring, pretending to fear its brilliance. "Shiny *and* practical—my favourite combination."

"When are you setting a date?" Liv asked.

"I have no idea. We're going to talk about it after we sort out the DD thing." DD stood for Dana's Dad. Rather than anyone knowing what we were talking about, we'd given him that nickname.

"Wow, love. That could take a while. We still have interviews to get through." Imani was talking about the captives we'd found in the basement of DD's factory. There was so much to record that they'd had to have days with just one victim to ask what they needed. It was definitely a huge mess. At least we'd gotten this far. It had been the biggest break through so far to finding out what happened to my parents. But I didn't want to bring that up here, and I was pretty sure neither did my friends.

I shrugged. "Whatever. It's fine. The fact that he loves me and asked is enough. It's not like I'm in a hurry to have kids or anything."

"Why not?" Liv asked. "You'd make such gorgeous babies."

I chuckled. "That's not a good reason to have kids, Liv. Ask me when I've travelled the whole of Europe and run out of things to do. I haven't got time to have kids right now… or for the next few years."

"Party pooper. I can't believe you're going to wait so long. I thought it would be cool if we had them at the same time. It would be amazing if our kids could grow up together."

My eyes widened. "You're not pregnant, are you?"

She snorted. "No! But, you know, I'm hoping it will happen in the next two or three years." She lowered her voice. "We've been talking about it."

"What about marriage?" Not that it mattered, but it was the natural thing to ask.

She shrugged. "I'm not that fussed, to be honest. After going through that whole engagement thing and the aftermath, it's kind of lost its appeal. I mean, if B asked, I'd say yes, of course, but it's not a priority. We've been living together for a while now, and it's the best thing in the world. I don't want anything to change—it's perfect just the way it is."

Imani raised one eyebrow. "And you think nothing will change when you have kids? Is that what you're telling us?" Liv opened her mouth to answer, but Imani's phone rang, cutting her off. "Sorry, love." She slid it out of her pocket. "Hello, Agent Jawara speaking." She listened for a minute. "Yes, of course. I'll be there as soon as I can. Bye." She looked at me. "That was your brother. He's called us in."

"Me too?"

"Yes." Her tone held enough gravity that Liv and I both knew what she meant—I was wanted for my talent. While it paid well, I was tired of being in the thick of crime scenes. There were some things I just didn't want to see.

I sighed. "Okay. What is it?"

We'd reached Angelica's. Imani kept her own counsel until we went inside. As we stood in the hallway outside the living room, she made a bubble of silence. "It's a murder scene—two of the slaves we haven't interviewed yet."

Liv sucked in a breath. "How did that happen? Aren't they living in PIB housing under agent protection?"

"Yes."

Yikes. That was scary and bad news. "Do you think they had information that could do lots of damage or is it a warning to the other slaves?"

She pressed her lips together for a moment. "Either or, neither nor. Who knows? The point is, we need to get to the bottom of it. Anyway, love, put your uniform on and grab your camera. We'll travel to headquarters and go with Will from there. It's safer."

"You don't have to tell me twice." Now we were closing in on RP, they were bound to become even bolder than they had been, and I'd almost been killed a few times. And, yes, we'd just been for a walk, but we'd had our return to senders on, plus Imani was with me, and James had organised for two other agents to tail us. If I'd thought things were serious before, I'd really had no idea.

Liv looked at Imani. "Do you think there are still rogue agents helping RP?"

Imani's grim expression said it all. "We all need to be extra careful. Keep your ears and eyes open, Liv. At the end of the day, when you go home, make a list of all the research Chad's assistant asks you to do. Maybe have lunch with her whenever you can, have a chat, if you know what I mean."

"Okay. Will do."

"Oh, and get B to protect your thoughts with a spell each morning. We're at the pointy end of things. Their guys or gals on the inside will take more risks now we're closing in on them."

"Okay, Imani."

While they talked, I magicked my uniform on, as well as a black coat—whilst it had been sunny, it was still only fifteen degrees. And for my final trick, I conjured my camera from my bedside table. "Ready." I looked at Liv. "You coming with?"

"Yeah, might as well. I'll grab a lift home with B later. There's some paperwork I have to finish for James anyway."

I made my doorway, and Imani made hers. I ushered Liv through mine. As I reluctantly stepped through after her, I shuddered. Murder scenes were my least-favourite place to be, and we had no idea what we were going to find. Would it be bloody, gory, stinky? *Please don't be horrible.* My stomach would be in knots until we arrived. *Just breathe, Lily. Just breathe.*

If only I had better advice to calm myself… because I was going to need it.

CHAPTER 2

The silence on the drive from the PIB to the crime scene was unnerving. Even the luxury and comfort of Will's Range Rover weren't enough to dampen the tightly wound atmosphere. If Will and Imani were preoccupied, this wasn't at all good. It wasn't as if they hadn't seen so much before. By the time we stood outside the second-floor apartment, my stomach wasn't so much in knots as it had already strangled itself and died. I rubbed it. Nope, that didn't help at all.

Will put his hand on my back. "Are you okay?"

"Yes." No. There was no use worrying Will with my stress. He had enough to deal with. Truth be told, I partly blamed myself for all this. I knew, of course, that it wasn't my fault that RP were evil slave masters, but if it hadn't been for me trying to find out what had happened to my parents, we never would've stumbled across these people. And even though being enslaved was horrific, at least they'd been alive. And what did it mean for our investigation? Had we driven RP further underground?

Will showed his ID to the policeman guarding the door. He pointed to three boxes sitting on the floor to the side. "Put those on first, and when you go in, don't touch anything."

We went to the boxes and grabbed gloves, plastic shoe coverings, and hairnets. It wasn't the full protective gear, but I supposed it would stop us contaminating things as long as we didn't poke into every nook and cranny. Once we'd donned our gear, the policeman lifted the police tape back and let us through. I hadn't had to deal with this before. Every time we went to a crime scene, the PIB were running things. Using spells to gather information was much more thorough and less likely to contaminate things. Maybe PIB crime-scene investigators had special spells to stop any contamination from happening too. I wondered if the PIB had used one here anyway, but they just couldn't tell the police.

Once we were inside, one of my stomach knots came undone. There was nothing in the living area I didn't want to see… at least not yet. I whispered to Will, "Why are the p involved?" I was pretty sure he'd know what I meant by p.

"A neighbour called them because they'd heard screaming. Whoever did this forgot or didn't care to make it quiet. We didn't get the call till after the police had attended." And even then, the PIB were here as a government agency—most of the police just didn't know they were magical.

"So why'd they bring you guys in?" Unless they knew magic had been involved, the PIB police implants wouldn't have known to call them.

"They have a list of our safe houses, and they knew about the warehouse slaves. We've tried to keep them out of it mostly, but we can't hide everything. As far as they're concerned, we're dealing with the case, but they're backing us up if needed… like now."

"Fair enough."

An agent—a dark-skinned guy in his thirties sporting a shaved head—appeared from a hallway just off the living area. He gave Will and Imani a nod. "Agents Blakesley, Jawara. Come this way." They strode after him, and I followed, feeling like a forgotten puppy. This tagging-along thing wasn't good for my ego. At a photography job, everyone looked to me as the authority… well, as long as it wasn't a wedding with a bridezilla or despotic mother of the bride.

I didn't follow them the whole way, just in case it was gory. If I was lucky, they'd magicked all the evidence to headquarters and cleaned everything. This was hopefully a site visit to show Will and Imani where everything had been and to check out the apartment to reference back to the evidence later.

Quiet talking came from the room they'd gone into—I assumed a bedroom. After a couple of minutes, the dark-skinned agent came out and walked past me without so much as a hello. Then Will poked his head out of the door. "You can come in, Lily. It's not too bad. They've taken the bodies away."

"Okay." I took a deep breath and went to the door. I'll admit my grip on the camera hanging around my neck made my hand ache. I forced my fingers to relax. Will moved further into the room, out of my way. Stepping inside, I gasped. The bodies were, indeed, gone, but the blood spatters weren't. Nausea clawed up my throat, and I slammed a hand over my mouth. After swallowing, I dropped my hand, the metallic scent in the room unmistakable. "What the actual hell? This is not, 'not too bad.' What are you? Nuts?"

"Sorry, love. We forget you're not a hardened agent. But

it's not like you haven't seen worse." Imani's words were sort of sympathetic, but her tone was all business.

"Normally it's through my camera. I don't think I've seen this much blood in person before."

"Pretend it's paint," Will suggested.

I gave him a deadpan look. "You can't take the facts back. It's too late. Can we just get this over and done with? How long have I got?"

"As long as you need. Imani and I have a few things to do here, and since you're taking our photos, you're free to do that. Just take as many as you can." His voice sounded in my head, and I jumped. *Take some real shots, too, just so we have something to show from that; otherwise people will get suspicious.* "There was a photographer on scene earlier this morning when the bodies were here. You're going to make sure they didn't miss anything."

"Right. I can do that." *Next time you're going to just jump into my head, a bit of warning would be polite.*

He smiled. *We'll figure it out later.* "Time to get to work. Just so you know, both victims were non-witches, and we haven't found a magic signature, so it might have all been done the normal way. The bodies showed signs of having been tortured. Just a warning." *Sorry, Lily. I really am. You know we wouldn't ask unless it was vital.*

Yeah, I know. And this is all because of me anyway. I need to help figure it out. Don't worry; I'll deal.

It's not your fault, but we'll talk about that later. The sooner we get this done, the sooner you can go home.

I nodded, fear scrabbling inside my belly. The photos I was about to take were probably going to be the worst I'd ever seen. Will was right though—getting it over and done with was the best idea.

The other thing I couldn't ignore—Will never spoke in my head, at least not unless it was the utmost emergency. We didn't want any of our enemies to know, and we weren't sure if they could pick up on it. Only some witches had the talent of being able to do this, and neither of us did—only when it came to talking to each other. It had saved me from the vampire witch—without Will's voice in my head, I would've given up. I'd have to talk to him about it later. Why was he risking it now?

"Love, come on. You've got work to do." Imani was staring at me, her head cocked to one side.

"Ah, yeah, sorry. Just thinking about what I need to do."

Her raised brow pretty much said, "Yeah, right."

I shrugged, lifted my camera, and gave her a sarcastic smile. I took off the lens cap and turned the camera on. "See. Working."

She rolled her eyes, but at least she turned and drew her magic. Whatever she needed to do was happening, and I was pretty much forgotten about. Phew. Or maybe not phew. I had to ask what had happened, and I didn't want to see it. Would my magic work if I didn't look at the screen? I was pretty sure I didn't want to see what had happened here to cause the mess.

I took a deep breath, coughed because of the smell, and drew my magic. "Show me...." Show me what? What did I need to ask for first? While I debated with myself, I clicked off a few shots of the room as it was. The blood, the messed-up bed, the window, and the fact it was closed. *Come on, scaredy-cat.* Yeah, yeah. Sometimes, I wished my inner voice would just be quiet. It wasn't helping.

"Show me the victims just before the killer came." The room darkened as the naked bulb became the only light source. Beyond the window was blackness. The bed was made, and a young man with curly brown hair sat on it, reading. I clicked off a shot and zoomed into the book cover and clicked. I couldn't understand the French title, but the spaceship against the black of deep space on the cover looked like science fiction.

I lowered the camera. Only one victim was in here originally. Had the other been killed in the second bedroom? I'd worry about that later. *Let's get this done.* "Show me the moment the killer entered the room."

The victim stood in the middle of the room, arm dangling at his side, book forgotten in his hand. *Click.* The window was open, and a man was climbing in. He wore a black jumper, black beanie, and black gloves. His large, round face was muscle and fat, two black, beady eyes staring from it. *Click.* Why hadn't the victim run? Maybe he was in shock from someone climbing in his window?

"Show me the victim as soon as the other guy is fully in the room." The victim wasn't visible from where I was, but I took a photo of the murderer standing next to the bed. He was six foot four or five and built like a brick outhouse. He was looking straight at me, so I must be standing where the victim was. I shivered. The fear his stare and size elicited was palpable even in photo form. I couldn't tell whether he was a witch or not, though. Add magic to the mix, and this guy would be a formidable enemy. I hoped I never had to face him in real life.

I swallowed the lump of fear lodged in my throat as I walked closer to the man. Then I turned around. The victim's back was to me as he ran through the doorway. Ah, so he finally unfroze. My hope at this turn of events was squashed as soon as my logic reminded me that he'd been killed.

The burn of tears mixed with the fear in my throat.

Damn all evil people.

I lowered the camera, then raised it again. "Show me how the victim was caught." I exited the bedroom and walked down the hall. Nothing… until I came to the living area. Another man, dressed the same as the first but a little shorter, had a gun pointed at another man—the other victim, I was guessing. The victim I followed was standing facing them. I clicked off a few shots and walked around to face him. His eyes were wide and leeching fear. *Click*.

In real time, voices came from the hallway. I lowered the camera and shook my head to clear it. I'd been deep in my alternate reality to the point that I'd forgotten I wasn't alone. If I wasn't careful, someone would think I was weird, taking photos of nothing in the middle of a clean space. The last thing we needed was for someone to tell me to leave or get suspicious.

Will and the other agent I didn't know came into the living room. The other agent looked at me, his brow creased. "What are you doing in here, then?"

I cleared my throat, but Will jumped in, saving me the explanation. "I've asked her to take photos of everything. You'd be surprised how many things get missed because they're subtle and unexpected." He looked at me. "Carry on. And don't forget the second bedroom at the end of the hall."

I nodded. "I won't."

Will looked at the other guy and gave a perfunctory smile. I wasn't sure who was senior, but the other guy seemed to be okay with that, and they walked to the front door. I figured I had enough photos out here—two murderers and two victims —that I could return to the bedrooms and take the rest of the photos. By the time I'd finished, I'd uncovered the total horror of torture and bloody murder. I had enough photos to identify both murderers and give me nightmares for the rest of my life.

We couldn't shut RP down fast enough. If it was the last thing I ever did, it wouldn't be too high a price to pay. And, as usual, this brought up more questions than it answered. Why torture them? Why kill them in such a bloody way and not even worry about someone calling the police? Was it to send a message to us and the other people we'd saved?

Well, if it was a message they wanted to send, it had come through loud and clear: don't mess with RP. Except, it was a message we were going to ignore. Whether that was to our detriment or theirs was yet to be determined. Like all things in my life lately, it was going to be a harrowing wait to find out.

CHAPTER 3

After the horror that was that particular crime scene, I went home and showered. It was as if the bloody tang had seeped into my hair and clothes. I magicked everything clean and infused a jasmine scent into it, which I got from a small bottle of essential oils Angelica had in the laundry cupboard. Once I was done, I grabbed a coffee and joined Will, Imani, and James in the living room. Normal procedure was to meet with Chad at the PIB, but James wanted to do it this way first because we still didn't trust Chad, and probably never would. There were things to be said privately so we could make our own plans.

I sat on one of the Chesterfields, next to Will, who had Abby curled in his lap. Ted was on the floor opposite us, at James's feet, enjoying a thorough head scratch. My brother was a total dog person. I loved cats and dogs, all animals, actually. If only I could have a pet squirrel, my life would be just about perfect.

James stopped scratching Ted and leaned back in his chair. He fixed a concerned gaze on me. "Are you okay, Lily? I've seen the photos."

I shrugged, tears deciding now was time to attack. Grr, I hated being unable to hide my emotions. It sucked. People worried about me more than they should. Stuff it. I talked through the crying. "I'm okay. I know it doesn't seem like it, but I'm dealing. It was horrific, and I'll have nightmares for a while, but it's for a good cause. I don't regret it." Will took my hand and rubbed his thumb soothingly along mine. I leaned into him, grateful for the comfort.

James's chest inflated with what I assumed was an aggravated breath. His mouth was a tight line, scoring his angry face. He swore. "Your efforts weren't in vain. We've identified the two murderers. They're non-witches from France. They've both been in and out of jail and are currently supposedly living in northern France. We're going to have to chase them up ourselves. I have no way of guiding our agents that way with no proof."

Imani, who was next to James, huffed. "Damned constraints. So, now what? Short of planting evidence, we're going to have to do our own thing."

James looked at her. "We can get away with chasing them up, but we can't do anything to them… unless we're provoked, but I don't want anyone getting caught with them because we can't explain it. We need to find some kind of link outside of the photos and work back from there."

I wiped my eyes and took a sip of coffee to steady myself. Time for crying was over; it was time to act. "Are you going to get Liv on it?"

"Yes, but from my place where I can block PIB eyes. If we can find out who they're attached to, we can look them up too.

Maybe we can trace it all the way to the top without PIB intervention. Once this all blows up, I don't care who finds out. We need them done away with."

My eyes widened. "Not arrested?" My brother was like Angelica—everything by the book.

He tilted his head to one side and wore his bossy-big-brother expression. "You think when we finally confront them to find out about where our parents went that they're going to tell us everything? Don't you suppose after everything they've done so far that they're not going to go quietly? Do you think they'll just hold their arms out and ask us to cuff them?" He shook his head, anger creeping back into his gaze. "This is all or nothing, Lily. This is war. We go in ready to fight."

I gulped and didn't comment on what he hadn't fully articulated: that we were also going there to kill or be killed. Why was I even surprised? Hadn't it already been that way for ages? Hadn't I been staying at home where possible, going out only with guards, watching my back for months and months? If I looked at it that way, this was no more frightening… well, not entirely. We were going into their territory and poking the viper's nest, after all.

James looked at Will, then me. "There's one more piece of information I think you'll be interested in. Those guys came from an area within ten miles of Mont Saint-Michel. One of them even did a stint at the hotel Mum and Dad stayed at… when they were still there." My stomach flipped nervously. "I think it's time you and Will had that little holiday you've been planning."

Imani regarded Will and me. She turned to James. "Are you sure that's a good idea? Won't they be expecting us?"

He shook his head. "Not necessarily. No one knows we've

identified those guys. No one else knows what's in Mum's diaries."

Imani wasn't giving in easily. "But we uncovered the warehouse. Won't they assume we might know other things?"

"Maybe. Obviously, they're going to be on the lookout because of what's been happening, but they have no idea exactly where we'll pop up. By the time they realise Lily and Will are there, hopefully they'll have some information and have returned."

Ha ha, *holiday*. "Sounds like the shortest holiday in the history of holidays. What have we got? Two, three hours tops?"

James chuckled. "Something like that. It won't take you long to grab some photos. Who knows, you mightn't even have to leave your hotel. I'm going to book you into the one our parents stayed at. I'm not sure when you'll go, though. I have Liv trying to get you into their room—we need to see exactly what happened there. She's going to get back to me as soon as she has something locked in."

"Has forensics turned up anything else from this morning?" Will asked. With no magic signatures to go on, it could almost pass for a non-witch crime. But we knew better.

"No," James answered. "They have a lot to get through."

Imani turned to my brother. "Have we beefed up protection on the other victims?"

"Yes. In light of Lily showing that they came in the windows, even though it was two stories up, we'll make sure we have someone onsite, both in the hallway and outside. If we weren't so short-staffed, we would've had a guy at their door at least. Maybe it will deter them from trying again."

"How can it be a safe house if there aren't guards?"

Maybe I was simple, but any old unit or house had locks on the doors. Was that supposed to make it safe?

"Normally we would have the resources to have agents at each property, but we had so many people housed, and they've been cutting the budget, that we're not coping. Also, the locations were supposed to be a secret."

I had to admit that we'd driven for an hour to get there, and it was in a leafy, quiet area, but still…. How could that be enough? "The PIB definitely dropped the ball on this one."

"Thanks, Lily." James scowled at me.

"Not you personally, but Chad… the people who run the place now Angelica is on leave and you're being dictated to."

He sighed. "Yeah, yeah, I know. But we can't do anything about that now. This conversation is getting us nowhere." He stood. "I'm going to go do some guard duty now, and Imani and Will have work to do. If you feel out of sorts, Lily, feel free to visit Millicent. It's her day off."

Wow, if my brother was pulling guard duty, things were dire. How long would the PIB last without an injection of funds? What would it be like with no PIB? A world where witch criminals ran rampant was not the kind of world I wanted to live in. Gah.

Abby stood and moved from Will's lap to mine. Once she was comfortably sitting, she nudged my hand, looking for a pat. "You're such a cutie!" I gave her a chin scratch with one hand and head pat with the other. "You cats live the life, don't you?"

Imani laughed. "You treat those animals better than some people treat their kids."

Will adopted a mock-offended expression. "They are our kids. What are you talking about?" Imani chuckled, and Will stood. He bent and kissed the top of my head. "Take it easy this afternoon. If you do feel upset, please visit Millicent."

My heart filled with warmth. "You're sweet. I will. Don't worry. Please just be careful out there. I'm not the only one they want now that the PIB are after them." If felt as if we were in an eighteen-wheeler thundering down the highway, our wheels were falling off one by one, and there was a gigantic tree waiting for us when we totally lost control.

Abby meowed, maybe reminding me she was there. "Listen to Abby. She knows what she's talking about." Will smiled.

"What did she say?" I still couldn't understand animal speak. To be honest, I'd given up.

"She said to pat her, and it will help you relax." He laughed.

I couldn't help but laugh too. I looked down at her. "You're so thoughtful! Cheeky kitty. I'm pretty sure you're getting some benefit out of this as well." I stroked from her head to her tail, enjoying the sensation of soft fur against my hand. "It does work, though."

"Okay, Lily. We're off." Imani gave me a wave, made her doorway, and left. James and Will both said goodbye and did the same.

"Right, kiddos, it's just you and me. Now what?" I hated being at a loose end. If it were safe, I would've taken Ted for a walk. I dropped my head back and stared at the ceiling. If only…. At least things were moving quickly now—both a good and bad thing. But none of us were going to squander this opportunity. Imagine the joy and freedom of a life without the shadow of the snake organisation hanging over us, ready to strike at any moment. I looked back down at Abby's fluffy face. "Not long now, Abby, and maybe we can have a normal life."

Okay, so "normal" was a relative term in a witch world, but it was my normal now, and I was happy with that.

Now we just had to make it happen and not lose anyone I loved along the way.

Unfortunately, that was going to be easier said than done.

Damn you to hell, RP. Damn. You. To. Hell.

CHAPTER 4

Later that night, when I was eating dinner by myself in front of the TV, Will came home. As soon as he came into the TV room, he magicked his jacket away and loosened his tie the old-fashioned non-witch way, then undid his top two buttons. "Why is it so sexy when a man loosens his tie?"

He looked at me, taken aback for a moment—it wasn't every day I called him sexy, even though he totally was. I was kind of shy when it came to verbalising that stuff. He finally found his cocky grin and sat next to me. "Maybe it's the guy rather than what he's doing with his tie." He waggled his brows.

I laughed. "Nah. It's totally the tie. You're not sexy anymore." I tried my best to stifle my grin, but it was too powerful.

"You always give yourself away, you joker, you." He was careful not to bump my plate as he gave me a passionate kiss. "How are you feeling?"

"I'm fine. I did some online Pilates and hung out with the fur kids."

"You didn't go to Millicent's."

"No. She was having lunch with her cousin. I didn't feel like crashing their party. I don't really know him well, and I didn't have it in me to be conversational with small talk."

He put his arm around me and squeezed. "Fair enough." He looked at my plate. "What's for dinner?"

"Chicken parmigiana, salad, and roast potatoes. Stand by." I'd made enough for both of us and magicked his plate into existence on his lap, then warmed the food with another spell. "Dinner is served."

"Thank you. This smells delicious." He took back his arm, picked up the cutlery on his plate, and started eating.

"So, how was your day?"

He gave me a "you don't want to know" look. "Just the usual."

"That good, huh?"

"Yes. That good."

We ate in silence and watched an episode of *Escape to the Country*. I loved that show, except for the fact that the people never bought any of the houses. Well, one person might have bought a house once, but that was it. Did anyone actually escape to the country, or did they all change their minds? Maybe they should change the title to *Trapped in the City*.

I ate the last mouthful of dinner and magicked my plate and utensils clean and away. I grinned. Gone were the days where I would've had to walk all the way to the kitchen and put them in the dishwasher. Not that doing that was terrible, but once you'd lived the lazy life, you never wanted to go back. First-world witch problems. I chuckled.

"What ridiculosity are you laughing about now?"

"Just enjoying that my witchiness enables me to avoid annoying chores."

"Living your best life, hey?"

I grinned. "You know it."

And just because we were having a relaxing moment, his phone had to go and ring. Stupid technology. "Hello, Agent Blakesley speaking." After placing his plate on the couch next to him, Will stood. He walked to the window and looked out at the darkness. He listened for a while, which wasn't a good sign. "Right. What do you want to do?" He ran his free hand through his hair and rubbed the back of his neck. I stared at him, hoping to pick up on whatever the convo was. Unfortunately, my eyes had no listening skills, and I figured magicking his phone onto speaker was too rude, even for me. So I suffered in silence as the people on *Escape to the Country* thanked the host for his help but didn't buy anything… yet again. Those house hunters were such teases. When was the host going to lose his mind and tell them to stop wasting his time? The British were way too polite.

"Yep. Okay. Bye." Will lowered his phone and looked at me. He didn't smile. "You might want to pack a bag. We're off to Mont Saint-Michel tomorrow." I knew we were only going to be there for a few hours, but I assumed taking the bag was so we looked legit.

I grinned because who wouldn't want to visit that place, but then I remembered I'd be seeing my parents, and sadness expanded in my chest until I couldn't breathe. "What time do we leave?"

The pain in his eyes told mc he was aware of what I was going through. "Not too early. We'll have an easy morning and travel there at nine thirty. We're going to a landing spot about a half-hour drive from our final destination." His expression had morphed to its work setting—as pokerish as they came.

"Okay. Um, that was a long conversation for just that. What aren't you telling me?" Even though going somewhere my parents had been was complicated and a mixed blessing, it was just a routine investigation. He seemed too quiet and preoccupied.

"One of the other people we rescued has been murdered. This time it was a woman. Not that that's better or worse. Just thought I'd clarify."

I shut my eyes for a moment, the bloody scene I'd photographed earlier splattering in vivid colour through my mind. I shuddered and opened my eyes. Will strode over and sat next to me. He wrapped a strong, comforting arm around me and drew me to him. I breathed in his scent and focussed on his warmth. "They're not going to stop till they kill every-one, are they?"

The silence stretched out.

Ted and Abby wandered in, Ted sitting at my feet and placing a gentle paw on my knee. Abby jumped onto the couch and sat in my lap. I leaned forward and patted Ted, then gave Abby a scratch under the chin. "You guys are gorgeous. Did you know that?" Abby meowed, and Ted gave a quiet bark.

Will laughed. "They said they know."

I chuckled. "What would we do without you to cheer us up? And you don't have to answer because I know you'll just be saying how awesome you are."

"*Meow.*"

"*Woof.*"

Will laughed again. "No translation needed."

"Ha, I knew it."

"Come on. Why don't we have an early night? I know just the way to cheer you up." He waggled his brows, but then serious Will came to the fore. "There's nothing we can do for anyone right now, and we have a big day tomorrow. Let's make the most of the peaceful time we have together."

He was the best man ever. "Sounds good to me." Abby hopped off my lap. Will and I stood, and I let him lead me to our bedroom, where we shut out the rest of the world. It couldn't last forever, but it was better than nothing.

Unfortunately, I couldn't slow time, and before I was ready, the morning had arrived.

"I smell hay." I crinkled my nose, then sneezed.

Will stepped out of the doorway, pulling his suitcase on wheels, and stood next to me. "Bless you. And that might be because you're standing on some."

I looked down. "Ah, thanks. I guess I am. So, where are we? I mean, it looks like we're in a stable, but I could be wrong."

"Yes, this is a stall in a barn in northern France. We're outside a town called Pontaubault. The farmer here is a witch. His family has supported the PIB for a long time. We pay a small fee to have a landing spot here and for his confidentiality. We don't want other witches to know our comings and goings, obviously. There are a few places like this spread over Europe."

"That makes sense, and it sure beats a public toilet. So, now what? Do we flag down a ride or call an Uber?"

He smiled. "No, nothing that uncivilised." He swung the

stall door open and walked into the main barn area. I grabbed the handle of my small trolley-style suitcase and followed. A couple of square hay bales sat against one wall. It was a typical barn—exposed ceiling beams, garden implements in one corner, horse tack hanging off large hooks in one of the stone walls.

"There's our ride." Will nodded towards the other end of the barn, near a large timber door. Two smallish cars sat there. An old red Peugeot and an old white Citroen. By old, they were probably fifteen to twenty years old. On closer inspection, they seemed to be in good condition—no rust, decent tread on the tyres. "Which one are we taking?"

"Which one would you prefer?"

"They both look pretty average. I don't care. You choose."

He shrugged. "Let's go with the Peugeot." He whispered something I couldn't make out, and his magic caressed the back of my neck. A key appeared in his hand. "Password protected." He winked.

"I'm surprised there isn't a spell to unlock the car door and start the car. Surely, you spy witches are capable of doing that."

"I suppose we are, but this is just the way it's always been done. It's not good to use magic for everything when being discrete is the name of the game. The more you use it for everyday things, the more likely you are to slip up and use it at the wrong time, in front of the wrong people."

I nodded. "Makes sense."

Will opened the boot and placed our suitcases inside, then he opened the door for me—always such a gentleman. I slid into the passenger seat, which was on the wrong side of the car. I put my hands up to grip a non-existent steering wheel. "I don't think I'll ever get used to driving on the wrong side of the road."

Will got into the car. "Lucky I'm driving, then."

I smiled. "Very." Hmm, something was wrong with this picture. "The barn door is closed. Are we going to do a James Bond and drive right through it?"

He laughed. "Aside from the fact that we're witches, I have this." He opened the glovebox and pulled out a small black controller, pointed it at the door, and pressed the button. The door slid across, revealing a sunny day outside.

I laughed. "Too funny."

We drove down a hard-packed dirt driveway and out onto a small main road. I tried to ignore my stomach, which gurgled unhappily—soon enough, I'd be staring through my camera at my parents. Seeing them was emotional enough, but what was I going to discover? The uncertainty had stolen my appetite this morning, and I'd only managed to down a cappuccino before we left.

I placed my hand on my stomach and stared out the window. A vast blue sky stretched over miles of yellow and green fields filled with crops. Soon we drove through a small village, stone houses flanking either side of the road, and then we were out the other side, back to sky and fields. "This is so pretty. There's just so much to see." I turned my head to look at Will and made a bubble of silence. Even though we both knew we might not live long enough, I couldn't help asking, "When this is all over, can we come back and drive around Europe for a few weeks? Surely the PIB will give you some leave."

He glanced my way before looking back at the road. His sad smile echoed my thoughts. "When we get through this,

Lily, I would love to take a holiday with you. Where would you like to go?"

"Everywhere?" I laughed. "I don't know, um…. Back to Paris, maybe see Nice, Switzerland, Venice, Rome, Florence… ooh, what about skiing in Austria?"

He chuckled. "I think the question is, where don't you want to go?"

"Exactly." I grinned.

We happily passed the time discussing everywhere we might never actually get the chance to go, but there was hope. And then I saw it.

My mouth fell open, and I gasped. "Oh my God! It's like a fairy tale."

Will glanced at me and smiled. "'Tis, indeed."

The grassy plain stretched into the distance, miles and miles of swishing greenery, feathered by the breeze, leading to something I expected to see in a movie. I shook my head in awe—even though it was in front of me, it was hard to believe it was real. I magicked my camera to myself from my suitcase and clicked off some photos as we drove.

Mont Saint-Michel sat on a rocky island, its grandeur rising above the flood plains, a whimsical silhouette against an azure backdrop. It looked more like a castle than a fortified town.

With every passing mile, the view became no less spectacular. "I can't believe we're actually going there. Wow." I sat quietly for the rest of the drive, just taking it in. "Cars aren't allowed on the island, are they?"

"No. We have a code to get through that boom gate, then we can park in a special car park—you get favours when you're booked into the island's hotels. We'll get a shuttle service to the island after we park."

As we got out of the car, I checked that my return to sender was up. Yep. Even though I'd been preoccupied with thoughts of my parents and the evil RP, I'd managed to get something right. Yay me.

Will and I grabbed our bags and caught the shuttle bus. Two-storey-high stone walls surrounded the town. Everything seemed to be made of the same stone—the protective walls, buildings, retaining walls. When the fortifying walls were built, back in medieval times, they'd likely had to take material from the closest possible place. I wondered if it had been from the island itself.

The briny scent of the sea freshened the air, and seagulls cried to each other as they wheeled overhead. We walked through the entryway, our bags rolling loudly over the pavers, the vibration of it travelling up my arm and through my body. Buildings crowded both sides of the narrow walkway leading to our hotel, their shopfronts forming inviting nooks in the shadowed pathway. Such a romantic setting. As I floated along in a haze of beauty and history, the delicious scent of food floated around me—pastries and pizza—a curious but heady mix. My stomach grumbled. I patted it. "Once we get settled, we'll grab something."

Will chuckled. "I'm thinking you're not talking to me?"

"You would be correct."

Slow-moving tourists crowded the laneway, their voices echoing off the stone as they wandered from shop to shop. When we reached our hotel—a gorgeous structure of granite, shingles with shutters on the windows, and fancy gold lettering proclaiming Auberge Saint Pierre—we had to wait for some people to pass before we could cross the short expanse of path and enter. The rumble of my bag on the pavers echoed in my ears. I stuck my finger in one ear to clear it, but it didn't help.

My arms and body retained the vibrating sensation. How funny. It was like when you got off a boat and could still feel the rolling of the ocean.

I let Will check us in, and to my surprise, his French wasn't that bad—well, he was speaking and the lady at the front desk could understand him. It could've been perfect French, but I didn't know my *chambre* from my *salle de bains*. Was it wrong that he became even sexier? I was going to have to learn some other languages to keep up with everyone. It seemed that I was the only one who wasn't at least bilingual.

As we climbed the stairs to our room… my parents' old room, I swallowed my rising nausea. Why had they come here? What were we about to find out? Would seeing them again hurt as much as it had every other time? Bittersweet didn't do the feeling justice. It was more like yearning and pain with love thrown in. Looking at something you couldn't ever have again, well, there wasn't much sweetness about it. I should be grateful to have those snippets of their lives, but the reminders of what I'd lost overshadowed everything. Avoidance would've been way better for my emotional state.

We reached our room, and Will opened the door.

The moment of truth. Such a cliché but so appropriate.

The room was everything you'd want a hotel room in a historic building to be—full of character, clean, pretty, cosy, and it even had a stunning view of the expanse of sand and water beyond the island's walls. I gazed at the polished parquetry floors, exposed timber beams, and inviting bed, and took a deep breath. It was the unwanted thing that also resided here that had my stomach somersaulting. Memories.

And they weren't even mine.

We placed our bags to the side—we'd likely never even

open them—and I took the lens cap off my Nikon. I hadn't bothered putting it away after the car ride. There was so much to see, even apart from what we were here for, that I wanted it at the ready, just in case.

"You're going to get right to it?" Will's forehead wrinkled.

"Yes. I'm okay. I think getting it over and done with is the way to go. We have more than this room to *sightsee* too." He nodded. I gave him a reassuring smile. "Here goes." I made a bubble of silence and stood near the door. "Show me the last time my parents were here." I jammed my back teeth together as the scene changed.

Night-time—the lights were on, and the window closed. I sucked in a breath, and tears blurred my vision. My parents stood together, holding hands, facing a man in a tuxedo, who had his back to me. My mother wore a sparkling, figure-hugging black halter-neck dress that reached the floor. My father was handsome in a tuxedo. Seemed they were off to a formal event, or had they already returned? *Click, click.*

I walked around behind my parents to get a look at the other man's face. But before I could focus on that, the nearness to my parents stole my breath. All those years ago, they had been here, in the exact spot I stood. It took all my strength not to reach out and run my hand down the back of my father's smooth jacket, to reach out and place my hand on my mother's warm shoulder. I blinked tears away, shut my eyes, and took another deep breath. When I opened my eyes, the weight of tears on my lashes became almost overwhelming.

The floor creaked as Will came and stood next to me. He placed a hand on the back of my neck. "It's okay, Lily. I'm here."

I nodded and sniffed. "Thank you." *Just get this over and done with, Lily*. I shook my head and refocussed on the stranger. He was in his late thirties, early forties. His dark, curly hair sat just above his eyebrows and just kissed the back of his collar. He had dark eyes, full lips, and the barely discernible yellow-greenish tint of olive skin, although he didn't have a tan. He had a straight nose, and I supposed he would be considered handsome, but there was something about him I didn't like. Was it his overly confident posture, or something in the way he was looking at my mother, as if my father wasn't there and she was his to bed? *Click, click.*

I lowered my camera, then raised it again. "Show me anything else I need to see." I turned on the spot, slowly taking in the whole room, but my parents were gone.

Hang on. I sucked in a breath and moved to the delicate writing table near the window. A postcard sat on it, writing side up. My stomach dropped to the floor as I read the first line.

To my darling Lily and James.

My heart raced. I clicked off a shot. But it was too much, and I lowered my camera, then plonked onto the bed. I blinked several times and shook my head. My voice came out in a whisper. "Look at this." Will took the camera from my outstretched hand and sat next to me.

Will's mouth fell open, and he turned to stare at me, but he said nothing. He must be just as floored as me. He turned back to the photo and enlarged it on the camera screen. "Have you read any of it?"

"Only the first line."

"Do you want me to read it out?"

If I had tried to read it, I probably wouldn't be able to see through my tears. I nodded. "Yes, please."

"To my darling Lily and James. Your father and I are

having a wonderful time on holiday. Mont Saint-Michel is enchanting, especially the abbey. Miss you both. Wish we could bring the Saint to us. I'm sure Tilly's brother would feel a real connection to it. Love you. Mum and Dad xx."

Hmm. "That sounds familiar." Had I seen this postcard before? If they'd sent it to us, surely, I would have. "It's all a bit weird."

"It is indeed. Who's Tilly's brother?"

I shook my head. "I have no idea. I don't even know who Tilly is. Maybe James knows? And why would she want to bring Mont Saint-Michel to us? I mean, I get that it's wonderful, but that's stupid. It could never happen. Why write it? My mother wasn't taken to being cryptic or whimsical, and it just doesn't sound like something she'd bother wishing for."

"It definitely looks like a clue to me."

"Agreed." At least coming here hadn't been for nothing. "Now what?"

"See if you can find anything else in here, and if not, we'll have a wander of the island."

"Did you see the other photos? There's a man in them. He looks dodgy."

His eyebrows rose. "No. Hang on." He bent his head and scrolled through. "Interesting. Okay." He passed the camera back.

I stood and switched the Nikon to photo mode. "Show me anything else I need to see."

Nothing.

Phew.

Okay, I knew we needed information, but I couldn't help not wanting to see my parents, or anything gory, for that matter.

"That's it."

He stood and enveloped me in a hug. "We're getting there. Just think back to when you arrived in London and knew nothing about what happened to them. You've come so far. My gut tells me we're close, Lily. So damn close."

"Me too."

And that's what I was afraid of.

CHAPTER 5

After we'd finished in the hotel room, we wandered the island, and I took photos, but nothing showed up. Because my mother had mentioned the abbey, we decided to venture in there. The more we strolled, the more it felt like an actual holiday, except that nothing could erase the emotional hangover of seeing my parents.

As we passed through a dimly lit room, the heaviness of granite walls feeling as if they were closing in, the vibrations from earlier intensified. I shook my head.

"What's wrong?" Will stopped walking and pulled me to the side of the room, away from the other sightseers.

"Our bags were noisy earlier, and they started some kind of vibration in my head. It's not as loud as it was, but it's ramped up a bit since we came in here."

He nodded and had an "ah huh" look on his face. He whispered, "The river of power sits close to the surface here, near the boundary between our world and where it resides."

My eyes bugged wide. It was an effort not to shout. "What? Since when is there another world?"

"Hmm, I've done a bodge job of explaining that. Maybe *dimension* would be better."

"I guess that makes sense. It's not like we can see it unless we're using our other sight, and even then, you don't really see the river anywhere."

"No, you don't. There aren't many places it's this close to the surface, for want of a better word."

"How do you make it go away?" It was almost as annoying as a mosquito zooming past your ear when you were in bed on a hot summer night.

"You can't. Just embrace it. You'll get used to it. The more you think about it, the louder it is. Why don't you take some photos, make the most of our *holiday*?"

I smiled. "If only we could be on holiday all the time." That comment was for the benefit of anyone from RP or the PIB listening in. I had no idea if anyone was, but chances were good that was the case.

I raised my camera and took a photo of Will. During the past few months, I'd taken so many photos, but most of them were to do with solving crimes. I'd hardly taken any of the people I loved, or Westerham. That was going to change today. I was scared of seeing if someone was going to die through my camera, and that was the reason, but that was kind of an excuse since I could turn my other sight off. Maybe it's just that the joy and freedom I'd had before I'd come to the UK had pretty much disappeared, and because I knew I couldn't roam and photograph, I'd stopped wanting it. Silly Lily. I'd wasted so much time. But not anymore.

"Smile." I clicked off a shot. "Do you want to take a selfie of us with your phone?"

Will looked at me as if to say "I'm not sure what the hell is going on, but I like it." He took his phone out of his pocket, and we posed. He showed me his efforts.

"Love it. One day when we're old, we'll look back at this and reminisce about what a hot couple we were." I laughed.

"Nah. We'll still be hot when we're old." He winked and grinned.

"You're so funny."

"I know."

I rolled my eyes and shook my head. "You just can't pass up an opportunity, can you?"

"Nope.

I took a deep breath and asked the question in my mind. *Show me my parents last time they were here*. Everything went almost pitch-black, and the people disappeared. The only light was from a small ball above my father's hand. He and my mother were dressed like burglars from the movies—black pants, black skivvies, black boots, and black beanies. My mother had her gun in one hand, and my father carried a leather bag. I snapped off a shot.

What the hell were they looking for?

I asked my magic, but nothing showed up—just this room as it was in the now. Hmm…. I looked at Will. "Okay. Next room."

He led the way to another room that was just as dark and granite filled as the last one. Nothing unusual showed up through my lens. We made our way up a narrow spiral stone staircase. This place had been a monastery and a jail in its former life. What secrets it must hold.

As we walked through, a shadowed movement flicked in my peripheral vision. I swung my head around, but there was nothing there. Had I imagined it? Probably. When your senses were on high alert, nothings could turn into somethings. I ignored the sense of being watched and kept walking.

After going up and up the staircase, we came out at a rectangular courtyard. A covered walkway enclosed it, giving us a view of the open grassed area through the stone archways that framed it. A cold wind swept through, and I shivered. I hastily zipped up my hoodie—we'd gone casual for this *holiday*. It was weird not being in uniform for an investigation, and as gorgeous as Will was in his suit, he also looked pretty damned good in jeans and a jumper. Truth was, Will couldn't look average in anything. If he wasn't an agent, he would've made a good model, although I couldn't see him keep a straight face strutting down the catwalk in some of the ridiculous outfits they had to wear.

I made another bubble of silence, raised my camera, and whispered, "Show me my parents." Another gust whistled through, and I shivered again. When we were done here, I was so getting a coffee and pastry. Just let Will try and stop me.

Daylight disappeared. Moonlight silhouetted three figures on the pathway across the courtyard from where I stood. I wandered around there, dodging a couple of sightseers who were here in real time. Will stayed at my side.

What the hell had gone on? It was hard to make out, but I was pretty sure it was my parents with the same man who'd been in their hotel room. The guy stood behind my dad and had him in a headlock. *Grrrr*. My father's hands were on the guy's forearms, likely trying to pry him off. My mother stood in front of them, feet planted wide, a gun pointed at the stranger's head. *Go, Mum!*

But hang on, there were two faint figures in the middle of the courtyard. They weren't showing up as solid as my parents. I snapped a couple of shots and zoomed in. My mouth dropped open. They had sandals and robes on... monks? What did they have to do with anything? One monk had grabbed the front of the other one's robe and had pulled him so their faces were close together—aggression if I'd ever seen it. What had that been about?

I shook my head, lowered my camera, and refocussed on where my parents had shown up—whatever was going on, I needed to deal with it one mystery at a time. "Show me what happened next."

Nothing.

I sighed.

I turned to Will, brought up the photo of my parents, and handed him the camera. "Check that out. I guess maybe nothing ended up happening? My parents returned from that *holiday*." I made air quotes. "I couldn't find anything else from afterwards. I'm assuming if they'd killed him, it would've shown up."

"You would think, but who knows how it all works—what the universe chooses to show you or not show you. In any case, it's intriguing, and we need to do some more digging." He went to hand the camera back, but I shook my head.

"Go to the next pic and tell me what you think."

"O-kay." He flicked across to the next one. His forehead wrinkled. He enlarged the picture. "They're a bit faded, but are they monks?"

"I think so, yes. But why? I'm thinking they weren't there the same time as my parents. I've never had that happen before—two time periods intermingling, two different crimes."

Will's eyes had a calculating look in them. "What if they're related?"

"Hmm, interesting." Way to make things more compli-cated. Fatigue washed over me at the prospect of doing more research, then piecing all this together. I walked to the edge of the space and looked across the water. The tide was out, and sand stretched into the distance. The tides here were crazy. At home, the water moved down or up between three and six feet with each tide, but the tides here sucked the water away for miles.

Will stood next to me and slid his arm around my waist. "Whatcha thinking?"

A blast of icy wind blew my hair away from my face. I slid my arm around Will's waist and snuggled into his side, soaking up his warmth. "I'm just tired. It's like, we find something, but then it raises more questions. How long can this go on? How long can *we* go on? I know our war with RP is coming, but if we have so many unanswered questions, will it come back and bite us later?"

Will stared out at the expanse of sand for a moment. "I don't know, Lily. I wish I could tell you it'll all be over in a couple of weeks, and there won't be any loose ends to chase up, but…." He shrugged.

I sighed. "I know." My stomach grumbled. "Yeah, yeah, I know I forgot to feed you before, and I promised."

Will chuckled. "Okay, Lily's stomach, let's hurry this up, and once we're outside, we'll go get you something yummy."

My stomach gurgled. "She said thank you." I grinned and pulled away from Will. "Let's get this done." I spoke with all the confidence in the world. But, hey, what did I know?

Even though we didn't find anything else in the abbey, Mont Saint-Michel wasn't finished with us yet. Not by a long shot.

After leaving the abbey, we visited the *boulangerie* next to our hotel and grabbed two sandwiches, two chocolate éclairs, and two coffees. We took them up to our room to sit and discuss our next move. Other than the drone of power constantly buzzing through my body, I liked it here. It would be nice if I could spend more time wandering around, exploring the narrow paths, nooks, and crannies of the island, maybe even have a romantic dinner before we went home, but we had work to do. I was definitely putting it on my list for us to come back and stay for real when this was over and done with.

I'd finished my sandwich, and it was coffee and éclair time. The first bite was even better than I could've imagined. "Mmmmmm." I spoke with a full mouth because all etiquette went out the third-floor window and died a happy death on the concrete. "This is soooooo good. Oh my God."

Will smiled as he ate the last of his. "Agreed. Hmm, maybe we should have an éclair wedding cake. Just a pyramid of them. What do you think?"

"I think you might be joking, but I'll hold you to it. Ooh, I know! We can do one layer of double-chocolate muffins, one layer of éclairs, and so on to infinity." I laughed.

"Whatever makes you happy." He grinned.

"You're the best. I knew I made the right choice when I said yes." I held my hand up and admired my sparkly engagement ring.

Will grabbed my hand and kissed it. "I'm glad you said yes, too, and not because we're going to get cake at the wedding." He leaned closer and kissed me senseless. He eyed the bed we were sitting on. "We could make better use of this before we go back." I was about to answer when his phone rang. Dammit. He frowned and picked it up off the bedside table. "Agent Blakesley."

Magic tingled my scalp. I narrowed my eyes and stood. Will gave me a brief quizzical look but had to concentrate on his conversation. I quietly walked to the door and carefully gripped the handle. Ready. Set. Go! I spun the knob and yanked the door open. Standing outside in the corridor, her eyes wide, was a young woman dressed in jeans and black jumper. I was about to ask her what she was doing when she turned and ran.

Should I go after her?

Stuff it. Yes. Yes, I should.

I bolted out the door and down the stairs. Her footsteps clapped a staccato beat to the bottom. I caught a glimpse of her heading for the front door. One of the waiters from the restaurant stepped out in front of me from a side door. I dodged him and sprinted for the front door. I burst into the street and jerked my head one way, then the other, as I gulped in huge breaths.

"Damn!" She'd disappeared in the crowd, or maybe she'd gone up nearby stairs. This place was a medieval rabbit warren.

"Lily!" Will said. I turned. He was standing just outside the hotel door. "What happened?"

I made a bubble of silence, something we hadn't done in the hotel room. "Someone was spying on us. Didn't you feel that magic when you were on the phone?"

"Yes, but it was so faint, and the call was important. I figured it was probably nothing—it could've been a hotel maid cleaning the room next to us."

"There was a woman, about my age. I didn't have my other sight on, so I don't know what spell she used, but she was standing in the hallway, likely spying."

Will swore and peered up and down the street. "Let's go

back upstairs. Things have changed." Without waiting for an answer, he turned and re-entered the hotel. I hurried to keep up with him. Whatever he needed to tell me was important, and in light of someone—likely RP—knowing we were here, danger was closer than we thought.

Will's magic tingled my nape as he set up a spell outside our room. "An alarm so we aren't taken by surprise again." He opened the door for me, then followed me in and shut it.

I checked, and my bubble of silence was still up. I'd managed to stay close enough to Will that it didn't break, which could happen. There was a point at which it didn't work if things changed too much from when you set it. "What was that call about?"

"One of the French men we'd rescued from the factory was due to give a statement today, but just as he came in, we received a call for him from one of his childhood friends. He rang to say that his parents and sister had been kidnapped, and that if he cooperated with us, they'd be killed." He took in a deep breath and huffed it out loudly. "He refused to talk, and being a victim, we can't force him."

"That's crap. Bloody RP." I growled. Frustration built inside me until I wanted to scream. "Argh!"

"Yeah, I know." Will ran a hand through his hair and placed his hand on his hips. "So, tell me about your girl. Do you think you could take a picture and we can send it to Liv?"

"Um, I can try. Not sure it's going to work."

"But it happened in the past, right?"

I shrugged. "I guess so. But won't someone find out my secret?"

"I don't think so. We can say we knew she was there, and you took a photo as soon as you opened the door."

I nodded. "Okay." I decided to use my phone since I could

just text the pic to Will, and it was more likely I would have my phone handy. I opened the door to an empty corridor, thank goodness. Whoever she was, she would confirm with whoever sent her that we were here. Maybe they were going to send more witches after us? I brought up camera mode and pointed it at the spot. Crossing my fingers, I said, "Show me the girl who was eavesdropping on us in the last hour." Yes! There she was. Long brown hair, slim, a bit taller than me. I clicked off a shot, then moved to another spot to get a side profile. Roman nose, a smattering of freckles, green eyes. *Click.*

I went back inside our room and shut the door. "Here." I texted the photos to Will.

"Thanks. I'll send them to Liv." He texted them.

"Now what? Do we stay and keep investigating, or do we go home where it's safer?"

He sat on the bed. "Maybe we're close to something; otherwise, why spy on us? And she didn't try to hurt us."

"Maybe she was working up to it?" I sat next to him. "Have you got any ideas on what my parents were looking for?"

"No. It could be anything—evidence for a crime, enslaved people like the ones we found, magical items. I'd like to know if our situation is linked with those monks in some way."

I rubbed my forehead. This was too much thinking with not enough information. "I'm guessing yes. My talent is never random."

"But it could just be that we're so close to the source. Maybe it's supercharging your talent, and you've managed to pick up on two totally unrelated circumstances?"

I shook my head. "I have no idea, Will. Absolutely none. Can you call a meeting at my brother's?"

"We might have to, but I think we're close to something

here. I'd hate to leave things as they are. That birthday dinner your mother's diary mentions, I bet it'll give us a lot to work with. I think we get some more photos, see if we can identify everyone who was there."

"Okay." I wasn't sure if I was happy to be staying or scared and tired. "What time are you thinking?"

"When everyone's asleep. One in the morning?"

I yawned just hearing what time I'd have to get up. "I thought you loved me?"

He grinned. "I do."

"So why are you trying to kill me with lack of sleep?"

"You'll survive. I promise."

I shivered. Lack of sleep might not kill me, but RP would if they got half a chance. We were in a strange place, just the two of us, and that worried me. But if we wanted to get to the bottom of everything, we had to push on. "I'll hold you to that, buddy. Now, where are you taking me for dinner?" If we had to hang around, I was going to do it in style. I just had to hope it wasn't our last supper.

CHAPTER 6

Dressed in black and under no-notice spells, we made our way to the hotel's courtyard. We'd had an uneventful night after dinner, thank goodness—the alarm had stayed quiet, but we both kept our return to senders up. At this point, doing otherwise was just stupid.

As we stepped outside, the frigid breeze stole my breath. Goosebumps sprung up along my arms. Man, it was cold. The shadowed shapes of tables and chairs sat along each side wall, leaving a path down the middle. Someone had a light on in a room above, but the window was closed. It gave us enough light to see by without making me feel too exposed.

Will stood guard, hand in pocket where his gun stayed hidden. I lifted my camera and whispered, "Show me my parents at Piranha's dad's birthday party." The night brightened to twilight. Fairy lights were strung up around the courtyard, and the tables and chairs formed a long line down the middle. People stood in small groups, chatting, and two men sat at the table, smoking. Those were the days… when you could be eating and have to breathe in stinky carcinogens. Thank goodness things had changed. I pointed at each elegantly dressed group and took photos, cataloguing everyone.

Grrr, there was Dana's father chatting to my parents. His wife stood near him, talking to the guy who'd been in the abbey and my parents' room. I had no idea who any of the other fourteen guests were, but we were going to find out. Were they all witches? Were they all involved somehow, or were some of them just innocent friends of Dana's dad's enjoying a fun night out?

Hmm, there were some juicy looking jewels among the women. If it was the real stuff, rather than costume jewellery, Dana's dad was mixing with the super-rich. That, of course, didn't surprise me. I was sure his ambitions were loftier than an eagle's nest.

After maybe five minutes, I was done. I lowered my camera and gave Will a nod. We'd agreed to stay the rest of the night and checkout like normal people. Now we had the alarm, I felt a bit safer.

We found our way to the door, and he opened it for me. I stepped through, and someone grabbed my arm, pulling me to the side.

Crap.

"Hey!" I would've screamed, but I didn't want to wake anyone in the hotel—anyone intervening was likely to get hurt or killed rather than help our situation.

A large hand gripped my upper arm, fingers digging in painfully. Another hand slammed over my mouth. My heart raced, and I did my best to push down the panic expanding in my chest. The man had his chest to my back, and something hard pushed against the side of my head. Double crap.

WITCH WAR IN WESTERHAM

Will stepped through the door, gun pointed out in front. He didn't miss anything, although my annoyed utterance was probably as good a warning as you could get.

The person holding me stepped back, dragging me with him—the person's strength and height gave it away. If it was a woman, I'd eat my engagement ring.

Will pointed his gun at the guy's head. "Drop the gun and let her go. You'll never get away, and if you hurt her, I will kill you. Give up now, and you'll only get jail time." Will's jaw was set, his eyes laser focussed on the jerk pointing the gun at my head.

"No. You drop the gun. I'm taking her with me, and if you're smart, you'll get out of my way." The gun barrel pushed harder against my temple. I tried to keep my breathing normal, but it wasn't easy. *No panicking, Lily. Just think.*

I had no idea if the man had a return to sender up, but since Will wasn't hitting him with any spells, I had to assume he did. The guy dragged me back a bit. "Don't follow me."

"You're not leaving here alive." Will kept his gun trained on the man's head.

I groaned and hoped my acting skills were on point. I mumbled through the guy's hand, "I think I'm going to be sick." The pressure of the gun lessened enough for me to know he was distracted. I made a heaving noise, and his hand dropped from my mouth. I put my chin to my chest and planted my feet. This was going to hurt, but it was the only thing I could think of. I made another gagging noise. I moved fast and put all my effort into thrusting my chest up and back, throwing my head back at the same time. I grunted with the impact. Pain smashed into the back of my head and radiated out. I fell to my knees—from the agony, and from the desire to get my head away from his gun.

"Argh!" The guy screamed out. Hopefully, I'd at least broken his nose.

Will stepped forward, then leapt at the man, tackling him. They wrestled on the ground. I was about to help Will—not sure how, but maybe kicking the guy in the head would make a difference—but the guy had lost his gun, and Will was gaining the upper hand. I crawled quickly to the gun and grabbed it, all the while careful not to hit my camera on the floor—it was still around my neck. I would've pointed the gun at the man, but I was just as likely to hit Will because moving targets were never easy to deal with, and I had no shooting skills to speak of.

The man grunted as Will turned him onto his stomach, put one knee on his spine, and bent his arm behind his back. He pulled out cuffs with his other hand and slapped them on, the gunman wriggling the whole time. But it was too late. He'd been caught.

I crawled over to them and put my face close to the ground, inches from his face. "Aw, bad luck, buddy. Have fun in jail." He pinned me with an angry gaze, then told me to you-know-what off. I just smiled and scrunched my nose in a cutesy expression. "Write me. Oops, I meant bite me." I stood, leaving the guy to spit on the floor. Ha, missed.

Will dragged him to his feet and looked at me. "Are you okay?"

I smiled. "Yep. Totally peachy." I resisted the urge to rub the back of my head, and to be honest, nausea was setting in, as was a headache, but I didn't want to give the craphead any reason to be happy. Let him think I was the queen of headbutts.

"Nice headbutt, by the way. You surprised me."

"I like to keep our relationship fresh and interesting. Who doesn't like to learn new, awesome things about their partner?"

He grinned and shook his head. Then he installed his poker face—back to business. "I'll have to take him to head-quarters."

The man shook violently. His mouth frothed. Damn, not again! His eyes rolled into the back of his head, and he collapsed into Will. Will lowered him all the way to the ground and felt for a pulse. He looked up at me and shook his head.

"Bloody RP have struck again."

"It sure looks that way." He pulled the collar of the man's jumper down to expose his neck. There it was—the snake tattoo. I shuddered. The snake's head was still on my arm, and we had no idea what that meant. Did RP have some control over me? Would they seize control of me at the worst possible moment? But then again, if they could force me to do whatever they wanted, why did they keep sending people to kidnap me?

Will nodded to himself, then stood. "I'll get you to take him to headquarters. I'll stay here and clean up—make sure any security cameras are wiped. I'll check out in the morning and drive back to the barn."

"But what about the fact we were supposed to be here on holiday?"

"That doesn't matter. He came to us. No one has to know what we were doing here. Looks like RP are going to find you any place they have spies on the ground. Maybe this is one of their regular haunts?"

"Maybe whatever my mother was after is still here?"

"It's looking that way, but we won't mention that to anyone at the PIB."

I saluted him. "Yes, boss."

He gave me a lopsided smile. "Only when it suits you."

I grinned. "Of course. I'll call James before I take this guy in." I pulled out my phone and dialled my brother.

He answered in a just-woken-up voice. "Lily? Is everything okay?"

"I'm about to bring in a dead snake guy. Can you meet me in the reception room?"

"On it. See you in a minute." He hung up. Being a witch, he only had to magic clothes on and make a doorway. So efficient. I looked at Will. "Love you. Stay safe. Maybe call me in the morning when you're on your way." I kissed his lips.

"You stay safe too. Love you."

And with that, I made my doorway to headquarters and stepped through backwards, dragging my prize by his shoulders. I felt like a lion with its prey, or maybe I was the gazelle who turned the tables on the lion. In any case, I didn't have to feel guilty about this one. This was all on RP and their stupid kill-people-to-stop-them-talking spell. Anyone branded with one of their tattoos had this hanging over them.

I arrived in the reception room. James was already there. "What have you got for me?"

I dropped the guy, and his head thunked loudly on the floor. I cringed. "Ouch. That would've hurt if he'd been alive."

James looked at me as if to say "you're an idiot." He knelt and checked out the body. "How did he die?"

"The RP spell that kills them when they're apprehended. Will managed to cuff him after a bit of a struggle, but he didn't do anything to him."

James's forehead wrinkled. "Then why is there blood on his face, and why does his nose look squashed?"

"Oh, that. I headbutted him and broke it. But that was

only because he'd grabbed me and had a gun pointed at my head. It kind of annoyed me." I gave him a sarcastic smile.

"Yes, I suppose I can see how that would irritate you. Right, well, he's definitely dead." He took the cuffs off and handed them to me. "Give these back to Will when you see him." He looked at my camera. "I take it you have some nice holiday snaps to share later?"

"Indeed I do. Maybe we can come over for dinner tomorrow night, or is that actually tonight?" Doing things after midnight but before 5:00 a.m. was so confusing when referring to the next day, at least for me. "Shame our holiday was cut short though."

"Yes." He looked down at the dead body. "Quite a shame." He buzzed the intercom while looking at me. "See you tomorrow at seven." A security guard I didn't know answered the door. James magicked a trolley bed into the room from the infirmary and hovered the body into position on the bed. He pushed it through the door and gave me a wave over his shoulder.

I guessed it was time to go home and hope that everything was okay with Will. What a disappointing end to the day when we could've woken up together at Mont Saint-Michel.

The way the universe was behaving lately, why would I expect anything less? But, hey, at least we had the opportunity to see a new day, something the guy with the gun wasn't getting. Did that bother me? Not. In. The. Least. My transformation to hard-hearted witch was almost complete. Somewhere, deep down, I knew it should bother me.

But it didn't. Not one bit.

CHAPTER 7

I'd managed to sleep okay, but worry woke me earlier than I otherwise would have. My phone screen showed 8:04 a.m. Abby stood from her spot at the end of my bed and stretched before coming up to my face and dipping her nose to mine. I smiled. "Good morning, sweetie. You're so cute." I kissed the top of her head. "Time to get up."

I slid out of bed, went to the bathroom, then wandered downstairs. Today, for some reason, I was really missing Angelica. Even though she worked long hours, I'd often run into her at some point, usually in the kitchen at breakfast or dinnertime. She'd been undercover for a long time, and with Liv gone and Will not home yet, the house was too quiet and empty. Yes, I had Abby and Ted, but it wasn't quite the same.

I sat at the kitchen table and magicked food into the fur kids' bowls, then magicked my cappuccino into existence. Mmm, the smooth, delicious fragrance always made me sigh. As I savoured my first sip, the sound of the reception-room door opening and closing had me placing my cup on the table and jumping up. By the time I reached the kitchen door, Will was standing there. "Yay!" I threw my arms around him. "I was worried."

He kissed the top of my head. "Back safe and sound. The rest of the night was uneventful, except that I missed you."

"Tell me about it. Let's not make a habit of spending the night apart. I'm getting used to you."

He smiled. "Good. Keep it up." He peered over my shoulder. "Is that coffee I smell?"

"Yes." I grabbed his hand and took him to the table.

He sat next to me and put a paper bag on the table. "Thought I'd bring you breakfast."

I gasped. "Chocolate éclairs?"

"You betcha. I stopped off at that patisserie we went to yesterday."

"Woohoo! Gimme, gimme." I magicked a cappuccino into existence for Will, and he magicked two plates onto the table. We quietly ate—there'd be time for talk later. I was just happy to have him home. Ted appeared at the door and went straight to Will for a pat. Ah, domestic bliss, at least I was pretty sure that's what this was.

We managed to finish breakfast before Will's phone rang. Of course it did. "Agent Blakesley speaking." He listened and made some grunting noises, the ones you make to prove you're still listening. "Okay, bye." He turned to me. "That guy who died trying to kidnap you was a man by the name of Julien Chevrolet."

"I thought that was an American car?"

"It is, but why does that matter?"

I shrugged. "It doesn't." He gave me a "you've got to be kidding" look. I grinned. "Don't forget that you love me. We're getting married. Remember?" I held my hand out and showed him the ring as proof.

He raised a brow. "Remind me why I thought that was a good idea." I made a huge *O* of horror with my mouth. He laughed. "You know I'm kidding. Still, you drive me crazy sometimes, and not in a good way."

"You'll get used to it."

He shook his head. "Anyway, as I was saying, Julien Chevrolet is from a town called Dol-de-Bretagne. It's not too far from Mont Saint-Michel. He has no living relatives that we can find. Liv hasn't had time to dive too deep, but it looks like his parents died in a car accident three years ago, and his sister drowned last year. Not sure about cousins, but Liv is working on it."

"Oh, wow. Do you think RP killed them all?"

"It's possible. The other reason could be that RP has a rival, and they intermittently kill each other."

"You don't sound convinced."

"I'm not. If there was an organisation the size of RP fighting with them, surely we would've heard about them by now. I'll liaise with our French office. They're only small, but they might be able to give us more information."

"Is there a PIB office in France?" Why was I always the last to know?

"Yes. We have satellite offices dotted all over Europe, and, of course, you know about our New York office."

"Yes, where your esteemed leader comes from."

He choked on air. "Ah, yeah."

"So now what?"

"We need to go to his house and investigate, but they might be expecting that, so James is thinking about what to do next. To be honest, as dangerous as it is, you taking some photos there might give us better clues about who we should be spying on."

My neck muscles tightened. "That sounds like a bad idea. If they're waiting for us to visit, why would we walk into a trap? They want to take us down, and that would give them the perfect opportunity to take two of us out. I'm surprised we survived Mont Saint-Michel."

"They're probably sounding us out. Seeing how strong we are."

"Come on. They already know all that." They weren't fooling me. Maybe they were just playing.

"Maybe they're not quite ready to face us full force. That's my best guess. But we got close to something they're protecting, so they couldn't ignore us. They can't know where you are all the time. I think they have people watching out at the abbey."

"I do agree with that… at least that's what I'm hoping. I still think going to this guy's place is a bad idea." My gut churned, and it wasn't because of our delicious breakfast. If I'd learned anything over the last year, it was to trust that little digestive pouch.

"Yeah, well, it's the next logical step. We can't ignore it. If it were a normal investigation, we'd be all over it. I'm afraid someone will have to go, whether you think it's a good idea or not." Will's phone rang again. He answered it. "Hey, James. Yeah, mate." He listened and nodded. "Okay. I'll be there in five. Bye." He magicked his uniform on. "Work calls. I'll see you at James's at seven tonight."

I sagged down into my chair, hoping one of the work things he had to do wasn't going to that French guy's place. "Bummer." Stuck by myself worrying all day again. Maybe I'd start learning French. That would be a decent distraction.

He stood and kissed the top of my head. "Love you."

"Love you too. Stay safe."

He made a doorway and left. Frustration had me gritting my teeth. Stupid RP. Would this ever end? Gah. Sitting around doing nothing wasn't helping anyone.

Time to think.

What other places had my parents visited when they'd been away on that trip. And where had they been before? Should I have been following their footsteps in order? Plus, we still had to work out what the postcard meant, but that could wait until tonight. I called James. "Hey."

"Hey, Lily. What's up?"

"I was wondering if Mill was home today. I wanted to look at those small books." Hopefully he knew what I was talking about. We kept them locked in a magical safe, and since Angelica wasn't around, the security fell to James. He was the only one who knew where they were—he'd moved them since Angelica had bowed out. She hadn't wanted to give anything away if she was captured and questioned. The universe forbid that happened.

"I'll let her know. I'll be home for lunch, so maybe come visit around one."

"Thanks. I'll be there. Ciao."

"Bye."

I opened my phone and checked out what apps were good for learning French. It was going to be a long morning.

I got to my brother's at 1:00 p.m. on the dot. Millicent answered the door and gave me a hug. "So good to see you. Sorry about yesterday."

"That's okay. You're allowed to have lunch with other people, you know." I laughed.

"Yeah, I know, but I haven't seen you much lately. Work's been crazy since the factory. My parents have been doing over-time with Annabelle."

I stepped through into the hallway, and she shut and locked the reception-room door. "How is my gorgeous little niece?"

"She's good. Down for her lunchtime nap."

I pouted. "Damn. I was looking forward to a cuddle. Maybe she'll wake up before I go."

"You never know your luck. Anyway, come through. James left those things on the dining room table." We were so used to speaking in vague terms that we almost didn't need bubbles of silence. I made one anyway and sat at the table.

I slid one of the diaries in front of me as Millicent sat next to me. "Did James fill you in on my little trip to Mont Saint-Michel with Will?"

"He told me a bit about what happened—mainly about the dead guy you brought in. What else happened?"

As I filled her in, Cinnamon and Bagel scurried in. I bent and picked them up. "Hello, cuties." They squeaked. Bagel climbed my arm and took her position on my shoulder while Cinnamon curled up on my thigh.

Millicent shook her head. "It sounds like you had a crazy trip. I'm glad you're both back in one piece."

"Thanks. So, what do you think about the abbey? Sounds like they were close to discovering something, doesn't it?"

"It does. Is that what you're looking for?" She nodded at the diaries. "More evidence?"

"Yep. There's so much we don't know. The more we dig into RP, the bigger the organisation gets, the bigger their reach." I took a deep breath and released it. "It's frightening." I swallowed and met her gaze. "I'm worried. What if we lose?"

She held my gaze, steel in her eyes. "That's not an option, Lily." Everything was at stake. To lose would mean we all died because I was sure RP wouldn't get away with things if even one of us survived the upcoming confrontation. At this stage, they had everything to lose. Being incarcerated for life was a big incentive not to get caught.

"No, it's not." I grabbed a diary. Where had they been before, and where did they go after Mont Saint-Michel? "Hmm, so, they'd been to another party at a chateau a week before they were at Mont Saint-Michel. Afterwards, it looks like they came straight home." I looked up at Millicent. "That just confirms that the postcard they sent to us was a clue rather than them keeping in touch."

"What postcard?"

Oops. I must've left that out of my recap on what we'd done yesterday. "Here. I found this yesterday when we took photos of their hotel room." I magicked my Nikon to myself, found the picture, and handed the camera to Millicent. "They sent that to us. I think James still has it somewhere as a keepsake."

Millicent read out the cryptic part of the postcard. "Wish we could bring the Saint to us. I'm sure Tilly's brother would feel a real connection to it." She looked at me. "Who's Tilly?"

I shook my head. "I have no idea. I was hoping James knew. With him being older than me, I figure he'd remember more." I looked down at the diary, then back up again. "I guess our next port of call is to this party they went to." I grabbed my phone and looked up the address. "Oh, crap. That might be difficult. It's a private address, and it's a chateau." I showed Millicent my phone.

"That's fancy pants. They probably have mega security too."

"Yes, because everything has to be as difficult as possible." Bagel nuzzled my cheek with the top of her head. I smiled despite my frustration. "You are the sweetest. Thank you." She squeaked. "Well, I think that's the place we start. There's no way I'm going to that guy's place, the one who tried to kidnap me. RP will be waiting."

"Agreed. They'll have no idea you'll aim for that chateau."

"Yep. I tried to talk Will out of it, but he seems to think the PIB have to go to follow up."

"He's right." Millicent installed her poker face. If things weren't so serious, I would've laughed. Far from hiding her feelings, it was a dead giveaway she had feelings… ones she knew I didn't want to know. James, Will, Beren, Imani, any one of them, or even all of them could end up there today or tomorrow.

I pushed that out of my head. I could only deal with so many stressful things at once. "Do you want to flesh this out with me? If we can come up with a plan by tonight, we can run it by James and hopefully get moving on that before one of them gets killed chasing up a lead we don't need." My rhyming game was strong today. Hopefully we could work out a plan that was even stronger.

"I'm in." She smiled.

"Yes! Let's do this."

After an hour and a half, we had a good—at least I thought it was good—plan worked out. Annabelle woke up, and I got to have a cuddle before Millicent gave her a feed. Once that was done, Millicent's phone rang. The shrill ringtone made me jump. Every time someone's phone rang recently, it was bad news. Was it possible to have PTSD—phone traumatic stress disorder?

Millicent handed Annabelle to me and answered the call. "Hey, darling." Her face fell. I let my head fall to my chest. Not more bad news. "Okay, I'll tell her. Thanks for letting us know. Bye." She looked at me with her best poker face. Maybe I should tell her it didn't work anymore. "Well, Lily, you were right. RP were waiting for our agents when they went to Julien Chevrolet's house."

My stomach dropped faster than a person with a faulty parachute. I couldn't find any words to ask who and what.

"Oh, honey, you've gone white. I should've led with the fact that none of our agents went. They sent two agents from the Paris office."

It was as if my heart started beating again. I found enough breath to ask, "What happened?"

"The place was booby-trapped. Shortly after they went in, it exploded. Both agents were killed."

My mouth fell open. "Are they crazy? They've basically declared all-out war on the PIB."

"They already had, Lily. Well, not in that sense, but they know we won't… can't stop until we've arrested them all. But by attacking our French co-workers, they've ensured it's not only the British headquarters that will be dealing with this. And Chad can't slack off now. He'll have the Paris guys on his back."

"Well, that's something. Quick question: if the UK branch is defunded, do the other branches survive?" It was something that constantly niggled at me. With everything that had been going on, all my loved-ones' jobs were threatened. Annabelle made happy gurgling noises. I smiled down at her and gave her a kiss on the forehead.

"No. The main directors make all the decisions regarding funding. It's government-funded. But they have to prove we're earning those funds. They're constantly schmoozing government officials, from what I understand. The directors have old money. I'm sure some of them make political donations from their own pockets."

"What a surprise. I bet those donations find their way back home in the form of government grants." I shook my head. The world worked on a stupid system that was always ripe for abuse. How could anyone doubt the PIB made a positive difference?

"Probably with interest." She rolled her eyes. "In any case, we have an escalating situation, and Chad's called a meeting for four o'clock today. James wants you there, but he said to say as little as possible about your trip. Make sure you frame everything as if you'd been on an actual holiday."

"Understood. There's a mole at headquarters. I don't think it's Chad, but you never know."

"No, you don't." Annabelle scrunched her face and made a straining noise. My eyes widened, and I gently grabbed her around the waist, ready to hand her to her mother. When the little explosions in her nappy started, I thrust her at Millicent and coughed. I was pretty sure my eyes were watering. "Gah, the smell."

Millicent chuckled and took her. "You're such a wuss."

"I know. And that's okay. We can't all be brave nappy-changing heroes." I grinned, then put my hand over my nose and mouth to block out some of the smell.

"You sure you don't want to be a good auntie and help? You can do it by magic, you know."

"Oh, that's right! I forgot. Still, no thanks. It would be like me to get it wrong and end up with a worse mess than I started with. I'll leave this to the expert."

Millicent shook her head. Her magic tingled my scalp, and she whispered something, then Annabelle's outfit changed from a purple onesie to a white one with mice on it. Annabelle smiled. And no wonder. The smell had been bad. I couldn't imagine how it felt to be sitting in it.

As the odour faded away, the outside world nudged into my thoughts. Those poor French agents. Had Will warned them? He must have. If only we hadn't gone digging around looking for evidence. I couldn't help but feel guilty about this too. The bodies were piling up, and the only way to stop it was to destroy RP.

Was that possible? I didn't even know anymore. But bad luck to me because I was still going to try. The course had been set. The only thing to do now was hoist the sail, point the tiller, and hope the next storm wasn't a hurricane. Those were deadly.

Just like RP.

CHAPTER 8

When I buzzed the PIB reception-room door at three fifty-five, Gus answered it. "Hello, Miss Lily."

"Hey, Gus! How come you're answering the door? I thought they'd found a replacement for the last guy." I didn't want to name the last guy—the vampire witch who'd almost killed me. The less I thought about that horrible time, the better.

"They have." My brother stepped into view. "Gus is my assistant, so he's coming to the meeting, too, but I wanted to be here to open the door."

I furrowed my brow. "Why?"

"Just wanted to make sure that Millicent passed on my message."

I stepped out of the room, and Gus shut the door. "Yes, she did. It kind of didn't need saying. Will and I have already talked about it."

"He told me."

I rolled my eyes. "And yet…." Gus looked around the hallway nervously, studiously avoiding looking at James or me. I shook my head. "You're making Gus uncomfortable."

Gus's eyes widened, but he stared at the floor. "Ah, I'm fine. I'd prefer not to get involved, Miss Lily."

James smiled. "Gus, you're a smart man and a loyal assistant." James folded his arms and gave me a "gotcha" look.

"It's okay, Gus. I understand. It's scary when you work for an ogre." I gave James a sarcastic smile, then headed for the conference room. James and Gus soon caught up. Thankfully, no more was said. When we reached the conference room, Gus knocked, then opened the door for me. I smiled. "Thank you, Gus. You're such a gentleman, unlike other people I know." As I stepped into the room, James grunted. Ha! I loved getting on his nerves. Who knew why siblings liked to tussle?

The table had extra chairs around it, and all but three were taken. Actually, they'd magicked an extension onto the table as well. Eight chairs were on either side, plus the two heads had a chair each, or was that the head and the foot. Ew, who'd want to sit at the foot of the table? Feet grossed me out. Why were they so ugly and smelly?

Someone cleared their throat. "I said, *hello*." Oops. Chad glared at me. What a great way to get started. Everyone at the table stared at me. Yikes.

"Oh, hello." Chad frowned, and James jabbed me in the side with his elbow. "Ouch." I gave him a dirty look. He gave me a dirtier one. Oh, right. I looked at Chad again. "Hello, Sir." I smiled as if nothing had happened. He wasn't my boss, for goodness' sake. He really only deserved a hello, but whatever. I didn't want to hold things up. This was going to be boring enough without dragging it out. While James and Gus made their appropriate, non-Lily-inspired hellos, I went around the table and sat in between Will and Imani.

James sat to Chad's left, and Gus sat next to James. Liv was here, as was Beren, but Millicent wasn't. Maybe she was getting things ready for tonight and catching up on some time with Annabelle? So, who were the other eight people at the table?

Chad leaned back in his chair, rested his hands behind his head, and clomped his feet on the table. "Right. Let's get started." Hmm, looked like I wasn't going to find out. James probably knew, and he could fill me in later. And if Ma'am were here to see this…. "Today, we've had an unfortunate event. Two agents from our sister agency in Paris have been murdered by the snake group." He looked at a short, balding man in a PIB suit sitting to his right. "Our deepest sympathies to you and their families."

The man nodded, his poker face in place. I imagined that if he didn't don it, he might cry, although maybe he was a toughened agent who'd dealt with this kind of thing before. Had he hardened himself to these tragedies? Or maybe he was just good at staying strong for his agents. That was one reason I'd make a terrible agent—I'd be bawling my eyes out if any of my co-workers had been killed. Hiding my emotions was my non-talent—I couldn't be worse at it if I tried. "Merci, Agent Williamson the Third. I will pass your message on to my colleagues." What was it about the French accent that made it so enjoyable to listen to? It was like I imagined a cappuccino would sound if it could talk—smooth, full-bodied, almost sensual. Yes, I knew coffee was more Italian than French. I reckoned an espresso would have an Italian accent if it could talk.

Chad looked around the table as he spoke. "The Paris

office is gathering evidence and will notify us when every-thing's been analysed. It was a non-witch explosive device, so we'll be looking at the materials and the way it was constructed. Now, moving on. I believe we have some leads to chase from the rest of the factory workers. In light of what's happened today, we'll be more than careful with our investiga-tions. We're also short on staff, so this is going to take longer than we originally anticipated."

Will raised his hand. Chad gave him a nod. "How long are we talking, Sir?"

"Months."

My eyebrows shot up, taking my eyelids with them. My eyes couldn't be any more open if they tried. Was he kidding? Did he plan on letting RP run around meting out death sentences for the rest of the year?

"Excuse me," said the agent sitting next to the French man in a delicious cappuccino accent. Seemed he was French too. He was maybe in his late thirties. His dark buzzcut hair, wide shoulders, and ramrod-straight posture gave him the air of someone in the military. "We need to act now. The longer this takes, the more time they have to wreak havoc."

"I agree." Imani hadn't bothered to raise her hand. That was my girl.

Murmurs around the table indicated Chad was alone in his opinion of how to handle the situation, but, as usual, he was dancing to the beat of his own drum, one that was being played by the directors, and badly at that. I wanted to snatch their drumsticks and shove them where the sun—

Chad jerked up and slammed his feet on the ground. "The decision's already been made." He pinned Will and Imani with a sly smile. The only thing he needed to look more like a croc-odile was some brownish-green lumpy things on his back and tail. Okay, so he didn't have a tail, but could've fooled me. "You're up first. Tomorrow, I'm sending you on an assignment. One of the first victims, who is still alive thanks to us, has a wife and two children. They live in a small village on the Italian border with France. The rest of the details are in the files in front of you." Chad's magic prickled my scalp, and two folders appeared on the table in front of Will and Imani. If anything happened to them during this investigation, I would kill Chad. Unfortunately, I couldn't tell him that—there were too many witnesses. Guilt stretched its arms behind its head and yawned as it woke up, but I smacked it on the head with the idea that Chad was out to get my friends, not to mention, he'd called us vermin that day he banned me from the PIB. Guilt promptly fell unconscious. Good.

My vindictive nature scared me. Since when had I turned into someone who threatened murder, even if it was in my own head?

Since the people I loved were in the line of fire. That's when.

"Find out what you can."

"Yes, Sir," they answered. Anger simmered in my gut.

Chad narrowed his eyes at me. "Have you got something you'd like to say, Miss Bianchi?"

Oops, I'd thrown a facial expression his way. "Yes, but I won't because, well, I know if Ma'am were here, she wouldn't want me to." So there. Your authority is not the one I answer to.

Liv mashed her lips together, trying not to smile. Beren studiously looked at the table, his face schooled into stillness. The two French agents shared a look that could have meant anything. Chad's reaction, however, was as clear as a newly cleaned window. He spoke through gritted teeth. "Well, she's not here, is she. And she never will be again, so get over your-self." I bit my lip, trying not to laugh. He was such a teenager sometimes.

"Lily," Will hissed out of the side of his mouth. "Please don't."

I sighed. Why I was even here, I didn't know. Oh, that's right, we were supposed to answer some questions. "Look, I don't want to be here as much as you don't want me here. Ask me what you want to know, and once I'm done, I'll be happy to leave." More than happy, actually. Plus, the longer I was here, the more likely I'd make things more difficult for Will.

With a flourish of his arm, Chad conjured a large screen on the wall behind him. The black-and-white picture of a woman's face was on it, larger than life, her eyes closed. "Is this the woman you think was spying on you yesterday at the hotel?"

"Yes. That's her for sure." Even with closed eyes, I could tell it was her.

Chad nodded. "Right, well, about two hours ago, her body was found floating in the sea off Mont Saint-Michel."

I swallowed. RP was leaving nothing behind. No one to question. If they kept that up, there'd be none of them left to arrest. Unless their army was way bigger than we imagined.

"Did she have a snake tattoo?" Will asked.

Chad magicked a yellow manilla folder to himself and opened it. He rifled through it until he came to the piece of paper he wanted. He slid it down the table to Will. We both looked at it. I placed my hand over my mouth.

The dead woman was lying naked on a stainless-steel table, likely at the coroner's office. There was no snake tattoo. She did have a pretty, colourful butterfly tattoo on the inside of her wrist though. Other than that, there were no other markings to speak of. Was she with RP and just didn't have a tattoo yet, or had they paid her to spy on us? "What was her name?" Seeing her helpless, dead, and naked gave her a vulnerability not evident yesterday. She looked more like someone's daughter, like a victim rather than a criminal out to get us.

"We don't know. She didn't have any ID, and the DNA results aren't back yet."

The bald French man spoke up. "We are sending two agents to the island to ask the locals if anyone had seen her recently. Maybe someone can identify her."

Not for the first time today, I missed Angelica and her steadfastness and confidence in the face of an almost-unsolvable mystery. Chad was fumbling along, and if he solved anything, it would only be because someone else actually did it or he'd tripped over it and fallen face first into it. "Is there anything else you'd like to ask?" Looking at a dead body, even if it was just a photo, was enough to take away the joy of needling Chad.

"The man who attacked you, have you ever seen him before?"

"No."

"Did he say why he was there?"

I gave him a "you've got to be kidding me" look. Was he there for a late-night supper or a drink at the bar? I didn't think so. "He was trying to kidnap me. That's it. He didn't say much else."

"So, it wasn't an accidental thing. You sure he wasn't there to rob the place, and you bumbled into him at the wrong moment?"

Oh, for goodness' sake. *Deep breaths, Lily. Deep breaths.* I shrugged. "Maybe? Maybe he saw me and forgot everything else and just had to have me? It's not the first time that's happened, so who can say?"

Liv's mouth made a small *O*, and her eyes shone with what might be excitement. She must be waiting for the fireworks sure to come. Chad was a few stubbies short of a six-pack, though. Maybe he'd disappoint us.

"Ah, right, Miss Bianchi. If you say so." Mmhmm, so disappointing, yet so predictable.

I smiled. "Yep, I do." *It's not my fault you asked a stupid question.* "If that's all, am I free to go?"

Chad stared at the desk for a moment, likely trying to activate some brain cells, but he must have failed. "Ah, yes. You can go."

I stood. "Thank you." I placed my hand on Will's shoulder and squeezed. Then I walked around the table and found a spot big enough for me and my doorway. I made my doorway and left. Will would fill me in on everything else I needed to know later. There was no use suffering and dragging everyone else with me. Life was too short. Who knew, I might only have a few weeks left, and I wanted to spend as little of it as possible in Chad's presence.

As I unlocked Angelica's reception-room door and went into the hallway, I considered the unidentified girl. Was she a criminal or another victim in this? Who was she, and where was she from? Was she even worth thinking about? Priority wise, she was low on the list. Getting into that chateau was likely to be way more informative.

Besides, Chad had the French agents on it. I mentally crossed it off my list. Oh well, that only left another two hundred and fifty-seven items—at least that's what it felt like.

I locked the door and bent to pat Abby and Ted. "Hey, cuties. It's so nice to have a welcome party come to greet me."

I made my way into the living room and magicked the fire on. It was time to prepare for tonight, go over the plan Millicent and I had come up with and look for any holes, because if we got this wrong, RP would make sure we paid the price.

And what a hefty price it would be.

CHAPTER 9

J ust after 7:00 p.m. and I found myself sitting at another table between Will and Liv. Beren sat at one end of the table and James at the other. Millicent and Imani sat opposite Will and me. The whole gang was here… well, everyone except for Angelica. I looked around the table and made a bubble of silence. "Has anyone heard from Angelica?" Everyone shook their heads, and I sighed. "I hope she's okay."

Will grabbed my hand and gently squeezed it. "She can take care of herself. Don't worry."

"I know, but I still do. And, crazy as it sounds, I miss her."

Millicent cocked her head to one side, her face sympathetic. "Me too. She's a hard taskmaster, but she's the best boss I've ever had. She asks a lot of us, but she asks even more of herself."

James nodded. "She does. Anyway, we need to focus on what we're doing. I guarantee that whatever she's doing, she's looking out for us at the same time. We'll hear from her if she thinks we need to. Now, I want to start with you." He turned a stern gaze on me.

I swallowed. "Um… what did I do?" It could've been for today's effort at the meeting, but then again, I might have done something else I wasn't aware of. I was special like that.

"Stop stirring up the hornet's nest. Why do you have to goad Chad every time you see him?"

I shrugged. "It's impossible not to. I try. I really do, but he's just so stupid and arrogant. And every time I see him there, I know it's because they pushed Angelica out for no good reason. In doing that, they've put all of you in danger. He's incompetent, and that's the nicest thing I have to say about him." As much as I was getting a small lecture, no one disagreed with my assessment.

James shook his head. "It's easier to beat your enemies if they don't see you coming. You're running at him, screaming and waving a red rag. Try subtlety, Lily. You might be surprised."

I laughed. "Yes, James, because my ability to be subtle is almost as good as my poker face."

Will chuckled. "She has you there, mate. I think we just need to keep Lily as far away from headquarters as possible, as often as possible."

I smiled at Will. "I'd like that. Thanks." I raised my brow at James. "See, Will gets me."

James stared at the ceiling and shook his head. When he recovered his patience, he gave me one final look, then turned his attention to Millicent. "You said you and Lily have come up with a plan?"

She smiled. "We have, indeed."

I sat up straight and raised my hand. "James, I have to ask you something." If I didn't ask now, I'd forget again. My brain was like a dog in a ball shop. No sooner had it seen one ball and picked it up, than another appeared that looked bouncier, chewier. It didn't hold onto any ball too long before it was dropped, drool-laden and forgotten on the floor.

He stared at me. "Okay, ask."

"That postcard Mum sent. Did Will show you the picture?"

"No. I vaguely remember it—I have it with some of their stuff—but I haven't looked at it for a long time."

Will looked at James. "Here's a refresher." He pulled his phone out, brought the photo up, and slid the phone to James.

James read it out so everyone could hear. "Well, that's a riddle," said Imani.

I nodded. "Yep. I'm sure it's a clue; otherwise, why would my magic show it to me? Mum was covering all her bases for the future, or maybe she thought things would come to a head earlier, and the clue would be needed before she and Dad disappeared." I looked at James. "So, who's Tilly?"

His forehead wrinkled as he thought. He drummed his fingers on the table; then his forehead smoothed over. "Our next-door neighbours, the Browns, had two guinea pigs. One was called Tilly; the other one was Gabriel. We used to feed them when the Browns went away."

"So," said Millicent, "that's the name we need to focus on. What has Gabriel got to do with the saint? And which saint are we talking about?"

Beren shook his head. "There are so many. Unless we took it in context of where they were—Mont Saint-Michel. The two must be linked somehow."

James magicked a large screen onto the wall behind him. Unlike this afternoon, however, there would be no dead bodies on there. "Will, do you want to link your phone pics to it?"

Will gave a nod, and his magic prickled my scalp. The first photo I'd taken at the hotel appeared on the screen. James gasped. I blinked tears away. Mum was incredibly beautiful and Dad so handsome. Both young and vibrant. Too young to die and leave two children alone in the world. Damned RP. *Your time is coming.*

As each photo came up, Will explained to everyone what they were. When it was over, James cleared his throat. "Two scenes in one photo, Lily. That's never happened before, has it?"

"No. Will thinks it's because of the river of power being close to the surface there. I have no idea if they're connected incidents."

Beren looked at me. "I think, based on the past behaviour of your talent, that they are related, although what long-dead monks have to do with what's going on today, I couldn't tell you."

Imani folded her hands together in front of her on the table and leaned on her forearms. "Maybe RP have a connection to the monks? Or maybe this has been going on way longer than we've been alive?"

I thought of the photo where my parents were obviously looking for something to take away with them. "Maybe the monks hid something at the abbey that everyone wants?"

"It's possible," said Will. "Or maybe something is hidden there that RP already owns and doesn't want anyone else to have?"

Hmm…. "That makes sense. Otherwise, why try and stop my parents? I'm pretty sure that's what the guy was doing with my father in a headlock at the abbey. Unless they managed to take whatever it was they were after?"

James shook his head. "I don't think so. There's no record

of them having handed anything in at headquarters that I know of." He looked at Liv. "Can you check that tomorrow? Go over all my mother's assignments for that year. Find out everything you can. If anyone figures out you're researching her and asks, just tell them you're doing me a favour because I want to know more about my parents."

"Okay. Consider it done." Liv smiled.

"Thanks. Once Liv does that, whether or not she finds anything, I think we need to look closer at the abbey and what might be there. RP obviously doesn't want us snooping around." Snooping was such a cute word. I felt like I was in an episode of *Scooby-Doo*, but instead of a trusty canine, we had rats, and we got around in a Range Rover instead of the blue-and-green Mystery Machine. Okay, so that was a weird visual. Maybe it was nothing like being in *Scooby-Doo* at all. "Which brings me to the plan Lily and Millicent have come up with."

Millicent gave James a smile. "Thanks. Okay, so Lily and I brainstormed this afternoon. It was Lily's idea to look at events in her mother's diary just prior and just after they were at Mont Saint-Michel. A week before, they'd been at an event or party held at a chateau. The address is about an hour and forty-five minutes' drive northeast of Mont Saint-Michel." She pressed her lips together. "Hang on. We only did half our homework." Her magic tingled my scalp, and a laptop appeared in front of her. She opened it and typed. After a minute, she looked up from the screen, excitement shining from her eyes. "Well, isn't that interesting." Gah, she was going for suspense. Just what I needed. It was like those stupid ad breaks in reality shows when there was going to be a big reveal.

I gave her a mock-angry look. "Get on with it! Haven't I suffered enough to get to this point?"

She chuckled. "Sorry, just having some fun with it." She winked. "The owner of the chateau is none other than a Gabriel Toussaint. He has links to a far-right political party in France, and he has a lot of money, according to the file we have on him." She looked at me. "I bet he's the Gabriel she cryptically referred to in her postcard. His last name, Toussaint, has a saint in it as well. Maybe your mother was researching him? It doesn't look like anything has been added to this file for quite a few years." She cast another spell, and his picture appeared on the screen that James put up.

Well, that was even more interesting. "It's him, the man my parents had in their room." And now it all made sense.

"The same man your mother pulled a gun on," said Will.

Imani sat back. "This plot is thicker than my mother's barley soup."

Millicent looked back at her screen and typed something else. After a minute, she looked up. "Seems he has properties all over Europe, including a three-bedroom apartment in Paris. If we're lucky, he won't be anywhere near the chateau for a while. He might use it as a weekender. We want to get in there as quickly as possible so Lily can take photos and move this investigation along."

James looked at Will. "You and Imani are off to France tomorrow. While you're there, make some noise, be obvious." I wanted to jump up and tell James he was crazy—I didn't want them in any more danger than what they already were, but their course was set, thanks to Chad. I frowned but kept my mouth closed for a change. "Hopefully, RP will be watching you and ignoring the fact that we might be somewhere else too. Beren and I can stake out Gabriel's apartment, get a read on whether he's there at the moment." He directed his gaze back to Millicent. "Does he own a company or work?"

She looked at her screen and scrolled. "Yes. And why am I not surprised. It's Arsenal Toussaint. They have a government contract and supply the armed forces. They're likely to have private contracts too. Have we got a guy we can trust who can hack into their systems? Chances are, he has an electronic diary, or his secretary manages one for him. I'd prefer that to ringing them with a story. It might raise suspicions, especially with what happened in Manchester."

I shuddered. That had not been the best day. Imani and I had been ridiculously fortunate to not get killed. If what that note I received ages ago said was right, part of RP wanted me alive, and it was probably due to them that I hadn't died. I knew Dana wanted me D.E.A.D. But she didn't always get what she wanted, and she'd never get that particular wish if I had anything to do with it.

Beren nodded. "Good thinking, Mill."

She smiled. "Thanks. In any case, we'll get that information, and in the meantime, you can pay his apartment an early morning visit, see what happens."

Beren gave her a thumbs up, and James nodded. "And what was your plan regarding the chateau?"

Millicent closed her laptop. "We'll need Will on security detail—taking out cameras, alarms, etcetera. It's also essential that we find out if any witches work there, or even if they have staff there when Gabriel isn't at home. With a bit of luck, we'll have the house all to ourselves. Once we know that, we can move ahead. If they do have staff, we'll have to get in there at night, when everyone's left, which also won't be too hard. If there's one or two people living on-site, they probably live in a separate cottage. We've snuck into harder places. Lily can get in and take the photos and get out again. While she's there, Will and Imani, you two can look for any obvious evidence of a link with Mont Saint-Michel or Lily's parents. It's a long shot—he has so many places, who knows where he keeps his most secret papers—but at least we'll have Lily's photos of that party."

Imani nodded. "It is what it is. If we can't work much out from that, we can always go back to Mont Saint-Michel. That sounds like a real hotspot."

Will shook his head. "Unless they've already moved what we were looking for."

James looked at Will. "They might be keeping whatever it is there because they can harness the stronger magic as a barrier. Moving it could be risky for them—we might not be the only people looking for whatever it is."

"The girl with the butterfly tattoo." Now *that* would be a whole other movie. I was glad it wasn't the tough chick with the dragon tattoo I'd come across. I dare say she wouldn't have run.

"Exactly, Lily," said James.

"Hmm." Will folded his arms. "I know who we can trust with the hacking."

James leaned forward. "Spill."

Will's smile was smug. "Agent… ahem, ex-agent Cardinal. He was one of our best. He's working internet security at another government agency, but his heart is still with the PIB. As soon as Ma'am's back, she'll offer him his old job, and he knows it." Clever man. Cardinal and I had never been best friends, but he'd always been helpful, was good at his job, and he was definitely on our side.

As much as I was okay with that, I didn't know if I wanted him to be a party to my secret talent. "We're not bringing him into this group, though, are we?"

James and Will shared a quick look. James moved his gaze

to me. "No. We can swear him to secrecy without having to make him swear on the book. We'll only tell him about this one person we're investigating. He won't even ask about the how or why."

Some of the tension in my shoulders faded. "Thanks."

James looked around the table. "Right, so we all have our jobs. Does anyone have any questions?"

I didn't actually have a job for tomorrow, so I put up my hand. "Um, is there anything I can do tomorrow to help?"

"Maybe brush up on some spells?" James suggested. "We have no idea what we're going to come up against in the next few weeks, and knowledge is power. Even if you find yourself fighting someone who has a return to sender up, hammer them enough with specific spells, and they might drop it, well, they will if you're stronger—all you have to do is outlast them. Find something that won't hurt you if it bounces back. Keep your fitness up, too, Lily." He looked at Will. "Teach her some pressure points."

"Okay. I'll go over them with her tonight."

James gave a nod. "Will, you guys check in with me tomorrow afternoon. We'll meet again as soon as we have more information on Toussaint's movements. Once we have Cardinal on board, we'll get him to delve into the bank accounts too. Any link we can find to RP and Dana's father is what we're after. Okay, folks. We're done."

Imani and I stood, and I faced her, the scritch of uneasiness in my gut like cockroach claws against skin. "Good luck tomorrow. Please be careful. I mean, I know you always are, but they'll be waiting. Look what happened to those French agents."

"We'll be extra careful, love. I promise. Will and I know

RP well—those other agents didn't go in there fully informed. We'll come home tomorrow night alive and well."

I wasn't a hugger, but I gave her one anyway. "You'd better." I said no more. She knew what I'd lost in my life. Going on about it wasn't going to make my point any clearer.

Will put his hand on my shoulder. "Come on, Lily. Let's go. I have to teach you about pressure points."

I turned and smiled. "*Pressure points*, hey? Is that what you're calling it these days?"

Beren laughed. "The best pressure points are where the sun doesn't reach… the more protected parts of the anatomy."

Liv smacked him. "Stop it!"

Will laughed. "Beren's actually right, and the sooner we get home, the sooner I can show you."

Well, I wasn't turning down that invitation. I hurriedly said goodbye to everyone, made my doorway, and left. It was time to learn about pressure points. Who knew? Maybe one day it would actually save my life, and in the meantime, I had Will all to myself. I'd call that a win any day of the week, even the day before he walked into danger.

I pushed that out of my head as I unlocked the reception-room door and Will arrived. Let the pressure-point lesson begin.

CHAPTER 10

Darkness claimed the day. It was just after six, but my time of looking out the window at the squirrels was well and truly over. Will and Imani had met with the ex-captive's wife with no dramas, which seemed like a miracle. I hadn't heard from anyone after the mid-afternoon update and had no idea what was going on with James's stake-out. It was time to continue the distraction with television. The news was on, and after that, I was going to watch *Escape to the Chateau*. Man, I loved that show.

Abby was ensconced on my lap, strangely enough, watching TV, too, as in paying attention. I supposed she could understand human speak, so why not? Out of nowhere, she growled, then stood and hissed at the television. "What's wrong, pussy cat?"

The screen blacked out for a second. When it came back on, my mouth dropped open. Abby yowled, leapt down, and ran to the TV. She sprung up and smacked it with her paw… right in the middle of Piranha's face, which took up most of the screen. The evil woman smiled. "Hello, Lily. Welcome to my evening news report, a special one, just for you."

I jumped to my feet. I opened my portal to the river of magic and donned a return to sender.

She laughed. "Oh, you're so funny. Surprised you, did I?" Her face twisted into hatred so powerful, I could feel the toxic waves. "Your death day is coming, you pathetic excuse for a witch. I have a message for you to convey to that man of mine."

I managed to get my crap together and wrestle my breathing under control. My heart rate was another matter. But as long as Piranha couldn't see how scared I was, it was all good. "You mean Will?"

"No, I mean Santa Claus. Idiot."

"Just making sure because, as you know, he hates you almost as much as I do. He's not anything but your ex. I guess you hadn't heard." I grinned and held up my engagement ring for her to eyeball. I waved it around and admired it, then gestured to it with my other hand as if I were a model on a game show.

Her eyes widened slightly before she reined herself in and became her hateful self once more. "Well, this is a development. I'll enjoy watching you suffer when I kill him. Tit for tat, as they say. But I'm getting off track. Make sure you let everyone at my favourite organisation know what I'm about to show you." The camera panned back, revealing Piranha standing in a nondescript room, which had a small Jesus on a cross hanging on the wall behind her. A woman sat at a red 1960s Formica table. "This is what happens to the families of everyone Will and his associates interview from now on." She lifted her arms and called down lightning, striking the woman.

I didn't want her to see how it affected me, but my hand

slammed over my mouth, and tears scorched my eyes. She was the most horrible witch. And if you replaced the w with a b, you'd get my drift. A gale of fury spun within me. "The only one of us who's going to die next time we meet is you." I bared my teeth in a corrupted smile that promised so much. "When I'm done with you, people won't call Karma down on their enemies; they'll be invoking my name." I grabbed the remote control, and before she could say anything else, I turned the TV off with shaking hands, then unplugged it, walked out, and shut the door.

I leaned against the wall and magicked my phone to myself. While dialling Will, I slid down the wall and sat on the floor. Abby sat next to me and pressed against my side. How could anyone do what she just did? She was truly psychopathic and the worst type of person that could ever exist.

Will's phone rang and rang. *Please don't go to voicemail.* Just as I expected it to click over, he answered. "Hey, Lily."

"Hey." My voice cracked. Gah. Damn my inability to push my emotions out of the way.

The concern in his voice came through loud and clear. "What's wrong? Are you okay?"

It was an effort not to cry. "Um, yes but no."

"Hang on. I'll be there in a minute." The true champion he was, in less than a minute, he was unlocking the reception-room door. When he saw me on the floor, he rushed over and knelt in front of me. "What happened?" He reached out and checked me over.

"I'm okay, but something happened." I told him about the interruption to the usual programming. When I finished, he stared at me blankly for a moment—likely taking it all in— then the thunderclouds moved in.

He sprung to his feet, opened the TV room door, and

strode in. His magic tingled my scalp. I had no idea what he was doing—maybe making sure it was safe?—and I was too upset to care. The worst was over for now, at least for me—she'd made her point. And there was nothing we could do. It would be impossible to protect every family member and friend of the people we'd saved.

His voice drifted out to the hallway. "Hey, it's me…. Yeah. Can you get over here now? There's an emergency. No, she's okay. Bye." He came out into the hallway and crouched in front of me. "Let's move this into the family room. It's cold out here, and I know how much you hate that." He gave me a gentle smile and held out his hand. I took it and stood.

As we made our way to the living room, there was a knock on the reception-room door. "I called your brother." Will saw me to a Chesterfield and went to answer the door. Abby and Ted had followed us in. Abby hopped into my lap, and Ted lay at my feet. I was so lucky to have them. I ran my hand over Abby's soft fur. I let her warmth comfort me.

Will had lowered his voice to talk to James in the hallway. It was a couple of minutes before they came in. Will must've taken that time to explain the situation. James's concerned expression when he came in confirmed it. He hurried over to me. "Are you okay?" He sat on the low coffee table in front of me.

I gave him a wan smile. "Yes, I'm fine. It's just a shock, that's all. That poor woman." I shook my head. "How did that witch break into our television? I know she wasn't actually in there, but you get what I'm saying. How could she see me? Are we safe here?"

James grabbed my hand in both of his. "If she could get in here, I'm sure she would've attacked you. Anyone with the know-how can hack into a smart TV and see the person on the other side. I imagine she's done it all with a spell. Not easy, but doable. You're safe here, Lily. I promise." He turned his head to look at Will, who stood next to the lounge. "If you guys are worried, you can come stay with Mill and me."

I shook my head emphatically. "No! I'm not going to bring more danger to Annabelle. No way. No how. As you said, we'll be fine here. She just took me off guard. That's all." Stupid Piranha was not going to intimidate me. We were obviously close, or she wouldn't have done something like that. Maybe she was scared too? And so she should be. I sat up straighter and lifted my chin. "I'm totally fine. Nothing a cappuccino and double-chocolate muffin won't fix. In fact, I'll order delivery from Witcheroo. Do you guys want anything?"

James looked at his watch. "Ah, no. Millicent's expecting me home for dinner soon." He stared into my eyes. "Are you sure you're okay?"

"Positive. She's not going to get the better of me now. If she wasn't just a little bit worried, she wouldn't have done that. We're so close. I know we are."

He squeezed my hand, then released it and stood. He turned to Will. "I'll call off the interviews for tomorrow. We won't give up on them, but we need to devise a different strategy."

Will placed his hands on his hips. "Agreed. Do you want to meet at your place, or do we involve Chad?"

"My place at eight. We have a lot to discuss. Chad, despite wanting to micromanage everything, doesn't need to know all this. He has his hands full with the French guys, to be honest, and he'll soon find out RP's murdered the woman you questioned today. That's enough of a warning. I'll let him call me about it. I need to fill everyone in on what B and I found out today, and hopefully, Cardinal's had a chance to get started as well."

"Okay. Lily and I will be there tomorrow at eight. See you then."

I gave James a wave as he made his doorway in the empty space between the couches and the door. And then he was gone.

Will sat next to me and slid an arm around me. We sat like that for a while before he said, "Are you sure you're okay?"

"Definitely. What about you?" He hadn't seen what I'd seen, but he'd met that woman, and I'd bet that even though he knew it wasn't his fault, he'd feel somehow responsible because he didn't see it coming and couldn't stop it.

"It is what it is. We have to put it behind us and focus on what's to come, but never for a moment will I forget. I'm keeping note of everything she owes—every injury, every lie, every death. Her reckoning is coming." He sat up straighter and turned to me. "Now, how about we order that food?"

❦

Here we were again, sitting around James's dining table, in the same seats as last time. I sipped my cappuccino—Millicent had decided to make it a breakfast meeting, which I was totally on board with. A selection of pastries sat in the middle of the table, and she'd magicked up bacon, eggs, cooked tomato, mushrooms, and toast for anyone who wanted them.

Once we'd finished the hot food, we magicked the plates clean and away, and we were left with the pastries and James's rundown of where we were at. "Okay, so yesterday was both a success and a failure. Beren and I saw Toussaint leaving for work at eight thirty, but we left before he returned. Whether he returned or not, we don't know, but we'll be visiting again tomorrow morning, and we plan to stay until late. In the meantime, Cardinal will keep trying to access what we need. He's coming in soon to let us know what he's doing." James had a sip of coffee. "Based on what he finds, we're still a few days to at least a week away from pulling the trigger on visiting his country house. Next up, our favourite ex-agent's stunt yesterday."

Imani gave me a sympathetic look. "When I get my hands on her…."

Will's calm voice had a distinctly heavy undertone. "I'm afraid you'll have to get in line, and this is a case where I won't be the gentleman and say ladies first."

I barked a short laugh. "Ha! I think it's whoever gets to her first won't be able to contain themselves. I'm not passing up my chance of cleaning her off the face of the earth, and I wouldn't begrudge anyone else the honour. As long as she's vaporised, I don't care who does it. I at least want to watch though."

Beren's eyes widened slightly. "Ah, Lily, since when did you become so bloodthirsty?"

"Since Piranha came into my life. She needs to die, and I'm willing to do whatever it takes to make that happen." I didn't have to remind everyone what she'd done in the past, let alone yesterday. How many people had she killed in her life? How many crimes had she committed? How many more people would she kill if we didn't stop her?

James cleared his throat. "We're getting off track. Back to matters at hand. Because of Dana's threat, we've postponed all of today's scheduled interviews."

Imani leaned forward, determination on her face. "Surely we need to continue those as soon as possible. We can't let her intimidate us and compromise our investigation. That's not how we operate."

James put his hand up in a placating gesture. "You're right —it's not. In light of that, our option to back off for good is out. That leaves us with a few other options. One: interview people and leave a trail of death behind us. Two: gather those we want to interview and keep them in a protected place until this whole thing is over. Three: interview them and keep agents there for protection. One is obviously not an option either, and out of the last two choices, I don't think three will be good enough. So that leaves us with option two."

Millicent gave an almost imperceptible head shake. "That would cost a fortune. Chad will never go for that. The scale of that is beyond what we're capable of. There are so many people."

"What if we choose a handful of people to interview and keep them somewhere secret and safe. We could manage that. Even if it's in the cells at headquarters."

I gave my brother an incredulous look. "That's hardly fair. You can't lock them up as if they're the criminals. And what about the RP ring-ins? They could get to them there. It's not safe."

Imani looked at me. "RP whats?"

I smiled. "Double agents, ones who are pretending to work for the PIB but are working for RP."

"Ah. You and your Aussie speak." She shook her head.

I turned back to James. "Just how important are these interviews? Will they help us find out what happened to Mum and Dad? Will they help us find answers we can't find ourselves? Maybe we should wait until I've visited the chateau. Maybe there's better ways to gather the evidence. I'd say some of the victims will provide more thorough information than others because they've been caught up in it longer. And if I can get some specific clues, we can at least target where to go more specifically, put fewer people at risk."

"Good point," said Beren.

James took a deep breath. "You've given me a lot to think about, Lily. I'm not sure how long we can hold Chad off for. You know what he's like—a bull in a china shop. If he thinks they should all be questioned, then, goddammit, he's going to question them, whether he's sentencing them to death or not."

Liv frowned. "That won't leave any witnesses for the trials."

"No, it won't." James rubbed his forehead. "In any case, I'll see what I can do in holding him off for at least the rest of this week. I might have to go and visit our French counterparts. I'm sure Chad's handling of things and lack of passing on information hasn't made him their favourite person. We can get them to help us and back us up in meetings. I don't know if it will help, but we can try."

The reception-room doorbell rang, and Will stood. "That must be Cardinal. I'll let him in."

He returned shortly with the redhead. Cardinal wore street clothes. He didn't look so serious or aloof out of uniform. He just looked like a regular young man. He gave a quick wave. "Hi, all. Great to see you again."

"Likewise." Beren stood. Cardinal came up to him, and they shook hands.

James smiled. "Thanks for coming, mate. I appreciate it."

Cardinal gave a small smile. "Happy to help." Beren gestured to the empty seat to his right, and Cardinal sat. "Thanks." He looked at my brother. "So, what do you want to know?"

"Whatever you can tell us. Have you managed to access any of their systems? Is there even a diary?"

"I was working on it last night, but I'm not quite there yet. They've got a couple of magical alarm systems on there. Once I work out how to disable those, I can tell you what you want to know. Do you want me to download anything else other than his diary?"

"If you can get access to bank records and employment records, it would help enormously. And emails. You never know what you can find in those."

"Okay. Consider it done. I'm off to work this morning, but I'll be home about six, and I'll get back to it then. I'll text you when I know something."

James nodded. "Hugely appreciated. So, how's the new gig going?"

Cardinal shrugged. "It's a job—I don't love it or hate it, but I do want back into the bureau ASAP. What's going on with Ma'am these days? Any news?"

James shook his head. "None that I can pass on at this stage, but she's doing all she can to get back there. I'll be sure to let you know when things have improved."

"I appreciate it. Thanks." He leaned back in his chair. "So, is that everything?"

James stood. "It is. Thanks for coming in."

Cardinal stood, walked around to James, and shook his hand. "I'll be in touch tomorrow."

"Excellent." James sat back down as Cardinal made his doorway and left. "Right, well, that about wraps up things for today. There's not much else w—" His phone rang. He looked at the screen. "I have to take this. Sorry." He put it to his ear. "Hello, Agent Bianchi speaking." As he listened, his jaw clenched, the muscles bulging. His firm voice held a note of anger. "Of course. Thanks for the information, Agent Roche…. Yes…. Bye." He hung up, placed his phone on the table, and stared at it for a moment.

Millicent's forehead wrinkled. "What's up?"

His mouth pressed together in a thin line. "Chad's up. That's what. He's just called the Paris office and told them we won't be needing their help. He's cutting them out of the loop."

Will growled. "That imbecile. That's criminal negligence. He knows we don't have the resources to wrap this up quickly."

I had to look on the bright side. "At least the French agents won't be asked to condemn their countrymen and women to death."

Beren grunted. "Yeah, that honour goes to us."

Millicent frowned. "What are you going to do? Can you just avoid Chad's calls and don't go into the office? Maybe we should all stay away? You can't get in trouble for not following orders if he can't give them to you."

"Well, he hasn't told me they're not in the loop, and I'm not going to cut them out. We need their help. The crime may have been discovered in the UK, but the victims are from France. We'll start a diplomatic nightmare if we try and keep them in the dark. They'll be forced to step in and halt our investigation."

Imani shook her head. "That fool is doing this on purpose. What's his endgame?"

Great. Something else to worry about. "None of it makes sense. On the one hand, he'll get you to question people who will get killed, but on the other, he doesn't want help doing it faster. He's helping and hindering the investigation at the same time."

Will placed both hands palm down on the table. "It doesn't matter what his endgame is. Let's not get distracted. What he's doing is about more than this specific investigation, and we don't have the time to deal with that right now. We need to plan our next move before this whole thing gets away from us."

James sighed. "Agreed. At this stage, we'll lay low until Cardinal gets back to us." He looked at Beren. "I think another stakeout today would be good, and I'll set up a private meeting with Agent Roche. We'll probably meet offsite, away from prying eyes." He looked at me. "Be ready to go to the chateau from tomorrow onwards, and stay away from the TV."

Crap. Could he narrow my world even further? Gah! I shouldn't blame him. It was Piranha's fault. James was just trying to keep me safe, but being stuck inside for the next however many days it took to get clearance to go to the chateau without TV was going to suck. "Can I get online for anything?"

He shook his head. "No. I'm sorry, Lily, but—"

"Yeah, yeah, I know." I just wanted this stupid thing to end. What a nightmare.

Will grabbed my hand and rubbed his thumb over the pad of my palm. "Not much longer. Once this is done, you'll be free."

Yeah, free or dead. But I wasn't going to say that. There was enough stress in the room, and unless I wanted to bug someone, I wasn't into escalation. So I nodded and smiled.

It was going to be a long wait.

But I could handle it.

I didn't have a choice.

CHAPTER 11

D ay two of no TV. I'd read a book, done Pilates, practiced walking on my hands, looked up some spells, and yet, I'd been bored enough to rope Abby into helping me pass the time. She'd been reluctant to comply with my request, but in the end, she'd caved when I'd promised her freshly cooked fish for dinner. Which was why I was sitting in front of the fire with a packet of salt-and-vinegar chips… okay crisps, with Abby on my lap and a squirrel on the chair arm.

"Would you like another one?" I held out another chip. The squirrel flicked its tail and took the chip. I looked down at Abby. "Thanks for being the go-between. You're the best." She closed her eyes in a kitty smile. If only I could speak animal. I was sooooo close to having a conversation with a squirrel. I wanted to squee, but I kept it contained because I didn't want to scare the little cutie. It finished the chip and looked at me, then reached towards me. "Awwwwww. You couldn't get any cuter. Here you go." I handed her, him, it—I had no idea—another chip. And I didn't care how long I'd lived in the UK; I wasn't calling chips crisps.

I ate another chip, then spoke to the squirrel again. "Next time you want some chips, feel free to bring some friends. The more the merrier." It held its paw out again. I handed it a chip. "Maybe I could set up a bed in here for you. Do you like it in here? I'm sure Angelica wouldn't mind." I frowned. "It's not like she's here anymore anyway." Gah, now I was sad. Things had changed so much since I'd gotten to London all that time ago. I chuckled when I thought back to our first meeting. She'd come across as a totally crazy person, but then she'd told me about James, and my whole world changed—for better and for worse.

I felt a tap on my arm. Oops, seemed I'd zoned out on my guest. How rude of me. "Sorry. Here." I gave it another chip.

Footsteps sounded from behind me. I turned, and the squirrel froze. We both stared at Will. He stopped and eyeballed us. He pointed at me, then the squirrel. "Um, what the hell have you got going on here? How did you get a squirrel to join you for afternoon tea?"

"Abby is a wonderful event coordinator. We really should pay her more."

"So, is that what you've done all day? Picnic with a squirrel?"

"And what if it is? It's not like I can watch TV. I'm making my own reality TV—except it's not being filmed. It's purely for my own enjoyment."

He put his hands up in a placating gesture. "No judgement from me."

"If you really want to know, I can also walk on my hands,

but my arms are sore because it took me a couple of hours of practice."

He quietly walked around my chair, careful not to startle my new friend, and sat in the chair next to me. "It's good to see that you're not entirely wasting your time."

I smiled. "Thanks. So, how was your day?" I gazed at the window. "It's not dark. What are you doing home?"

"I have news."

My heart beat harder, the thud reverberating through my chest. "And?"

"The chateau is a go."

"When?"

"Tonight."

"Wow, give a girl some notice. I haven't had a chance to get my hair done. And whatever will I wear?"

"Ha ha, very funny. Ponytail and black. There, done."

"Don't ever give up your day job to become a stylist."

He pouted. "You're so mean, crushing my dreams like that."

I turned to the squirrel. "What do you think? Am I mean?" It chittered. I blinked and turned to Will. "Was that a coincidence, or did Grayson really speak to me?"

"Grayson?"

"It's better than calling him or her it. I have no idea what gender it is."

"I can't believe I'm having this conversation." He put his palm to his forehead. "Seriously."

I grinned. "Are you saying it's crazy that all your dreams are coming true?" I waggled my eyebrows.

He looked at Abby. "Help me out here. You started this." She meowed and gave him an irritated look.

"Tell me what she said. Come on."

He rolled his eyes. "She denied starting anything." He looked at her. "If you hadn't pandered to Lily, the squirrel wouldn't be here, and I wouldn't be having this ridiculous conversation." He sighed dramatically, and Abby flicked her nose into the air and turned her back on him.

I laughed. "I don't need to read minds to know she just told you to you-know-what."

He laughed. "Yep." His joviality disappeared. "Are you prepared for tonight?"

"There's not much I need to do other than grab my camera and go. I know what we're looking for."

"Okay. I know I don't need to say it, but I will—don't forget your return to sender, and if anything happens, make your doorway and come straight back here." I met his serious gaze. How could I promise to abandon him and Imani if things went pear-shaped? "Lily...." His gravelly tone had that warning I'd heard a million times before... from Angelica and my brother.

"I don't want to just leave you if something happens. You might need my help."

"Please, please, please, just promise."

A deluge of sadness drowned my previous squirrel-induced good mood. "Why can't you ask me to promise something else? It goes against who I am to ditch my people in times of need. How would you like it if I asked you to do the same thing?"

"It's different. I'm an agent. It's my job to protect you and everyone else. I've trained years for this, Lily. Why do you have to make it so hard? I hate putting you in harm's way in the first place."

"This is my battle, Will. RP did need taking down, obviously, but we wouldn't be here if it weren't for my parents going missing. I've been on this journey since I got here. I've placed myself in this, and, in fact, I'm putting you in danger." I folded my arms and my forehead tightened as I gave him my best concerned angry-person glare.

"Please." It came out as a desperate whisper.

A person was only as good as their word, or so the saying went. I was about to become the biggest opposite of good there ever was. "Okay. I promise." ...*to always love you*. Okay, so if I finished the sentence in my head, was it really a lie? I was at least telling myself the truth. *Hmm, semantics, Lily.* If it was a battle I thought he and Imani could handle, I'd be out of there faster than a racehorse out of the gate, but if not....

"Thank you." The way he gazed at me with those gorgeous grey eyes, trusting me.... I sucked.

Time to change the subject. "So, do you think Angelica would mind if Grayson moved in?"

If guilt kept someone warm, I'd be sweating up a storm rather than shivering. Clouds obscured the stars as we hid in the bushes outside the stone walls of Gabriel's chateau in eleven degrees Celsius—I'd checked the weather app on my phone. It had just gone 1:00 a.m., and the security guard service they used had driven in there ten minutes ago. Surely they'd be finished soon. Apparently, they visited twice a night at random times. This was the second time, according to James, who'd done the shift from ten when the security guards went on duty. There must be a few rich people out here who used their services. And thank you to Cardinal for getting all this infor-mation. There was a lot more, apparently, but it would take time to sift through and make sense of.

"Are you shivering?" Will asked from behind me.

"Yes, but it's okay. We'll be inside soon."

He moved to stand behind me, then pressed his chest against my back and wrapped his arms around me. "See if this helps." If we weren't about to break into someone's house, it would be so romantic. Come to think of it, it was romantic anyway.

"Argh, you guys can't keep your hands off each other for five minutes." There was a hint of mirth in Imani's tone. Sigh. Things just got way less romantic, but at least I was warmer.

"If you're feeling left out, come here, and I'll cuddle you." I snorted.

"That's not a bad offer. I'll consider it."

I laughed. Then stopped. Headlights shone through the wrought-iron gates, and the quiet hum of an engine reached us. Will dropped his arms from around me, and we all crouched. The car drove through and turned onto the road. Once they were out of sight, Will's magic tingled my scalp. "Okay, perimeter cameras and alarms disabled." He reached down and grabbed the ladder James had magicked there earlier. He leaned it against the wall. "Once you get to the top of the wall, just hang from your fingertips and drop. It won't be far at all."

"Yes, boss." I scaled the ladder and stayed low as I reached the top of the eight-foot-high wall. I slid to the other side on my stomach, my legs dangling over the chateau side. I gripped the top of the fence and lowered myself, then dropped the rest of the way. It had been a damned sight easier than last time Will had helped me get over a fence when we were trying to catch Liv's fiancé. Gee, time went quickly. Where the hell did it go?

Imani dropped over next, then Will. His magic tingled my

scalp again. "Ladder, back to where James got you from." He and Imani pulled their guns out, and I checked my return to sender was up for the fourth time since we'd arrived. It was becoming a nervous habit. "We'll get to the tree line, then I'll have to disable the home security system, so once you get there, just wait for my signal before moving to the chateau."

"Okay," we both replied.

As we walked, old leaf litter crunched underfoot, and I cringed at each crunch. Every now and then, Will stopped to listen. The third time we stopped, leaves still crunched. My heart galloped, and I held my breath for as long as I could. Whoever was coming towards us, still came. *Rustle, rustle, crunch.* Will pointed his gun into the gloom. Then a few feet away, from behind a large tree, a deer appeared. I let my breath out in a whoosh. The deer stopped and jerked its head towards us, then turned and ran the other way. Will swore quietly.

"I second that," I whispered.

"Come on." Will started walking again.

Finally, we reached the border where trees met lawn and pool. It was still a good fifty metres to the house, a gorgeous three-storey neo-Gothic chateau that was the size of a hotel. Man, this place was huge.

Will closed his eyes. His magic tingled my scalp again, and an owl hooted. If I wasn't a witch, I'd be even more scared, but I supposed I was in my natural environment. I swallowed a giggle. I'd never seen myself as spooky before, but perhaps I was. Time to own it, maybe?

After a couple of minutes, Will opened his eyes. "We're clear. Let's go."

We sprinted across the lawn. Instead of going to the front doors, Will headed around to the back of the chateau. If the security guards happened to do a third check, they wouldn't see us before we saw them. At least, that's why I thought Will was headed around the back.

He stopped at tall french doors, which he unlocked using something he pulled out of his back pocket. "Why aren't you using magic?" I asked.

"I've disabled all the alarms and cameras, but what if they've got a subtle one that detects magic? I'll know more once we're inside."

"Fair enough."

The lock clicked, and we were in.

Trespassing was not on my list of favourite things to do. My back itched, as if someone were watching and we'd be sprung at any time. Will and Imani entered first, guns drawn. Once they confirmed the room was clear, I went in.

The sweet, dusty odour of old books folded me in a heady embrace. Dim light from Imani's phone revealed wall-to-ceiling shelves filled with books on three walls. The furnishings were as you'd expect in an expensive French chateau library—numerous leather and fabric chairs, rugs, dark timber shelves, parquetry floors, and ornate ceilings.

Imani turned to Will. "I'll clear out this side of the house; you clear out the other." He nodded, and they went through different doors. I stayed and turned my camera on. "Show me my mother at the party the week before she was at Mont Saint-Michel."

Nothing changed. She probably hadn't been in this room. I took the route Will had taken and walked into a living room, then repeated my question. This time, the room changed from dark to light. Electric wall sconces were on, as were two chandeliers. Twenty-seven people dressed in evening wear stood in groups, most with drinks in hand. Two butlers with serving trays filled with full glasses were also in the shot. I wandered around and made sure I got everyone in at least one shot. When I was done, I went back to my mother's group. She stood with three other women, none of whom looked familiar. My mother, dressed in a strapless red gown that hugged her figure to her waist, then fell in soft folds to the floor, was stunning, as always. My heart filled with the infinitely painful spikiness of love, yearning, and loss that always hit me at these moments. "Miss you, Mum," I whispered.

I moved to the next room—another large entertaining space, filled with plush furnishings and more people. I asked the question and took more photos of the numerous guests. Gabriel made an appearance in this room, as did three young women in servant's attire. They held trays of hors d'oeuvres. Even though my mother was here, my dad was nowhere to be seen, and there was nothing suspicious about anything. I took photos of everyone and kept going.

And so it continued through the rest of the ground floor. I ran into Imani at the bottom of the staircase in the grand foyer. "Lily, I've found his study. I'm thinking this is the most likely place we'll find something."

"Okay. Lead the way."

At the top of the stairs, Imani took a left and hurried along the corridor. We passed three doors before she stopped at the fourth, which was already open. Another huge room awaited, with a timber desk in front of a shuttered window. Imani shut the door and turned on the light. "No one will be able to see the light with the shutters closed. I've used a small amount of magic to cast a no-light-leak spell."

"Is that specific to the PIB?"

"Yes. You end up with an interesting cauldron of tricks when much of your job comprises sneaking around. Anyway, best get going. We've been here for twenty-three minutes."

"Crap. That went quickly." I raised my camera. "Show me my mother the night of the party." Hmm, that was odd.

"What's wrong?"

"I'm not getting anything. Hmm…." Maybe Mum stayed at the party and acted like a lookout for Dad? "Show me my father at the party the week before he was at Mont Saint-Michel with Mum." I smiled. "Gotcha!" The light was on in the past. My father stood behind the desk, going through the top drawer. I took a photo of him, then walked over to the desk and took a picture of the document face up in the drawer. "Is there anything else I should see?" That was kind of a broad question, but I had a feeling I wasn't getting the full story. It was akin to asking my magic to show me more. After all, showing me one piece of paper wasn't much. I doubted my father risked being found out snooping if there hadn't been something important here.

The light was on, and my father held a piece of paper in his hand, but his gaze was on the door. I snapped a pic of him, then turned. Oh, crap. Toussaint stood in the doorway, my mother behind him, her hand on his upper arm, maybe trying to stop him? Her frantic gaze met my father's. Toussaint's eyes radiated anger, and his mouth was pinched closed. He gripped the door handle so hard, his knuckles protruded alarmingly. I snapped off a shot. *But hang on a minute.* I'd caught him the moment he was looking slightly to my father's right and up. The only thing there was the window. I carefully shuffled a few steps to where my father had been and photographed the paper in his hand… a map. Interesting.

I lowered my camera. "I've got some good info, but there's something else I want to check out. Look at this. Toussaint isn't quite looking at my dad." I showed her the shots from the beginning. When I reached the one of Gabriel, Imani screwed

WITCH WAR IN WESTERHAM

up her face. "What are you talking about, love? How can you even tell? All I see is a man looking across the room."

Damn. I was the only one who could pan across the whole scene and understand the context. I lifted my camera again. "Show me what Gabriel was looking at." Nothing. Damn it. I lowered my camera and made my way behind the desk. I turned my head to look at Imani. "Can you kill the light? I need to open the shutters."

She shrugged. "Okay." She turned the light off, and I drew my sleeve down and opened the shutter on my left—as amateur as I was, I was not going to leave fingerprints behind. The shutter had covered a thick windowsill decorated with ornate timber panelling. I tapped it. I had no idea what I was looking for, but seeing as how they did this in movies all the time, maybe it would reveal something. Imani came over to me. "What are you doing?"

"Looking for something."

She grinned. "Why don't you try pulling the sconces next to the fireplace?"

"Oh, can you while I do this?"

"You numpty. I was kidding. Seriously, what are you doing?"

"There might be a cavity or something hidden here. I swear Toussaint was looking at this."

She sighed. "Fine. Let me put you out of your misery. At least you'll know we looked." She grabbed gloves out of her pocket and put them on. Then she gave me a gentle push to move me out of the way and placed her palm on the thick timber covering the wall of the window nook. She used a breath of magic that only just feathered the back of my neck. I shivered. There was a small click. She looked at me, her eyes widening as if to say, would you look at that? She slid the timber panel across so it stuck out more and more, until it stopped.

"There's a cavity here."

I jogged around the desk to look over her shoulder. She reached into the hole and pulled out a small metal box. This time, she held it and shut her eyes.

"I'm checking for booby traps…. Looks clean." She magicked a lock picking implement to herself and got to work. "I don't want to leave more magic signatures behind than I have to. The less magic I use, the fainter the signature. Hopefully, the one I've already used will fade by the morning." She slid the implement into her inside jacket pocket and flicked the lock across.

The lid opened, and she reached in.

"What's in there?" It was hard to see in the gloom, and I knew she didn't want any lights on because someone might see it shining from outside, not that there was anyone within cooee of the chateau in its massive grounds.

"A skeleton key and a small stone. I'll show you when we get home." She pocketed the items, shut the box, and slipped it back into the wall. She returned the timber panel to its original position and closed the shutter. "Let's check out a couple more rooms, just to make sure we haven't missed anything. Then we'll grab Will and get out of here."

"Okay." We went back to the three rooms we'd passed earlier. Each was a bedroom. The first two we got nothing, but in the third, Toussaint had his arms around one of the young women who'd been serving food downstairs. He looked down into her eyes, a lascivious, sly expression on his face, while her eyes emanated fear. She had her palms against his chest, as if trying to get away. *Click.*

"You got something?"

"Yeah, and it just helps build a case proving Toussaint is the world's biggest di—"

"Hey, how are you two going?" Will asked as he walked in.

I jumped. "Can you not scare me like that every time?"

"Sorry. It wasn't intentional."

"Lily's gathered a lot of evidence. What about you? Anything interesting?"

"I'm not sure. There was a notebook in one of the bedside tables that had names and phone numbers. I took photos, and I'll follow it up later. Not sure if it's relevant, but you never know."

"Right, well, I don't think we should push our luck. What do you think? Should we call it a night?"

Will turned to me. "Have you been in every room, Lily?"

"No."

"I really think we should keep going, just in case."

My stomach flip-flopped. I wanted to get out of here as soon as possible, but we'd come this far, and we needed to make sure. "Okay, let's hurry it up." We rushed from room to room until I'd covered them all. Only one more scene showed up on my screen, and that was in one of the bathrooms on the top floor. A shirtless, overweight older man was in the middle of slapping another young serving woman across the face. He also had a snake tattoo on his neck. By the time we made our doorways to come home, anger was like boiling acid in my veins.

When we arrived home, Imani didn't show up. "Isn't she coming?"

"No, Lily. It's too late. We'll meet in the morning at James's. Not with everyone there, but we'll show him what we found and throw some ideas around."

I yawned. "Fair enough." I looked at my phone. It was

after three. Yikes. I'd forgotten what time it was. "Bed is calling my name."

As I drifted off to sleep, I couldn't help but be relieved we hadn't been discovered. Unfortunately for us, good news only came in ones. Why was it only the terrible stuff that came in threes?

CHAPTER 12

Will was kind enough to let me sleep till nine, then it was quickly magicking my clothes on and hopping over to James's. At least coffee was waiting for me there. James answered the door and took us through to the dining room. Millicent and Imani were already there, sitting next to each other. Imani turned and waved. Millicent stood and gave me a hug. "Morning. I hear last night went well."

"Yes. At least I think it did. Maybe the stuff Imani took out of the wall won't amount to anything, but why hide it if it's unimportant?"

"Why, indeed," said Imani.

Will and I made our way around the back of James's seat and sat opposite Millicent and Imani. James magicked the screen on the wall again. I handed him my camera, and he hooked it up via magic. I really had no idea sometimes, not that I was good with non-magical technology either.

A picture came up on the screen. "Is that the first one?"

It was one of the crowd in the second room I'd been in. "Yes. I've taken these for reference—so we can identify the people and see if they're worth investigating further. It doesn't get super interesting till we come to Dad going through Gabriel's drawers—and, no, not the underwear type of drawers."

My brother rolled his eyes. "Not funny, Lily."

I shrugged. "Meh." Oftentimes, I was the only one who thought I was funny, so it was no froth off the top of my cappuccino if he wasn't laughing. As he clicked through them, he was oddly quiet. He was probably thinking about Mum and Dad. It was difficult for both of us, but I didn't say anything. We were there to work, and I knew he would find it easier to keep it together if I didn't make a big deal out of it. Eventually he got to the photo of Dad, then of him being discovered rifling through the desk. He kept going with the photos, but when he realised that was the last of Mum and Dad, he turned and looked at me. "So, what did you find in that room?"

"Well, I noticed Toussaint wasn't quite looking at Dad—he was looking towards the window, which I thought was super odd. Turns out, he was looking at the wall next to the window. It had a hidden cavity that Imani so kindly found. Inside it was a locked box." I looked at Imani. "So, let's see the spoils."

"It would be my pleasure." She pulled the key and a small, smooth black rock out of her pocket and placed them on the table. Iridescent blue lines swirled through the stone. It was quite pretty. "I'm thinking that maybe the map Lily took a photo of has something to do with this."

"But we don't know that for sure," James said.

Imani's answer was to the point. "No."

I looked at the screen. "Can you go back to the picture of the map? We don't even know what it's a map of, but I think we can assume it's the abbey on Mont Saint-Michel. The fact that our parents were there the next week is telling."

James nodded. "It is."

Will stared at the screen. "Hang on a sec." He pulled out his phone and pulled up the internet to search. He gazed at his phone, then back at the wall screen, then at his phone. "Looks like we have a match, folks." His magic tickled my scalp, and the map on the screen halved in size. Another map appeared next to it. Will stood and went to them. "It's definitely a map of the abbey, but the interesting thing is this." He pointed to what seemed to be an extra room taking up part of the area on the internet map that was marked as *rocher*.

"What's a rocher?" I had only just started the French lessons from my app, and I hadn't encountered that word before.

Will looked at me. "It means rock."

Interesting. "So where everyone else thinks there's a rock, there's actually a hidden room… at least according to Gabriel's map.

Millicent smiled and looked at Will, me, then Imani. "You three have done excellent work. I wonder what's hiding down there."

Will left the maps and sat next to me again. "Whatever it is, Lily's parents might have been killed for it."

It was as if someone ran a piece of ice down my back. I shivered, and goosebumps sprung up along my arms. I swallowed the unexpected burn of impending tears. All this time, I had some kind of hope that maybe they were still alive. But of course they weren't. RP didn't play around—their attempts to kill me and all the murdering of the last few weeks made it more than apparent.

My parents were dead.

This was now, and probably always had been, about confirming the worst, and finding justice for my parents and everyone else who'd had the misfortune of getting caught up with RP.

I looked up. "When is Toussaint due back at the chateau? Surely it's only a matter of time before he discovers that stuff is gone, and then they'll be waiting."

James's steady gaze met mine. "Tomorrow."

Will ran a hand through his hair. "Looks like we need to go back there tonight, then, when the abbey's locked up. At least we won't be announcing our arrival by staying at the hotel." He looked at Imani, then Beren. "Care to come with?"

I sat up straight like a kid who'd just discovered they were missing out on going somewhere awesome because they were too young. "Hey, what about me?"

"You don't need to be there, love. We need you for the final showdown. You know that I *know* this."

She'd had dreams, that was true, but…. "Who says this isn't the final battle?" I was pretty sure it wasn't, but let nothing get in the way of me trying to persuade them to let me come. "Even if it's not, how will you know exactly how to use the stone? The key is pretty self-explanatory, but where does the stone actually go? And the entrance is obviously hidden. You'll need me to speed things up. You could search for that all night. And I doubt you'd want to use loud magic for that. It's probably booby-trapped with a way more complex spell than the box last night."

James pressed his lips together. Ha! He knew I was right, and he hated having to let me go. Yes, he was scared for me, but how many times had I shown that although I didn't know all the spells, I was one of the strongest witches here? I believed in myself, even if they didn't quite trust me to get through everything. I didn't plan on dying until I knew exactly who had killed my parents, and I certainly wasn't dying before Piranha.

I had goals.

I folded my arms. "This isn't nearly as dangerous as being locked in an apartment with a vampire witch, and I survived that. Stop underestimating me. I know you're worried, but stuff it, James. This is us doing everything we can to wipe RP from the face of the earth. Risks must be taken by all of us. I'm here to see this done. Don't deny me my place in avenging our parents. We both have a right to do what we feel we have to, and I'm more than up to the task. Besides, you don't think I'm scared to death every time you're on a dangerous assignment? But I never say anything. Know why? Because I know you have to do what you do to be happy. You've chosen your path, and I'm here to support you. I'm just asking for the same."

James gazed at me, the fire in his eyes dimming somewhat as realisation set in. He knew I was stubborn and right. "I'm sorry, Lily. You're my little sister, and I've been both brother and parent to you since Mum and Dad died. I sometimes forget you're a fully-grown woman with strength, skill, and determination. Also, I don't want to let Mum and Dad down, you know? They would've wanted me to protect you."

I smiled sadly. "And they would've wanted me to protect you too. I'm sure Dad worried about Mum, but instead of fighting her on being an agent, he teamed up with her. How awesome is that? Maybe we should do the same?"

His smile was slightly less sad than mine. "Deal." He reached out, and we shook on it.

I grinned. "We've got this."

"We do." He looked at Will. "What time do you want to go in?"

"We're going to need a way to get in once it's locked up. I think we should send in someone they wouldn't suspect. I imagine RP has a database of all our agents. We'll need to use someone that's not on it, someone we can trust to magic a lock to open at a certain time."

"Have you got anyone in mind," James asked.

Will grinned. "I sure do. Lavender."

Imani clapped her hands together. "That's an excellent idea. He'd love that. He fancies himself as a potential agent." She laughed.

I smiled. "He's definitely capable, and we can trust him. Noice choice." I put my hand up, and Will high-fived me.

"Noice?" asked Imani.

James grinned. "It's ocker for nice."

Her brow wrinkled. "Ocker?"

I laughed. "An uncouth Australian. Like, the rougher ones."

She shook her head. "I swear I'll have to get down there one day. You can show me around and explain everything."

"I would love to show you around! As soon as this is all over, we'll plan a holiday. Will, Liv, and Beren can come too."

Millicent raised her brows. "What about me?"

"You're welcome. I wasn't sure you'd want to travel with Annabelle, but it would be awesome if you came!"

James cocked his head to the side. "There'll be no one left at the PIB if we all go."

Beren, who'd smiled at the prospect of visiting Australia, frowned. "If things keep going the way they have been, there won't be a PIB to worry about."

Liv rubbed his back. "Ma'am will figure out a way to save things. Don't write her off yet."

"And before all that," James said, "we have an evil cesspool of an organisation to bring down." James's phone rang. Talk about good timing. We'd just about finished. "Hello, Sir…. Yes?" As he listened, his eyes widened, then narrowed, and his lips pinched together. His nostrils flared. I gave Beren and Liv a worried look across the table. They responded with concerned looks of their own. What was Chad up to now? "I thought we'd agreed not to do anything for a few days?" James listened for a while longer, my stomach speeding through a roller coaster. What the hell was that man stuffing up now? He was going to get us all killed. When James finally spoke again, his voice was barely civil. "Right. Well, I warned that this might happen…. What? You're kidding?" He huffed a breath. "I'm advising against this, Sir…. No." He spoke through gritted teeth. "I understand. Bye."

We all stared at James, and it was almost a minute before someone summoned the courage to ask what happened. To be fair, James needed time to cool down enough to speak if his reddened face was anything to go by. Will was the brave one. "What was that about?"

"He sent two agents to interview another family this morning, early. The family was killed as soon as the agents left. A video was sent to headquarters. It doesn't show who pulled the trigger, but it shows the three family members being shot."

I sucked in a breath, incredulous. "Oh my God. What a piece of sh—"

"That's horrific." I'd never seen Beren so angry. Hot sparks were practically shooting from his eyes.

Millicent's voice was quiet but sharp. "Barbaric. Truly barbaric."

James clenched a fist. "That's not the end of it. He's insisting Will and I interview the parents of another of the forced workers this afternoon. When I said no, he said if I didn't, it was immediate dismissal."

I placed my elbows on the table and buried my face in my hands. There was no way James would do that. I had to hope Will wouldn't either. How could they pander to Chad and still sleep at night? Surely a job wasn't worth sacrificing all their ethics. They were supposed to protect people, and, yes, there were sometimes casualties in that, but this? This was mass murder, and if they condoned that, they weren't much better than RP. I looked up.

Imani tapped her nails on the table. "So, gentlemen. What are you going to do?"

James shared a meaningful look with Millicent before turning to Will. "As I see it, we have two choices. Take them to a safe location, question them, and guard them with our lives, or refuse. That's it."

Will donned a poker face, his gaze steady. "Agreed. Which one do you prefer? Whatever it is, I'm in."

"If we have to guard them, I guess the safest place would be at Angelica's. But is the information they can provide really going to help? We all know this thing isn't going to get as far as a trial. If this doesn't work, we're still after RP, and I've got plenty of money saved for a rainy day. Maybe Cardinal can find us jobs." His mouth quirked up on one side.

Millicent reached across the table and grabbed his hand. "Whatever you decide, I'm with you 100 percent. Besides, the rest of us will still be on the inside if we need information, and as you said to Cardinal, we can't count Angelica out yet. Things will come good." Her closed-mouth smile and kind eyes gave away her love, but also the fact that she knew

Angelica coming through was maybe a fifty-fifty proposition at best.

James gave Millicent a smile. "Right, well, I'm not going to phone in my resignation. Let him find me to fire me."

My brother was awesome, and so was Will. "I love both of you. You're two of the strongest people I know, and you have all my respect."

James cocked his head to one side. "Thank you so much, Lily. I appreciate it."

Will gave my hand a squeeze. I grinned. "Just a favour, if you would. Can one of you maybe get a job at Costa so I can get discounted double-chocolate muffins?"

Will's magic tingled my scalp, and something pinched my bottom. I jerked up from my chair. "Ow!"

He laughed. "If you're going to be cheeky…."

"Ha ha. I'll let you have that one since today you're doing such a noble thing. At least we can concentrate on tonight. So, who's going to call Lavender?"

Will grinned. "I would love to."

Funny how quickly things changed. Well, actually, it wasn't funny at all, but you know what I meant. You wake up expecting one thing, but you get another, and it's something that can change your life forever. Hopefully one day we'd all wake up and those changes would be for the better.

I was counting on it because what else could I do?

CHAPTER 13

Lavender was a true champion. The make-up artist had set up a landing spot for us in a hotel room he'd rented out—not the one we'd stayed at earlier. We donned return to senders and no-notice spells before we left home. At midnight, we arrived at the island. Lavender was waiting for us in his room. As soon as I stepped through my doorway, he jumped at me and enveloped me in a massive hug. "Gorgeous girl. So brilliant to see you."

"So good to see you too. How's it hanging?"

His eyes widened, and he laughed. "You're such a naughty thing."

"We use it a lot in Australia. It's not naughty at all." I winked. "So?"

"Fabulous, as always. I was so excited when Will called. This espionage stuff is so much fun."

I laughed. "It can be, but don't forget that it's dangerous."

"You don't have to tell me. I still have nightmares about

that horrid vampire witch." He shook his head. "That was a close one."

I shuddered. "Tell me about it." Tommy was one witch I wanted to forget about.

Will came through and interrupted our mini-reunion. "Hey." He shook Lavender's hand. "Let's not muck around. What do we need to know?"

Imani, Beren, Will, and I listened closely as Lavender explained how the spell on the abbey door worked. "So you don't have to use magic when it's quiet out there and nearby witches might notice, just place this in the lock, and it will unlock." He handed Will a thin metal rod. "The spell I used just mimics the locking mechanism and is attached to it. The rod will trigger an unravel spell, so one touch of this will unlock my spell and therefore the door, all with no new burst of magic."

Will blinked. "That's very clever. How is it you aren't already working with us?"

He shrugged. "I do love the drama of the fashion world, but you never know. I might fancy a career change one day soon."

Will looked at Beren, Imani, and me in turn. We'd ditched the PIB uniforms for all black and no ties. "Who's got the map?"

Imani put up her hand, the map in it. "Right here."

"Good. No dawdling. We get in, we see what's down there and possibly transfer it to the barn, and we get out." We all nodded. Will turned to Lavender. "Thanks again. I'd prefer it if you checked out early and left. No telling what could happen when Toussaint finds out his key's gone. They might come for any witch on the island, and they could easily link you to us with a small amount of digging."

"I can hand my key in the after-hours box as soon as you leave. No skin off my perfectly powdered nose."

"Good." He turned to the rest of us. "Let's go." We dragged our balaclavas over our heads and filed out—if someone caught us on security video, we wouldn't be identified. Will didn't have time to look for and disable whatever cameras there might be.

Elephantine butterflies stampeded through my stomach as we jogged out of the hotel and down the narrow thoroughfares of the island. It was as if I were flying as my feet glided along the empty streets. The silence, except for the intermittent distant cry of gulls, cast an eerie pall over our mission. In the still night, salt air settled in a haze around us, filling my nostrils and seasoning my tongue.

When we reached the door, Will got to work while the rest of us watched for any interlopers. "I'm done."

I turned. "That was quick."

He opened the door and gestured for us to go through. He was the last inside and shut the door. We each pulled out a small torch, and Imani consulted the map. When she set off, we followed. Beren was in front of me, and Will behind. Even though we were alone, I did my best to walk quietly—I couldn't shake the paranoia that came with trespassing. But I needn't have worried. The thick walls absorbed most of the noise we made, deadened it. Gah, why did I have to think about that word? Dead.

The abbey had been used as a jail at one time, and it seemed as if the oppression and despair from that period stained every surface. It hadn't felt like that during the day, but now.... Fear scratched its way up my throat. In an effort to fight it off, I concentrated on Beren's back. He was real. He'd keep me safe, and Will was behind me. We were going to be okay. We were the only things alive in here—well, other than a few spiders and grubs—and it was just a building. Just. A. Building.

Imani stopped in an unremarkable, smallish room. She looked at the map again. "This is it." She looked at one of the inside walls. "It's here somewhere." She approached the wall and placed a palm on it, feeling around for... I didn't know. Beren joined her.

Will made his way to one of the thick columns that supported the curved stone ceiling. He slapped a few spots with his palm. "Nothing. I think it's time for Lily to do her thing."

"I thought you'd never ask." I pulled out my phone and switched on the camera app. Doing something helped me feel like less of a target, but the faint scritch, scritch of fear down my back made me wary. I ignored it and said, "Show me Toussaint activating the secret doorway."

The lighting of the scene didn't change much, except a female witch with a ball of light floating above her hand stood next to a crouched Toussaint. I took a photo, then stepped close to where he was and leaned down. I took another picture. He'd lifted a small, loose piece of stone from the floor near the wall and had inserted the stone into a divot underneath it. The adjoining stone slab in the floor had begun to open. Wow, nifty. I handed my phone to Imani. "There you go."

"Nice. We would've been searching a long time to find that. Thanks, love." She handed my phone back and crouched. It took her a moment to find where the stone lifted. She pushed it, then *click*. She took the small piece out, which revealed a matching-sized hole. She placed the smooth stone into it. I held my breath and waited.

The grinding of rock against rock raised goosebumps on my arms as one stone dropped slightly, then slid across into the other. It worked! What were we going to find? Would it be weapons, a magical artefact, artwork? Okay, so artwork was a long shot, but it could be anything. Hopefully it wouldn't be more slaves….

The stone opened the whole way, and the grinding stopped, plunging us into near silence again. Will drew his gun and pointed it at the hole while Imani shone her torch into it. "It's a manhole with rungs. Time to climb." Without pausing to consider the intelligence of her decision, Imani swung her legs into the opening and descended. Beren went next. I looked down. "Should we wait till they find what's down there?"

Imani called up. "There's a door, and what do you know… the key works."

Will raised a brow. "Does that answer your question? Come on. In you get."

Unfortunately, it wasn't a bath he was requesting I hop into. The small space did not look inviting. "What if I get stuck?"

He took a deep breath and sighed. "Beren fit, and you're way smaller than him. Since when do you have claustrophobia?"

"Since it's a tunnel into the earth. It kind of feels like I'm getting into my own coffin."

He grabbed my hand. "It's safe, Lily. Beren and Imani will be waiting for you. Don't you want to know what's down there?"

"I thought I did, but I'm not getting good vibes."

"Just go down, and I'll stand guard here. Okay?"

"Okay." I swallowed and crouched. One foot, then the

other. *Come on. You can do it. What happened to the warrior for the downtrodden? You're close to getting the answers you've been searching for.*

And maybe that was the problem.

While I didn't know for sure, I could pretend that maybe I'd get a happy ending.

The ladder only went down about nine feet. I turned around, an open doorway greeting me. There was a light on inside—how convenient. I stepped inside, and my mouth fell open. It was like something out of an Indiana Jones movie.

Imani and Beren stood in the middle of a large, low-ceilinged space, each with hands on hips, maybe trying to work out what to do next. Gold bars, four rows deep, were stacked to the ceiling against the far wall. On one other wall, a stack of timber-slat boxes also reached the ceiling. Along another wall were four long boxes shaped like coffins stacked two by two. I shuddered. Surely, they weren't. I had no idea what could be inside, but, of course, my brain wanted to go down the most macabre path possible. I soon got over it, though, because I had to touch the gold. There must be millions and millions of pounds' worth, maybe hundreds of millions. I'd never seen so many gold bars. Well, I'd never seen any in real life. There were enough here to make into a doghouse, one bar stacked on another, or maybe I could give one to each of my friends to use as a doorstop, for front and back doors. I snorted.

Beren approached the high stack of non-coffin boxes. "Before we start magicking them away, I want to see what's in them and make sure there are no tracking devices on there. Would you give me a hand? And don't use magic, just in case there's an alarm we don't know about."

He'd been talking to Imani, but we both stepped up to help. Beren reached for the top box and worked it loose. He braced himself and grunted as it came free and he took its weight. He placed it on the ground. "Lily, can you drag that over there and open it while we unstack a few more?"

"Can do." I dragged it to the middle of the room, out of their way. The lid had been nailed on. Seriously? How was I supposed to undo that without tools or magic? I relayed my issue.

Imani came and had a look. "Maybe there won't be any alarms set off if we magic a crowbar to ourselves up where Will is. They must use magic for small things in this place all the time. Hang on a sec." She hurried out and up the ladder. I didn't feel her magic, if, indeed, she had even used it. Maybe it was all the stone?

Boots clanked dully as Imani came back down. Except it wasn't Imani who entered but Will, a crowbar in one hand. "I wanted to come and see what we have—" His eyes bugged out at the gold. "What the hell?"

Beren had just grabbed another box, turned and put it down, then straightened to look at Will. "I know. It's crazy. I'm wondering, though. What if it's not stolen? Can we really take it? Should we take photos for evidence, just in case, and leave it here?"

"I can solve that problem for you." I waved my phone. "I can just ask my magic."

Beren smiled. "You're always full of good ideas. Go ahead."

"Show me any stolen goods." A beefy man had his back to me as he stacked the gold bars. Another spindly man was working with a stocky woman to stack the boxes Beren had started to get down. The coffin-like boxes weren't in the photo. I took some pics, then showed the guys. "Looks like this is all stolen, but that isn't." I nodded at the long boxes. "So there's your answer."

Will gave a nod, then crouched to jimmy open the box I'd had trouble with. The timber creaked and cracked, then opened. Will gripped the lid and pulled it all the way off. A pile of different sized black-velvet pouches filled the box. Will picked one up and pulled the top open. He poured the contents into his hand and whistled his surprise. "Woah." A handful of large—what I had to assume—diamonds crowded his palm.

I reached in to grab another pouch. It didn't feel like separate gems. I opened it and pulled out a couple of Rolex watches. I had no idea what they were worth, but I knew Rolex ran into the thousands of pounds. Will snatched out another pouch. This one contained rubies and a couple of gold rings. "Right, well, we can be pretty sure they all contain more of the same. Let's get this lot out of here."

"Before we do"—Beren looked at the long boxes—"can we see what's in there? If we don't, I'll always wonder."

I nodded. "So will I." I didn't want to have nightmares about dead bodies if there weren't any in there. "Maybe they're witches' brooms?"

Will laughed. "That's a fallacy. We don't ride brooms, and you know it."

"Yeah, but I like to tease. Maybe they do exist, and no one told you guys about them?"

Beren grinned. "Just open them so we don't have to listen to Lily hassling us."

Because they were only stacked two to a pile, Will didn't have to move any to get the lid off one of the top ones. His trusty crowbar quickly did the job. He slid the lid off and stiffened. Wary, I moved closer to peer in.

I gasped and slammed my hand over my mouth.

My worst fears had come true. A skeleton lay in the box,

dusty, bloodstained clothes draped over its wasted frame. Normally I wanted to be right. This time, however, was a massive exception.

Crap.

Will placed the lid back on. "B, help me lift this one down so I can get to the next one." Beren did as asked, and then Will opened the next box. There were no surprises this time.

Except, maybe there was.

The skeleton in the box had a hole in the front of its skull. But it was what was sitting in its bony hand that blindsided me. I blinked. Maybe I was wrong? It had been years since I'd woven the colourful wristband for my father and attached a cheap golden-coloured metal heart onto it. I swallowed the nausea threatening to suffocate me. It couldn't be. I shook my head.

Will grabbed my arm. "Lily, what's wrong?"

I lifted my phone and called on my magic with a shaky, quiet voice. "Show me the person in the box before they wasted away." The body fleshed out, and my worst nightmare came true. I clicked off a shot before my jelly legs gave way, and my bottom collided with the ground. Somehow, I managed not to drop my phone.

No. No. No. No. No.

Will fell to the ground next to me and grabbed my phone. He took a moment to look, then passed it to Beren. "Lily, who is this?" Surely, he knew. Maybe he just wanted confirmation?

My voice sounded as if it belonged to another person as the enclosed space swallowed it up.

"My dad."

Will swore. Without saying another word, he and Beren opened the other two boxes. My stomach clenched, and I heaved. If my mother was in one of them, I didn't know how

I'd cope. This was not what I'd expected. I knew they were probably dead, but until now, it was a distant concept. Being the positive person I was, I'd let hope lull me into some kind of fantasy world where I'd find them alive… maybe imprisoned and desperate, but, nevertheless, alive.

It wasn't to be.

I stared at my phone, at the picture of my murdered father so when someone sighed in what sounded like relief, I didn't know who it was, but then Will crouched next to me. "The other two bodies are men, Lily. Your mother isn't here."

I wasn't sure what to do, so I cried, and when Imani helped me upstairs and made a doorway for both of us to go home, I didn't stop as I stepped through.

I was about to find out that a person could cry long after their tear ducts ran dry. It was as if with every tear, I felt less capable of continuing our search for answers.

All I could think of was, what was the point?

They were dead.

So. Damned. Dead.

And now someone had to tell James.

That someone had to be me.

CHAPTER 14

James and I sat on his couch holding hands. Will sat next to me with his arm around my shoulders, and Millicent sat on the other side of James, holding his hand. My brother's immediate reaction was to freeze. He just stared at me, probably in shock—that was the last thing he'd expected us to find, and that made two of us. We'd sat here for the last hour just processing.

James wiped his eyes with the back of our joined hands and cleared his throat. "It's devastating, but at least we know for sure, and we can lay him to rest like he deserves." James looked at Will. "So, you got everything out of that room?"

"Yes. We've transferred the material things to the barn, and Imani and Beren will guard it overnight. As for the bodies… well, skeletons… I've gotten in touch with the French agency. They've agreed to store them in their morgue and have their man look over them without informing UK head-quarters."

"They're being exceptionally helpful," said Millicent.

"Yes, well, Chad cut them out of an investigation that they should at least be going fifty-fifty on, not to forget they've lost two agents in all this because of Chad's lack of disclosure." Will shook his head. "Chad's good at making enemies."

"I'll say." James gritted his teeth. "He emailed me and told me I was on forced leave, to be looked at again when this investigation is over. If I do anything to look into RP, it's an automatic firing. To be honest, I couldn't give a rat's bum."

I smiled sadly. "And that's putting it nicely."

James grunted. He looked into my eyes, grief and care clear in his gaze. "What about you? Are you okay after seeing that?"

I swallowed. "No, but it is what it is. As crappy as it is, at least we know, and we can say a proper goodbye. I want to know who shot him."

Will rubbed my back. "We may never find out. You need to be prepared for that."

I nodded. "I know, but I thought I was prepared for this." I sniffled. "And where's our mother's body?" Acidic anger ate into my stomach until it ached.

James squeezed my hand. "We may never discover that either, but before this is over, we'll do our best to find out. You have my promise."

I leant my head against his. I wanted to say so much, but what could I say that hadn't already been said? And I knew what was going on inside him—the same thoughts were likely swirling in my head, and voicing them would change nothing. This would be a matter of processing things.

"Oh, I grabbed this for you." Will put one hand in his pocket and let go of my hand to place his find in it.

I sobbed. "Dad's friendship bracelet."

"It should probably be in evidence, but I knew you'd want

it, and, honestly, I don't see how it being with the agency is going to help anything."

"Can I see it?" James's voice was heavy with loss.

We released hands and I gave it to him. "Remember when I went through that phase? I made one for you, about ten for Mum because you wouldn't take any more than you absolutely had to, and I had my own collection. I only have a couple left. I actually have the one I made you, but you left it when you came here."

"Sorry, Lily."

My heart, so battered by grief, still filled with affection at the regret in his voice. "It's okay. I know you love me. I love you too. Maybe I can grab it next time I go back, and we can give it to Annabelle." I smiled.

"That would be great. I'll hold you to that." His mouth curved up in a reluctant smile.

"Right. I know this has been a night of shocks, but we should get home and try and get some sleep."

"Oh, crap. I forgot you had to work." Poor Will. Yes, I was going through something huge, but I couldn't forget he had commitments. Life had to go on, as the saying went.

"I don't, actually. I got the same email as James—in all the running around, I forgot to tell you. I still have to get up by ten, and it's three forty now. I want to pay the French office a visit, and someone has to relieve Imani and Beren." He looked at James. "I might have to call you in to do that. I haven't told Agent Roche what else we found and where. He told me it's okay for now, but there would come a time when he would ask, and he would expect me to answer. I just don't want anything leaking to the wrong people."

I pressed my lips together. "Stupid Toussaint will find

things missing soon enough and start asking questions. Who knows what friends he has where?"

"Exactly. Anyway, let's head off." Will stood, gently pulling me with him.

James and Millicent stood, and we gave each other sad gazes before putting our arms around each other in a goodbye group hug. Will made a door for us, and we stepped through. Bed sounded wonderful because I was beyond exhausted, but would I be able to sleep?

I was about to find out.

I woke up to an emotional hangover the size of Sydney Harbour and a ringing phone. Huh? Oh, it was my phone, and it was on the pillow next to me. Where was Will? I grunted and wiped the drool off my face. I put my hand on the phone, and it stopped ringing. Dammit! They never gave you enough time to answer it before it took a message. Stupid phone companies. I looked at the display. Will. Oh, God, it was lunchtime. Funny how I could happily go back to sleep for the next few weeks, till the shock of what I saw last night wore off.

The phone rang again, and I flinched. This time, I managed to answer it before it stopped. "Hey. Is everything okay?"

The smile in his voice came through loud and clear. "Did I wake you, sleepyhead?"

"Of course. It's the kind of day where staying in bed oblivious would be preferable." I lifted the blinds and checked outside. Yep, raining. What a surprise… not.

"How are you feeling?"

"About as you'd expect, but I'll survive. Thanks for asking."

"It's my job, fiancée." I couldn't help but smile at that. Yes, life went on. "I'm also calling because I'd like you to come to a meeting I'm having with Agent Roche. Millicent and James are minding the… stuff."

"Um, okay. Is it at headquarters?"

"No. We're meeting at Roche's house. I'll come get you. Can you be ready in fifteen minutes?"

"Yep. See you soon. Love you."

He hung up, and I dressed, then had breakfast. Just as I magicked the dirty dishes clean and away, Will's footsteps came down the hall. "Hey, Lily." He had small bags under his eyes, and his hair was a little mussed up, but that made him even more sexy.

I gave him a huge hug. "Hey. You look tired. How are you going?"

"Just like you, I'll survive." He smiled. "Come on. They're waiting for us. I gave Roche a couple of the things we found in the boxes, intact pieces of jewellery. He says he has some very interesting information on them."

"Okay. That sounds… interesting." I waggled my brows.

"Come on." Will made a doorway, and I stepped through. He was right behind me. We came out to a small white-painted room with light-coloured timber parquetry flooring. The only furnishing was a pretty French country-style chair upholstered with cream-coloured fabric, which had blue flowers all over it. Hopefully, I wouldn't need the chair because Roche would answer the door promptly. Will knocked.

The door swung open, and the bald agent I'd met briefly stood there. He was dressed in his uniform, as was Will. I'd opted for jeans and jumper since I wasn't an agent, and I wasn't actually investigating anything. Okay, truth be told, I hadn't thought to wear the uniform, and Will didn't ask. Yep, it was totally his fault. "Agent Blakesley, Miss Bianchi, lovely to see you again." Agent Roche stepped back and gestured for us to come in. "*Veuillez entrer.*"

I smiled. "Merci." Since we were in France, it was only polite to use whatever French I knew, which wasn't much, but still.

Agent Roche led us through a small foyer to a large lounge-dining room, richly furnished with ornate upholstered furniture. It was very French, but it also looked slightly uncomfortable. Will and I sat next to each other on an apricot-coloured chaise lounge. It wasn't really my style, but I wasn't here to critique his designer skills. The head of the French PIB dragged a black Louis XV chair close to us and sat, then cast a bubble of silence. "Thank you again for coming today. These are fearful times, the worst I've seen in all my years with the PIB."

Will sat forward, leaning towards our host. "May I speak frankly?"

"But of course. I was hoping you would." He looked at me. "Earlier today, we both took a vow of honesty, sealed with a spell. Whatever we talk about today to each other will only be the truth." He turned back to Will. "Which I was more than happy to do. We need cooperation now more than ever."

"Yes, we do." Will rubbed his five o'clock shadow. "I must let you know that Chad… Agent Williamson the Third, has stood me down because I refused to interview any more people in relation to the Regula Pythonissam case until we could ensure their safety. So anything we talk about now is strictly off the record. I expect the same courtesy. If you feel you can't provide it, we can shake hands now and go our separate ways."

WITCH WAR IN WESTERHAM

"Please, no. We need your help, and I fear we have lost the support of your head office. I am more than happy to speak *off the record*. Oh, and forgive me for not asking, but would either of you like a tea or coffee?"

I shook my head and smiled. "No, thank you. I just had a coffee before I came."

"Are you sure?"

"Positive."

"Okay, then, let us get into what I have to tell you about the jewellery you gave me earlier." His magic—steadfast, quietly powerful, and self-assured—tingled my scalp, and a small, round table appeared to his left. A golden-beetle brooch and a ruby-and-diamond necklace were sitting on it. His magic tingled again, and two A4 photos materialised in his hand. He held them up for us to see. "Fifteen years ago, a woman by the name of Lucile Dupont reported having jewellery stolen. This picture of the brooch is enlarged and is a copy of what she sent us."

I sucked in a breath. "They're identical!"

"Yes, they are." He handed the pictures to Will to study. "The necklace was reported stolen five years ago, from a pawnshop in Paris—we have the name of the person who sold it to them on record as well. The interesting thing about these items is that they both belonged to families caught up in this slave trade you uncovered."

Will looked up from the pictures. He had his most professional poker face on, so I had no idea what he was thinking. "Are you sure?"

"Yes, positive. The brooch belonged to the grandmother of one of the men who was murdered in the apartment, and the necklace belonged to the great aunt of one of the women you still have under protection—her family has not been interviewed yet, but this great aunt disappeared after she sold the item to the pawnshop. No one knows what happened to her."

I frowned. I had a pretty good idea what had happened. If she was in any way involved with RP and she did something they didn't like, she was not of this earth any longer.

Will handed the photos back. "I can bring you more of the pieces if you like. You can cross-check them against your records."

"Three more pieces would be helpful. I think if we can identify them, we will establish a pattern."

"Agreed." Will sat back and folded his arms. "What do you think is going on here?"

"I'm not sure, but in the report about the brooch, when our agents went to interview the woman who reported it stolen, she refused to talk to them."

I scrunched up my forehead. "That's weird. Why would you report it in the first place and then not help the police later?"

Agent Roche waved his finger forward and back. "And that is the question, is it not? Maybe someone got to her, threatened her?"

My eyes widened. "Threatened to kill her?"

Agent Roche tipped his head to the side. "It is possible. And this is what we must find out, among other things. If they did threaten her, she knew who they were. She died five years ago, so we may never know."

Will scratched his neck. "But maybe her descendants know. I think we should track down her children and grandchildren and see if they can remember anything. But we'd have to protect them afterwards."

Agent Roche deflated, his shoulders drooping. "I don't

know how that is possible. I can't take them to our cells, in case we have a mole, and I don't have anywhere else to put them."

I looked at Will. "The other option is that we cut the head off the snake and find out the specifics later. God knows we have enough evidence to put Dana and her father away for life."

His intense gaze burned through me. He knew as well as I did that we weren't looking to arrest them. There would be no way that Dana would come willingly. I had a feeling that she'd rather die than be incarcerated—not that she'd ever believe she could possibly lose, especially if she was fighting against me.

Did I have news for her.

Somehow, she blamed my mother for her mother's death. I didn't know if it was true, but she had one up on me: the snake group had killed both my parents, and she still had her criminal of a father. As upsetting as it was, I wouldn't have blamed her personally if she was a nice person whose father happened to be involved. Yet, she carried a vendetta against my mother and all her descendants. It was utterly crazy. And what was I supposed to do? That's right—I wasn't going down easily. I might be a nice person—at least I used to be—but I didn't have a death wish.

"But what about the rest of them?" Agent Roche asked. "Are they really the only two at the top?"

Argh, why did he have to complicate things? "Um, we don't really know."

Will stepped in, thank the universe. "We've been investigating them for a long time, and it appears that way. We do know that when we go for them, that it will expose most, if not all, of the people at the top. Everything they've done so far is to protect Dana and her father. Anyone who works for them is murdered as soon as we start questioning them, sometimes even before." Will looked at me briefly before turning back to Agent Roche. "Lily's parents were investigating them years ago. They both disappeared, and from the clues her mother has managed to leave behind, it points to Dana's father running the show. We have another man who's featured prominently though."

Understanding sparked in Agent Roche's eyes. "The man you have been watching—Toussaint."

Will licked his lips. "Yes. Those jewels come from his stash." Roche leaned forward and opened his mouth to speak, but Will shook his head. "Not yet. We're not quite ready to tell you everything." It was an effort not to sag with relief. I wasn't sure how we were going to explain how we'd gotten to the point of stealing the key. There would be too many questions about how we discovered it.

"Well, I will be asking you to explain things before this is all over, and I expect an answer."

Will nodded. "I understand."

Hmm, I had a thought, although it was probably stupid. Ha, what was I talking about? It definitely *was* stupid. "I know a way we can confirm who's running the group."

Both men stared at me, disbelief loud and clear in their expressions. I should be used to it by now, but it rankled. "I can't explain now, but I'll run it by Will when we leave. If he finds it acceptable, he can fill you in later, when we've done what we need to."

"That's all very, how you say, wishy-washy, Miss Bianchi."

"Sorry, but it's the best I can do. But rest assured, when we take them down, we'll have all the major players."

Roche looked to Will for confirmation. He gave him a nod.

Then Will's phone rang. He looked at the caller ID. "Excuse me a moment. I have to take this."

When Will was gone, Agent Roche pinned me with a shrewd gaze. "So, you suspect they had a hand in your parents going missing?"

My brows drew down. "Didn't Will tell you about my father?"

"No."

"Can I trust you not to pass this on?"

"Yes."

I was hoping the truth spell they'd both sworn to would extend to me. "The skeletons in the boxes…."

His eyes widened. "One is your father?" I nodded, not trusting myself to speak as a wave of grief swamped me. He nodded, a thoughtful expression on his face. "*D'accord*. I understand."

Will walked back in and gave me a quizzical look. I shook my head. I could explain later. Right now, I didn't want to cry in front of a stranger. Will looked at Agent Roche. "I'm afraid we have to leave. Agent Bianchi needs some help, but I'll be in touch in the next day or two."

Agent Roche stood, and they shook hands. He then turned to me and enveloped my hand in both of his—they were oddly smooth. I guessed even men had ultra-smooth hands when they didn't perform manual labour. Did he get manicures? Pedicures? A scalp massage? Oh dear, now a smile threatened. I kept it in check because I didn't want him to think I was hysterical. "We'll get to the bottom of this, Miss Bianchi. Have no doubt that I am on your side, and Agent Williamson the Third will not hear of anything from me. When you need them, my agents are at your disposal, but we must tread cautiously. As in your head office, we may have Regula

Pythonissam spies among us." He released my hand. "Good luck, and God speed to both of you.

We thanked him and left.

Will made the doorway, so I had no idea where we were going until I stepped out into the barn in France. We exited the horse stall and made our way over to James and Millicent, who were sitting on a couple of plastic chairs in the middle of the barn. They both stood. Large bags had settled under James's eyes, and he hadn't bothered to shave. I knew just how he felt. Since seeing my father lying in that makeshift coffin, a heavy dolefulness had attached itself to my heart. Everything was harder, more effort, especially breathing and smiling. I went to him and gave him a massive hug. I didn't bother saying anything. Asking how he felt was a waste of time. He knew I knew, and I knew he knew. We both just… knew.

He was the first to pull out of the embrace, and he turned to Will. "It's been pretty uneventful for a change. I relieved Imani early this morning, but I haven't had much sleep. If you could do a few hours with Millicent, I can be back with Imani to take tonight's shift."

"I can do that. Get some rest."

"Thanks, mate. It won't be easy, but I'm ready to collapse." He gave Millicent a quick kiss on the lips, made his doorway, and left.

Millicent smiled. "I'm just going to the loo. Be back in a sec. Then it's you and me, Will. Fancy a game of gin rummy?" She magicked a pack of cards into her hand.

He smiled. "Sounds good to me."

Millicent handed the cards to Will. "Be back in a sec." She headed for a door on the other side of the barn, where I assumed the toilet must be.

I planted my hands on my hips and cocked my head to the side. "Hey, I want in if you're just going to socialise all day."

Will's brow furrowed. He was such a worrywart. "It would be good if you were safe at home."

"I know, but if I'm there, all I'll do is think about the last couple of days, and it'll do my head in. Can I at least stay for an hour or so? Then I might be ready for an afternoon nap." I gave him a cheesy grin.

He blew out a big breath. "Okay."

"Yay!"

His phone dinged with a message. "Why does it never end?"

"I have no idea."

He opened the message and blinked. "It's the coroner from the Paris PIB. He has some news on the corpses." He looked at me. "I don't want to leave, but this shouldn't take too long. I'll be back soon. If I'm going to be longer than twenty minutes, I'll message."

I smiled even though disappointment settled in amongst the other crappy feelings running around inside me. "That's okay. I'm sure Millicent will still play cards with me."

"Of course I will!" She called out as she hurried over. She sat on one of the plastic chairs. "Why isn't Will playing?"

"I have to go to the Paris PIB for a little while, but I'll be back soon. Even though you're playing cards, stay alert. Okay?" He handed the cards back to Millicent.

Millicent nodded and patted her jacket pocket. "I'm ready for anything."

"Good. I'll see you both soon." He made his doorway and left.

Millicent's magic tickled my nape, and a foldout table

appeared between the two plastic chairs. She put the deck of cards on top. "Time to play." She smiled.

"Get ready to lose, baby. I used to play with Mum and Dad all the time. We had family game night every Friday night." I sighed, trying not to make it into a negative. I'd been lucky to have that time with them. *Remember them with joy, Lily.*

Millicent grinned. "We'll see about that." She winked. "Okay. Cut the cards."

I reached over to cut them, and she slammed her hand on the top of her chest. Her face twisted. "Are you okay, Mill?"

She blinked, and her magic tickled my scalp. Handcuffs appeared in her hand. She looked at me, alarm in her widened eyes. Crap. Were we under attack? I jumped up and looked around—I already had my return to sender up, so I was as ready as I could be.

Something cold hit my wrist. *Click.* A gut-wrenching void opened inside me. Millicent stood, pushed me around, and forced my arms behind my back. She clamped the other hand-cuff on my wrist.

What. The. Hell.

"Millicent, what in the name of all that's squirrely are you doing?"

She blinked. Her mouth dropped open as her glassy eyes resumed their normalcy. "I— I don't know. Oh my God, let me get those off you."

The door burst open, slamming against the barn wall. Dana and a tall herculean man walked through.

Crap.

"Hurry up!" Oh, God, I didn't want to die today. Why had she done that?

But she wasn't hurrying. She stared at our enemies and pulled her gun—they probably had return to senders up, but I couldn't tell because I couldn't access my other sight. Damn. She groaned and shut her eyes as she slowly lowered her gun, although it seemed like she was fighting it. Dana laughed.

Soft footsteps sounded from behind me. "What's going on here?" Will swore. I spun to look at him. What was he doing back? Not that I was unhappy to see him.

"I think they got control of Millicent somehow. She cuffed me."

Will pointed his gun at them and kept his gaze on them as he approached me. Dana stopped halfway between us and the door and planted her hands on her hips. "You're not going to make this *difficult*, are you?" Her lap thug kept moving towards us, albeit slowly.

Millicent, still gripping her gun, had dropped to her knees in her fight against whatever they were doing to her. Why wasn't her return to sender working? I assumed she'd had one up—she was a seasoned agent. There was no way she'd make a mistake like that.

Dana smirked. "Uncuff Lily, and I'll kill Millicent."

I swallowed my protest. Begging would only make her more excited. Evil witch. If there was something I could do with my hands cuffed behind my back and my magic not working, I'd find it. Hatred, anger, and fear were great motivators… at least in my case.

Will stopped, and the thug took two steps towards me. Millicent had curled into a ball on the ground. What the hell were they doing to her? I stared at Dana. I wanted to wipe that smirk off her stupid face.

"Ooh, Lily, you look angry." Her tinkling laughter reminded me of doing a number one on the toilet. She was gross even when she wasn't trying to be.

"You remind me of wee." Her smirk dropped, and I

laughed. "I also love that you're so scared of me that you had to disable my magic. Feel like it wasn't a fair fight before?"

"She doesn't like to lose, and she knew she'd lose if you had all your magic." I loved it when Will joined in. Maybe if we prodded her enough, she'd make a mistake out of anger.

Her hand flicked out. I couldn't feel any magic because mine had been cut off, but she was up to something for sure. "Watch out, Will!"

A zap of magic hit the dangling light fitting above Millicent, and it came crashing down. Will deflected it just before it hit my sister-in-law, and she didn't even flinch, still caught up fighting whatever was in her head.

With Will distracted, the thug shot at him, the crack sending a mouse scurrying across the floor.

I screamed.

Will must have had a shield up because the bullet deflected and hit the barn wall.

My breath came fast, and my heart raced.

Millicent groaned. I spared her a glance. She clawed at her chest. What the hell was she doing?

"Enough!" Dana approached Millicent and put her hand on her head. She looked at Will. "Let Lily go peacefully, and I won't kill Millicent." I didn't know what she was doing, but Millicent cried out, then whimpered. Adrenaline warmed my throat, and it was all I could do not to run over there and slam Piranha out of the way with my body.

There was only one other option—going with them. Surely, I'd figure something out on the way. I refused to believe I couldn't work out how to escape later. Goodness knew I had a talent for accidentally killing people... and she couldn't be worse than someone born to kill other witches, aka the vampire witch. I'd survived him, and I'd survive her.

WITCH WAR IN WESTERHAM

"It's fine, Will. I'll go with her. She's got nothing on that vampire witch I killed last month." I gave Piranha a self-satisfied grin, as if nothing was too hard. It gave me pleasure to see her eyes widen before she quickly resumed her snarly demeanour.

"Please don't, Lily."

"Have a little faith, future husband of mine." I grinned. Anger singed Piranha's gaze. He he, I sure knew how to push her buttons. I looked at her. "What are you waiting for? Are you still scared of me, even with my hands cuffed?" I stomped a step towards her, and she flinched. "Ha! I knew it. Scaredy-cat."

"I'm not scared of you." She let her hand slide off Millicent's head and took a step closer to me.

"Great, nice to know. I don't believe you, though. In any case, I'll come with you on the condition that I get to give Will a kiss goodbye and Millicent a hug, well, as best I can with these cuffs on."

"Since when did I say I was taking last requests?"

I shrugged. "You didn't, and I guess I'd expect it from a loser like you. I bet your mother would be so proud." Bingo. I'd hit the jackpot.

A crazed flash lit her eyes. "Don't you dare bring my mother into this. She loved me, and if it wasn't for your mother, she'd still be here."

"Blah, blah, blah. Whatever you want to believe. You're a horrible person, and your mother, had she still been here, would agree with me."

"She has got a point," Will said. Wow, it surprised me that he'd cottoned onto my line of needling. It was all I had left. "I have no idea how any mother could love someone as depraved as you." Ooh, low blow, but I highly approved.

"It's probably good she's dead. You would've broken her heart."

Her nostrils flared. She shook her head slowly. I couldn't tell if she was drawing power, but she raised her arm, and her associate shook his head.

His deep voice was measured. "Remember what your father said." Hmm, interesting.

She clenched her fists. "Argh! You'll pay for that comment, William. Once I have Lily, I'll torture her and film it, just so you can watch later. I might even keep her alive long enough so you can watch some of it in person."

"Well, in that case, I'm not going with you. Screw that." I couldn't be too agreeable, or she'd figure out I had a plan. Okay, so it wasn't a great plan, but the fact that it existed was a bonus, considering how my brain wanted to flake and run from the situation.

She snarled and gripped Millicent's hair and yanked her head back. A knife appeared in Piranha's hand. She placed it at Millicent's throat. My normally fairly unflappable sister-in-law's eyes were filled with terror. "Oh, yes you are. You pull out and this witch gets it." She sneered. "Just to prove I'm a good sport, have your idiotic kiss and cuddle, then. I can wait another two minutes for victory."

Will watched his adversaries warily as I made my way to him, my cockiness squashed by fear. If Piranha cut Mill's throat…. If it wasn't for my plan, I'd be a screaming mess. But I only had one chance.

Will gave me a fierce hug, and I whispered, "Make a bubble of silence." He did, although my nape prickled at the thought of pissing Dana off further while she had a knife at Millicent's neck. "I'm about to free Millicent's magic."

"But how?"

"You'll see. Just be ready."

The thug was yelling at us, but we couldn't hear him. Will dropped the bubble of silence. "Sorry, but Lily and I wanted to have a few private words goodbye." He looked at me. "I don't like you doing this. Please don't." I was sure he meant it but was also putting on an act for Dana's benefit.

I shook my head. "I have to. If anything happens to Millicent, James will never forgive me. She's a mother now. I'm not. It's better I go than she dies. Besides, you know I'll figure it out. They won't hold me for long." The bravado was important, lest Piranha figure something was up. She wasn't the sharpest tool in the shed, but she wasn't stupid either... cunning was a kind of intelligence, and she was all over that personality trait. Plus, she had no conscience. I didn't doubt she wanted to kill Millicent. The only reason she didn't is it gave her leverage. Even she knew all bets were off if Millicent died.

Piranha barked a laugh. "Yeah, right. Dream on. You're the weakest witch I know." She flicked her gaze at her henchman. "And that's saying something." He gave her a deadpan look but said nothing. Way to make friends and influence people. Hmm, maybe I was a bit out with the *cunning* assessment. Upsetting your hires was bound to cause resentment. I'd file that information for later use.

Thankfully, Dana dropped Millicent's hair, but she kept the knife. I had to walk close to Piranha on my way to Mill, and I did my best not to flinch, but it wasn't easy. Hate radiated off her, and it was all for me. Deep down, I knew I could beat her, but it would also take a bit of luck... and magic. She had way more experience than me, especially at attacking people. Without my magic, it was as if I walked naked. I'd never felt so vulnerable, and I hated it. *Add that to the reasons you want her dead.*

Those reasons were piling up faster than a multi-vehicle accident on an icy highway.

Millicent had curled back up in the foetal position. This was going to be tricky. I looked around in an automatic precursor to asking for help. Piranha's evil gaze met mine. Ah, yeah, nah. I'd have to do this myself. I dropped to the ground, slamming onto my knees. Pain speared through them. I ground my teeth together rather than cry out. I took a deep breath, trying to regain my concentration. "Millicent, honey, it's Lily. Can you sit up? I want to say goodbye."

She curled in tighter to herself like an armadillo. I turned an angry gaze on Piranha. "For goodness' sake. Stop torturing her. I want to say goodbye properly, dammit."

She grinned. "Ooh, cranky, cranky. What if I don't?"

"Well, don't, then. I'll just add it to the accruing list of stuff I have to take revenge for. Be my guest. Oh, and I'll tell your father how cruel you've been. From what I understand, he wants to use me for something—he doesn't actually hate me." I cocked my head to the side. "Hmm, are you jealous of me? That your dad wants something from me you can't give him?"

Sparks flew from her eyes as rage stiffened her shoulders. I swear she wore a button on her forehead that said *Push me, Lily*. It totally wasn't my fault. Who could resist that kind of temptation?

"Enough!" Her raised voice told me I had hit a bullseye. I held back my grin—no need to push her over the edge so that she said no goodbye cuddle for me and Millicent. Let no one say there was no finesse to this.

Millicent relaxed enough to look up at me through teary, bloodshot eyes. It looked like the real Millicent was there.

"Can you sit up? I want to say goodbye."

A tear rolled down her face as she uncurled. She groaned and shut her eyes for a moment. What had they done to her? Finally, she sat up, then made it to her knees and met my gaze. "No, Lily." Her hoarse voice was quiet, and I had to lean in to hear. "Let her kill me. We need you."

I shook my head and gave her a meaningful look. "I just need to give you a hug. Please? We don't have much time. I have to go, and I'll be devo if I don't get to say goodbye properly."

"Devo?"

"Devastated. It doesn't matter. Just put your arms around me. I'm kind of tied up." I gave her a "whaddaya gonna do about it" smile.

Her brow wrinkled, but she said, "Okay." She shuffled closer and put her arms around me. I buried my face in her neck, burrowing like a pig searching for truffles. I had to get my tongue under the collar of her sweater. *Please don't react to me licking you.*

There, got my tongue under. I resisted the need to blow a raspberry—having wool in your mouth wasn't fun. I dug around a bit, and she shifted slightly, probably wondering what the hell was going on, but she said nothing. She trusted me, and that meant everything.

There it was, something textural and cold. I gathered it with my tongue and placed it between my teeth. Then I chomped down and pulled back. It silently snapped, and Millicent relaxed against me. "Thank you," she whispered.

"Any time. Now, be a good sister-in-law and make a shield around us so you can unlock my handcuffs."

"It would be my pleasure." We each sat back, and she gave me a nod. I had to assume her shield was up because I couldn't feel anything. We stood, and I turned my back to Millicent so she could free me.

Piranha's mouth dropped open. She must be able to see Mill's shield. Yay! This time I allowed myself a smug smile, all for her.

Will grinned and gave me a nod. He turned and shot twice at the thug—he would've had to drop his shield to do that but would surely have snapped it back in place. Both bullets rico-cheted, but the thug bent at the waist, as if someone had punched him. His magic had taken a real hit.

Millicent's cold hands on mine were reassuring. I felt more than heard the tiny *click*, and then I was free. My magic was back! "Woohoo!" I grinned and looked at Piranha. "Care to play?" I drew as much magic as I could hold—she likely could see the ridiculously bright glow of my aura and realised I wasn't mucking around... even though I was. I assumed she'd run. If she didn't, maybe I'd blow her up. "Mill, drop the shield on three."

That's all it took for Piranha to hiss and make her doorway. Before she left, she pointed at one of the boxes we'd brought back from Mont Saint-Michel. Her magic stabbed icky fingers into my scalp, and the box disappeared. Crap. "One, two, three." As the shield fell and I let loose a bolt of lightning, she stepped through her doorway. Damn! My lightning kept going and blew a hole in the side of the barn. Timber fragments exploded everywhere. Oops.

Her thug gave Will an angry glare. Will shot at him again. The man staggered backwards, scrambled to make his door-way, and jumped through.

Will swore. "What the hell?" I looked at Will and shook my head. What had they wanted that was in that box? We hadn't gone through everything yet. Grrrr.

Millicent grabbed my arm and turned me to face her. "I'm so sorry, Lily." She shook her head. "I— I don't know what happened. I was being compelled. Oh, God, I almost got you killed." Her face collapsed in sorrow and shame.

"You were almost killed too. It's the necklace from your cousin. He's one of them, Mill."

She dug under her sweater and pulled out the broken rose-gold chain, the little heart still attached. She stared at it, her brows drawing down.

Will strode over and looked at me. "How did you know?"

"She was clutching her chest, and last time I saw her cousin, he was making sure she was wearing it. He doth protest too much, me thinks. And I know you had lunch with him the other day. I bet he made sure you were wearing it."

She stared at the necklace in her hand for a moment, then looked up. "He was there with a colleague… another witch. But I can't remember much."

Will and I shared a horrified look. He swore again. "They must have coerced you to wear it. Show me your phone." She unlocked it and handed it to him. "Damn. Look at the message you sent."

She's here. Hurry.

Millicent paled. "I— I— Oh my God, James is never going to forgive me." She started hyperventilating.

Will put a firm hand on her shoulder. "Look at me, Mill." He waited until she'd complied, her panicked gaze meeting his reassuring one. "James is going to do nothing of the sort. He loves you. This isn't your fault. I fell for it too. I went to the morgue, and there was no one there. I was a bit pissed, but then I figured maybe they had to rush out, so I came back… and just in time, it seems."

"And, hey, everything turned out okay. Plus, we know

about the necklace now, and you won't be wearing it anymore."

She shuddered and held it out to Will. "Please take this. I never want to see it again. As for my cousin…."

Will's predatory grin almost made me feel sorry for her cousin, but not quite. "James and I will take care of him when this is all over. Don't you worry about that, Mill. We'll leave him for last so he can rot in jail later. I'd hate for him to die as soon as we arrest him. Once we're done with RP, he's the first priority on our list."

She nodded and sniffed, another rush of tears trailing down her face. I slid my arms around her and pulled her to me. "You're just as much a victim as me, Mill. You are *not* responsible, and I love you. Please forgive yourself. Don't let them break you. We stand together now and always."

She spoke through her tears. "But I'm an agent, Lily. I'm supposed to be aware and capable. I've failed spectacularly this time."

"You haven't failed. Your cousin set you up. They knew the only way to get to you would be through someone you trusted. Don't beat yourself up about trusting a relative. You can't be on guard 24/7."

Will put his hand on my back. "Come on. Why don't you take Mill home? I'll hold the fort here. I might call Agent Roche and see if there's anyone he trusts to provide back up. Once you've spoken to James, go home, and stay safe. We need to rethink everything. We can't leave this stuff here—we're too exposed." He didn't need to voice his concern over what they'd taken. Had all this just been a ruse to take what was in that box? Surely not. If it was, why did they wait till I was here without Will or James?

"Hmm…. I might have just the person." Someone owed

me a favour—not that I thought they owed it to me, but they thought they did, so same thing. I hated asking anything of anyone, but things didn't get any riskier than this, and it could be my last chance to ask anything of anyone, so I might as well take it. Who knew? It might just help protect my loved ones. The fewer distractions we had right now, the better.

"Since when do you know people?"

"I wouldn't want to give anything away." Will had cast a bubble of silence earlier, but I had no idea if there were any privacy wards on the barn. In light of what just happened, I wasn't going to blurt things out in a place I didn't know well. "I'll tell you later."

His forehead lines deepened. "Don't go anywhere without me, James, or Imani."

"I won't. Don't worry. I'm thinking I can probably call this person to come to me, and before you panic, it's someone I trust."

He shook his head. "I don't like this."

I rolled my eyes. "I'll tell James who it is, okay? I'll even get them to come to his place. Does that make you feel better?"

"Yes. Since you're taking it all away, I'll make sure it's all catalogued. I'll need another twenty-four hours; after that, we'll store it. Now, you both look after each other. I'll see you later." He gave me a firm hug and a fierce goodbye kiss on the lips. Even after everything that had just happened, he made me feel like it was all going to work out, and even if it didn't, he gave me butterflies and made my heart happy. Whatever the future brought, I was still the luckiest girl in the world.

"Come on, Mill. Let's go." I took her hand, made a doorway, and pulled her through.

Thankfully, James managed to talk some sense into Millicent, but she wasn't fully recovered. Every time she looked at me, her eyes were apologetic. Hopefully it wouldn't last long because it would drive me crazy. She'd look at me like that and I'd feel compelled to tell her it was fine. I guessed whatever it took to make her feel better, and if that meant I was telling her for the next few months, well, so be it.

James had okayed me calling Mr Sorokin, the father of one of Tommy's victims. Alena had been an agent, yet she'd succumbed to his attack. Killing the vampire witch had come with a huge thank you and an offer that if I ever needed him, he'd be there to help. I wasn't sure exactly what he did. I think someone had mentioned something about owning a successful business, and I didn't think he was into anything criminal, but I got the feeling he commanded respect and people would do anything for him. Which meant he probably had strong witches on hand to protect his stuff. He'd promptly answered my call and was now sitting on James's couch, a cup of tea in hand.

I'd just finished giving him a rough rundown. I didn't want to tell him everything, of course. He also let James ask him a couple of questions and judge his honesty. If James was happy, I was happy. I drained my cappuccino and magicked the cup away. "So, these are the proceeds of crime, and we'll need them for evidence later, but we know the people we stole them from want them back. And we don't want to store them at head office because…." Gah, how to say it without insulting the PIB, seeing as how his good friend was one of the directors.

He smiled. "Say no more, Miss Bianchi. I have somewhere very safe to store your goods. We have the latest non-witch tech, and I have a security department of witches that rivals the world's best. If anyone tries to steal these goods, they'll get a nasty surprise." He laughed. Hmm, seemed he had a similar sense of humour to Angelica.

"Thank you so, so much, Mr Sorokin."

He waved a dismissive hand. "No. How many times do I have to tell you; call me Maxim."

I smiled. "Only if you call me Lily."

He tipped his chin up. "Okay. It's a deal." He held out his hand, and we shook on it.

"Agent Blakesley, Will, will be in touch tomorrow, and you can discuss where you'll be moving everything to."

"Excellent." He drained the last sip of his tea and turned to Millicent. "Thank you, Mrs Bianchi."

She smiled, albeit it gingerly. "My pleasure, Maxim."

Maxim stood, as did we all. James held out his hand to shake Maxim's. "Thanks again. You're saving our skin. Resources are rather limited at the moment."

He frowned. "So I've heard. In any case, lucky you're on the job."

James cleared his throat. "I'm not, actually. I'm doing this in my spare time. I'm on… leave."

Maxim gave him an assessing gaze. "Well, that's good of you, then." Maxim turned to me. "If you need anything else, give me a call."

"I feel bad about putting you out, but we really need your assistance. Hopefully, I won't have to call on you again. You're really saving us."

He smiled. "It's my pleasure. I will see you soon." He made his doorway and left.

James turned to me. "He seems like a good bloke."

I nodded. "He does. I guess I should go home. It's been a long day. I'm going to have an early dinner and get to bed. All the *excitement* has made me tired." I gave Millicent another hug. "I hope you feel better tomorrow. Love you."

I didn't think she'd had dry eyes since we kicked Dana out of the barn. "Thank you, Lily. I love you so much. I don't know how I can ever make it up to you."

I shook my head and smiled. "You're the mother of my gorgeous niece. You've given James and I the gift of family. I can never pay you back either, so why don't we call it even?"

"You're too good to me."

"Ha! I wouldn't go that far. Anyway, let's forget today ever happened, except for the part where I'm holding an extra huge grudge against Dana witchface. She'll get hers soon enough." I gave James a hug, made my doorway, and went home.

This week had been some of the most painful and scary times of my life. If only I knew it was all behind me, but, somehow, I knew it was just the start.

CHAPTER 15

I yawned and rolled over.

"Good morning." Will grabbed my hand and kissed my palm.

"Mmm, what time is it?"

"Just before eight. I got in at midnight, but you were fast asleep." His magic tingled my scalp, and the blinds opened just a smidge, letting enough light in to see without blinding anyone. Although, the sky was so grey, I didn't think we were in much danger of it being too bright. I still blinked and shut my eyes because I wasn't quite awake. Will grunted.

"What's wrong?"

"You've still got the head of that damned snake on your wrist."

I sighed. "Yeah, I know. I've been pretending it's not there. Maybe it can't do anything without the rest of its body?"

"After yesterday, let's not underestimate their ability to control people from a distance."

Damn it. How could I not be awake now? I opened my eyes and looked at Will. "If they get control of me, kill me."

"What? No!"

I hurriedly sat up and looked down at him with way too much intensity for first thing in the morning. "You have to promise me. I'd rather die than be forced to kill any of you. Seriously, Will, you cannot let them use me like that." I didn't know what they could do, but if I were them, I'd use me to kill my friends. That would be the ultimate control and revenge. Piranha would just love that. Crap. Maybe I should go into hiding and stay away from everyone? Gah. Why did it feel like I was back to when I first got the tattoo and everyone was worried about saying anything in front of me in case RP were spying via the tattoo?

Will sat up and swung his legs over the bed. "Let's get dressed and have this discussion over coffee."

Mmm, coffee. I wasn't going to say no to that. We magicked our clothes on and went downstairs, Abby and Ted following. Abby always slept on the end of our bed, and Ted in his dog bed in our room.

"Sit, Lily. Let me make breakfast."

I smiled. "Okay. Thanks!" Yes, he didn't have to put in as much effort as a non-witch, but it was still nice that he asked. He magicked cappuccinos into being and a plate of pancakes with all the accoutrements—chocolate sauce, strawberries, cream, sugar, lemon, jam, butter, ice cream. My mouth watered. "Who's going to eat all this?"

He grinned. "Us. I'm sure I can finish it off if you get full quickly." Ted looked up at Will and wagged his tail. "This stuff isn't great for you, buddy. I tell you what, I'll give you a tiny bit, then you can have a lovely bone." Will gave the dog a bite of plain pancake, then his magic tingled my scalp. A huge raw bone appeared in Ted's bowl and fresh chicken in Abby's dish.

I put a couple of pancakes into my plate and heaped strawberries, ice cream, and chocolate sauce on top. "Mmmm. Yum!" The first bite was divine. I shut my eyes and savoured it. My stomach was cheering. "You're so good at pancakes."

He gave me a cocky grin. "I know."

I laughed. "You're lucky modesty isn't on my list of partner must-haves."

"And you're lucky that compliance isn't on the list of my partner must-haves."

Gah. I made a bubble of silence. "Which brings us to the fact that RP could use me against you. You really know how to ruin a really good breakfast." I frowned. He gave me his best sad face. What hurt most was that I knew he meant it. If anything happened to me, it would break his heart. "I don't want to die, you know. I'm going to do everything in my power so that doesn't happen, but how would you feel if they made you kill everyone?"

"Well, if I have to kill you, it will be their fault." He shook his head. "I'm a trained agent. I've done things I wouldn't wish anyone to do, things that have stopped me sleeping at night, but I could never do that, Lily. I don't know that any of your friends could. And James certainly wouldn't."

I put my knife and fork down and placed my elbows on the table. They made a comfortable stand for my head, which didn't feel like holding itself up anymore. What the hell were we going to do about the tattoo?

"We could get Millicent's dad to try again?"

I shook my head. "He said it's too deeply embedded. Trying to remove it could kill me, although…."

"No!" He ran his fingers through his hair and made part

of it stick up the wrong way. I chuckled and smoothed it down. He looked at me with so much love that I just had to return it and not say anything for a moment. I hoped he could see in my eyes how I felt... would always feel. "I know." He gave me a sad smile and linked his fingers with mine.

"So, what are we going to do about it?"

"I don't know. We'll call a meeting. This needs to be dealt with. We can't go into this fight with any unknowns. We have to prepare for every scenario imaginable."

"I don't know that that's possible. There will always be surprises." And we all knew how much I loved those, but dealing with things on the fly was normally my strong point... except for when I found my father. I sagged back into the chair.

"Come on. Enjoy your breakfast. There are enough things to worry about when we're finished." He leaned over and kissed me.

When Will was right, he was so right. I tried to push everything out of my mind so I could enjoy my ice-creamy, chocolatey pancakes because letting food go to waste was a sin. Okay, so it wasn't, but it should be. The rules according to Lily. I smiled. At least I could still find the humour hiding around the place. Sometimes I had to dig deep, but it was always worth it.

I didn't need a psychic to tell me that I was going to need a lot of it in the coming days. Bummer.

The next morning, we all sat around James's dining-room table. Thankfully, Millicent seemed to be almost back to normal. She'd only apologised once in ten minutes, which was an improvement.

James smiled. "So, we've managed to inventory everything that was left, and it's safely in Maxim's hands. Well done for that one, Lily."

I grinned. "Thank you. I guess it was lucky that I got kidnapped by Tommy."

Imani screwed up her face. "You're so twisted, love."

"Gotta look at the positives." I winked.

She shook her head. "Seriously, love. You're a nutter."

Will stared at me. "Unfortunately, she has another major issue, and we need to discuss it."

Liv giggled. "Are they picking on you? Do you want me to make them go away?"

"Yes please." I smiled, but then it disappeared. "Will's actually not joking." I held my arm up and lowered my sleeve so they could see the snake head. "We have no idea what this is going to do, and not trying to put Mill on the spot, but we know they're exceptional at controlling people from afar. I'm worried they might force me to kill one, or all, of you next time we come face to face."

Beren blew out a huge breath. "Wow, that's heavy. But you're right. Damn."

"That's about it." What else could I say? At least I'd thought to bring it up before it was too late. Millicent looked at me and opened her mouth. I put my hand up to stop her. "If you're going to apologise, don't. You have nothing to apologise for."

"I wasn't going to apologise." I gave her an "are you sure?" look. Her chagrined expression said it all. I laughed. "Okay, so I was. You'll just have to get used to it."

I shook my head. "Nope, I won't because you're going to

stop. Now, instead of that, why don't you give me a good idea so I don't end up killing you all."

"Hmm, let me think. Maybe one of us could have the job as babysitter, so to speak. We can be ready to slap the cuffs on you if something happens."

I raised my brows. "That's actually a great idea!"

Will and James shared a satisfied nod. "That is a good idea," said Will. He looked at Imani. "I think it should be our job. One of us will be next to her at all times."

"Maybe we should both be next to her at all times?" said Imani. "As extra protection as well as caution."

"Well, since I'm not working at the moment, I'll volunteer to be with Lily at all times except when she's here or at home. Our wards have proven to be strong enough to withstand what they have. Other than that television incident, which proved they can't touch her physically, we've had no breaches."

"I'll get Dad over to check the wards if you like."

Any extra checks to our security made me feel way safer. "Thanks, Mill. That would be awesome."

"So, how close are we to weeding them all out and arresting people?" Ah, Beren, always the sweetie. Surely, he knew deep down that they weren't going to go down without a fight and that a lot of them would end up dead.

James took a sip of water. "We need to find out who the main players are. Dana's father and Dana, obviously, and likely Toussaint, but who else? We don't want to miss any of their leaders. We need to squash the potential for them to restart. I have some interesting information, though." His magic tingled my scalp. A piece of paper appeared in his hand, and a picture of a brunette woman wearing a pink designer suit and walking along the street talking on a mobile phone popped up on the wall screen. "Cardinal has dug very deep into Toussaint's affairs. Other than having close contact with Dana's dad—who's been buying weapons in bulk from him over the last ten years—there's another person involved. A woman… Katrin Brandt." He pointed at the screen. "She's a multi-millionaire witch who runs a manufacturing company. She has factories in Germany, England, and France—interestingly, she used to operate in China, but eight years ago, she closed that down. She's also bought weapons from Toussaint, and from email correspondence, it appears she and Dana's father regularly meet with Toussaint. Unfortunately, the German and French governments also buy weapons from Toussaint's company, so we can assume he may be protected in some way. Whatever we pin him on, it's gotta stick. We have the skeletons and gems from his stash, but until we have hard proof he was involved, we really have nothing. There were no fingerprints, no magic signatures. We can only hope for some DNA. What we really need are some witnesses."

Damn. Typical that this wasn't going to just happen easily. "Yeah, well, considering witnesses tend to die en masse, that's not going to be easy."

Imani pressed her lips together. "There has to be a way. This is ridiculous."

James turned to Liv. "If you could do some more research into Katrin Brandt, it would help immensely." He magicked a file onto the table in front of Liv. "There are the details on what we already know. I want you to dig out info on her friends, family, what she does on the weekends… everything."

Liv nodded. "Okay. I'll get started as soon as we're done here."

James smiled. "Excellent."

Will's phone rang. "Hello, Agent Blakesley speaking." He listened for a moment. "Okay, thanks. I'll be there soon." He hung up and put his phone in his pocket. "That was Agent Roche. He's tracked the phone that sent that message yesterday back to an Agent Fontaine. He's in custody, but it doesn't look like he has a snake tattoo, and since he's not dead, looks like he's not a member of RP. I'm going to help interview him."

I didn't want to get my hopes up, but…. "This could be the breakthrough we need."

Will looked at me. "It could, but maybe it isn't. Let's not get our hopes up."

James said, "Be careful, and let me know what happens."

"Will do."

"In the meantime, I'm going to go through Mum's diaries again and see if there's any mention of this German woman. If there is, Lily and I will do further research." Yeah, further research meant putting ourselves in danger, but whatever. I didn't think there was a time where we weren't in danger anymore. I just hoped I didn't get killed while I was on the toilet. How embarrassing would that be? James looked at me. "What's wrong?"

"Uuuuuuuum. Nothing."

He gave me a weird look, then shook his head, dismissing the comment. "When everyone leaves, Lily, please stay, and we'll get started."

"Okay."

Imani looked at Beren. "We have PIB work to do. Let's go and pretend we're on the job. Maybe we could spend some time surveilling Toussaint's place?"

Beren smiled. "Sounds good to me." He turned to James. "If you need anything, just buzz."

"Will do, mate."

"Okay, I'm off. I'll be back when I'm done." Will made his

doorway and left, taking a piece of my heart with him. What a cliché, but still…. What if something happened to him? I hoped it wasn't another scam call. Although we were pretty sure Roche was on our side, what if someone had stolen his phone and was impersonating him?

Deep breaths, Lily. Deep breaths.

One by one, everyone said goodbye and left, and then Annabelle started crying. Millicent went to feed her. And then there were two. James magicked Mum's diaries onto the table. "Okay, so Mum hasn't been obvious about the information she's given us. Why don't we look for code names for people?"

"Could you do it using magic?"

"Not unless I knew what spell she used to create the code, if she even did. That one about Gabriel was your garden-variety clue." He opened one of the diaries and slid one over to me.

Hmm. "James?"

"Yes?"

"From what we can see, back when Mum was investigating this, the PIB knew about it. Right?"

"I think so. From what Angelica said, it was a PIB assignment, but after our parents disappeared, they swept it under the rug."

Suspicious much? "That's just weird. Why wouldn't they look into it?"

He shrugged. "Apparently they did, but another agent went missing, and then it all got shelved. One of the old directors died… not under suspicious circumstances, and a new one was appointed. There was a fair bit going on at that time, so they decided to leave it alone."

"That's crazy. Agents were killed! Didn't they care? So much for protecting their workers."

He shook his head. "I don't know, Lily. Anyway, why ask?"

"Well, maybe we should go through Mum's old files. She might've had something in there. If it was an investigation, she must've had evidence in some files at work?"

"I've already looked for it. Everything to do with that case was destroyed."

"What?"

He sat back and looked at me. Eventually, he said, "You're right. It's all too weird." His eyes widened. "There were records of when it was destroyed too. Hang on a minute." He magicked his laptop to the table in front of him and typed away. When he was done, he turned the computer so I could see the screen. It was separated into two images. One showed a document with a date: Two thousand and fourteen. The other was a screen with a small picture of Dana's face in the top left corner. Employee start date: 2nd February, 2014.

My mouth dropped open. "Well, well, well, someone started working there at a suspicious time. So she was never there because she wanted to be an agent."

"Doesn't look like it. She must have destroyed those files." He swore. "RP must have information on everything from our operations to evidence in multiple investigations. Jesus. This goes back further than I could've imagined. Did they have someone in there when Mum and Dad went missing?"

"Your guess is better than mine. I didn't even know the bureau existed until last year."

He rubbed the back of his neck. "Stuff it. I can't find out anything about that now anyway. Let's just focus on accessing those files." He looked at me. "Ready for some snooping?"

I grinned and magicked my camera to myself. "Always."

He stood. "We'll just get in and try our luck. Chad won't

be wandering the hallways. He's probably holed up in his office with his feet on the table eating cheese from a can."

I laughed. "What?!"

"He gets it sent here from the US." James imitated sticking his fingers down his throat and gagging.

"What do you have to put in cheese to make it come out of a can? Is it even cheese anymore?"

"I have no idea. I've never tried it, and I'm not about to. Give me a good brie or feta any day."

My stomach grumbled. Damn. I'd just had breakfast. Was it too early for a mid-morning snack? "Mmm, me too."

"As much as I'd prefer to chat about cheese all day, we need to get a move on. Mum's office now belongs to Agent Fairweather. She's quite nice, actually, a good agent, and she started two years before Mum left. She's only a few years younger than Angelica, and I'm pretty sure she's one of her supporters, but still, don't say more than you have to."

"Of course. I don't trust anyone outside of our little circle."

"That's what I like to hear. Hang on a sec." He pulled his phone out and sent a text. One came back within a minute. He looked up at me. "See you in the reception room."

I stepped through my doorway. James stood in front of the intercom, but he didn't press the button. "What are you doing?"

He smiled. "Waiting for Gus. I texted him before we left."

"Ah, good call."

We didn't have to wait long before the door opened. Good old Gus. He shook James's hand. "So good to see you, Agent Bianchi. We've missed you around here."

"I've missed you too. Just keep it quiet." James tapped the side of his nose.

Gus nodded, a gravely serious expression on his face. "Of course. Here. I thought you might need this." He handed James something small and hairy, then looked at me. "Hello, Miss Lily! It's awfully quiet around here without you."

"Aw, thanks. I miss stirring things up." And it was true. I disliked Chad immensely, but he was fun to rile up. No one else quite gave me the fodder for fun that he did. While I said hello to Gus, James had attached the stuff Gus had given him. I blinked and laughed. "I'm not sure if that's a great disguise or it's going to make people stare." He'd put on a moustache, short beard, and thick eyebrows. "Where's mine, Gus?"

His mouth made an *O*. "I'm so sorry, Miss Lily, but I didn't think to bring anything for you. To be honest, Agent Bianchi forgot to mention you were coming."

I rolled my eyes in mock offence. "Hopeless. I don't know why I bother." Gus looked at me in horror. I giggled. "It's fine. I was just kidding. You need to lighten up, Gus. You know I'd never get upset with you."

He gave me a shy grin. "True. You're always happy to see me."

"I am. You're awesome. I guess I just need to walk behind you guys and try not to be seen, although I haven't been banned from here, so I suppose if someone sees me, we can just tell them, I'm your assistant, Gus. Oh."

"What?" asked James.

"You won't be able to use your magic here now that you're not on the *approved* list."

"No, I won't, but you still have yours. Hopefully, I won't need it. And on that note, let's hurry this up. The longer we're here, the more risk we're taking. You lead the way, Gus. We're going to Agent Fairweather's office."

"It would be my pleasure, sir."

As we walked, James, in all his wisdom, decided to engage Gus in small talk. "How's the family, Gus?" *Noooooooooooo!* I magicked my earbuds to myself and programmed my phone to play some Thirty Seconds to Mars, and it was just in time if James's disgusted face was anything to go by. I gave him a cheeky grin meant to be interpreted as "sucked in." His response of a dirty look made me smile. He understood. To be fair, I'd warned him about this before, and if he hadn't listened, it wasn't my problem.

We got in the lift and went down one level. I bopped my head up and down to the music while Gus talked, and James plastered a pretend smile on his face. It almost looked like he had gas. I quietly snorted. They both looked at me. Oops, it mustn't have been as quiet as I'd thought. Maybe my music was up too loud? I shrugged.

The door opened, and Gus led the way to the left. I took my earbuds out as the gravity of the situation seeped in. We were going to Mum's office. I was going to see her through the lens again. I swallowed, memories of my father raw and stinging. My stomach had turned into a tempestuous sea of queasiness—a quea-sea. Ha ha. It wasn't even funny enough to make me smile. Prognosis—not good.

"I'm sorry, Miss Lily. I forgot I wasn't supposed to mention vomit."

I did my best to smile. "It's fine, Gus. It actually wasn't your story. I think I ate something this morning that didn't agree with me."

James looked at me, concern in his gaze. I gave a short shake of my head. He nodded, then turned to Gus as we slowed and stopped in front of a door. "Are you going to wait around, or do you want me to text you when we're done?"

"I have a couple of things to do downstairs. Just text me."

"Okay. Thanks, mate."

"Any time…"—he lowered his voice to a whisper—"Agent Bianchi." Gah, seriously, Gus. He should know better. My brother looked up and down the hallway, but thankfully, no one was coming.

"I'll text you." James turned and knocked on the door as Gus gave me a wave and walked off. I kept my mouth shut. James and I could whinge to each other later, when we were safe at home with our information.

"Come in!" The voice was loud, as if the woman was in the hallway with us.

James must've noticed the surprise on my face because he said, "An amplify spell."

"Ah, cool."

He opened the door and waited for me to go in first. I walked through the empty reception area and stopped at an open doorway. A slim woman in PIB pants and jacket, her straight auburn hair in an angled bob cut, stood behind her desk. She smiled at me. "Hello." She stared at me through her red-framed glasses for a moment. When James stood behind me, she looked at him; then her mouth dropped open. She created a bubble of silence. "Oh, my goodness! Lily Bianchi! I'm Miriam Fairweather. Lovely to finally meet you." She came around her table and gave me a bright smile. "You look so much like your mother, it's not funny." I knew I looked a bit like her, but I could also see traces of my father. I guessed everyone perceived things from their point of view. "It's lovely to meet you." She shook my hand, then turned to James. "Agent Bianchi. A pleasure, as usual. Why are you wearing that ridiculous facial hair?"

He rolled his eyes. "I figured I'd visit incognito. I've been stood down." Maybe she was just really good at recognising people? We had to hope no one else was that observant.

She shook her head. "So I heard. Ridiculous. This place has become a right old circus." She gestured to the chairs. "Please, sit down. So, what can I do for you?" She walked around to the other side of her table and sat.

"This used to be my mother's office, didn't it?" Hmm, this was going to be an interesting conversation. He hadn't explained to me how we were going to get the information without disclosing my secret.

"Yes." She rested her arms on the table in front of her and interlaced her fingers. She was a bit like Angelica in the sense that she was calm and gave the impression that she could wait patiently for you all day to spit it out. She was unlike Angelica in the way that her demeanour wasn't scary at all... just measured. Hmm, come to think of it, Angelica would be giving off flinty vibes by now, and you'd feel the pressure to just spit it out. Maybe she wasn't like Angelica at all.

"You were one of my mother's best friends here, weren't you?"

"Yes." She cocked her head to one side. "Your mother was one of our best agents. It was very upsetting when she disappeared. I'm just sorry that I didn't get more involved in trying to find her." Sadness emanated from her gaze. "I failed her... and both of you. I'm sorry."

Wow, that was unexpected. James and I had suffered so much over the years, missing them and not knowing what had happened, but I hadn't realised that maybe other people missed her or felt guilty for not doing enough. I couldn't lie, though. It would've been nice for someone to have stepped up and called us, checked in to make sure her kids were okay. I looked at James. Maybe they had, and he'd told them we were okay?

"It's okay. And I know you and Angelica called a few times to make sure we were okay. I appreciate it."

I raised a brow and stared at James. He ignored me. It would've been nice to know, but I guessed it wouldn't have changed anything. "For what it's worth, no one blames anyone but the people who killed my parents." Anger pulsed behind my temples. Those people were going to go down sooner rather than later, and I couldn't wait.

Her brows drew down. "We don't know that for sure."

James put on his best poker face. "Would you be willing to swear to secrecy and agree not to do anything that would hinder our investigation or Lily's safety?"

Her eyes widened. "What's going on, James?"

"Will you swear with a witch oath?" His determined gaze didn't waver.

"Yes."

James grabbed my hand. Huh? "Lily, I can't draw power in here at the moment." Ah, stupid Chad. "Could you give me yours for this spell?"

I blinked. "But…." Was he going to give away one of my secrets? There weren't many or any witches left who could just give and take power, whether the recipient wanted it or not. It wasn't my biggest secret, but if this got out, I'd gain the wrong type of attention, and not to forget that the less RP and Piranha knew about what I could and couldn't do, the better. Surprise might be the only thing that gave us the upper hand in the days to come.

"It's fine, Lily. Once she swears, she won't be able to tell anyone or try and sabotage us. And she answered honestly in the first instance." Ah, because it was his talent, he could use a little bit of his own power to figure out whether or not she was telling the truth. The ban they'd put on him here mustn't be as strong as handcuffs. But even still, he could only use the tiniest amount of magic, so it wasn't like he could do anything much, even with access to his internal reservoir.

I looked at Agent Fairweather and back at James. "Okay." I kept my eyes on Fairweather, just in case she tried something. I didn't really think she would, but you never knew. I also put up a return to sender and drew more power. My arm and hand warmed as the magic flowed to James.

"Repeat after me," he said. "I, Miriam Fairweather, do swear on my life that I will not tell another living being about anything said in this office by James or Lily Bianchi in the next hour. After that, I promise to support them by never telling anyone not already sworn to secrecy about anything they tell me. I also promise to never purposely interfere with their investigation into Regula Pythonissam or help Regula Pythonissam in any way. I promise to never disclose what Lily's talents are to any other living person, and I promise to protect her in all things if it is in my power. I promise never to harm Lily or James Bianchi. This I solemnly swear. If I break my promise, I understand that death will be swift, via a massive heart attack."

Oh, wow, that was pretty heavy, but we needed her total agreement, or we'd have to walk out right now without any photos. We could try and lie about why we were taking photos, but this woman didn't strike me as the stupid type. She might put two and two together. Even an assumption would be enough to start others looking into my history. It would not end well.

Funnily enough, she didn't flinch the entire time she repeated James's words. When she was done, a bell rang, the note clear and loud, but, of course, there were no bells in the room.

Agent Fairweather smiled. "It is done, then. Now, let me hear all the news." She rubbed her hands together, and I couldn't help but giggle. We'd been so serious, and she'd promised so much; now she just wanted to know.

James started by going back to when I arrived in the UK. He told her everything, from the diaries to what we'd found at Mont Saint-Michel. "They've done the DNA testing, and one of the skeletons is our father."

Sadness moistened her eyes. "Oh, no. I'm so sorry. It's good that you have closure, but I'd hoped that somehow, they were alive somewhere and were in hiding, waiting for the right time to come out and expose everything. I knew it was a fanciful wish. I'm so sorry for both of you."

I blinked, banishing my own tears. "It is what it is. But we still have to find out what happened to my mother. If we can lay them to rest together, I'm sure they would appreciate it… not that it really matters—they're not here anymore—but, I don't know…."

She nodded, understanding in her eyes. "It's all right, Lily. I get it. And what about Regula Pythonissam?"

Anger crept into James's gaze. "We're dealing with that right now, which is why we're here today in this particular office."

"Your mother's office."

"Yes." James turned to me. "You can explain this part, since it's about you."

I licked my lips. It was never easy to spill my secrets because I was so used to keeping them inside for fear of what might happen. I took a deep breath and told her about my talents, the seeing who will die, the seeing the past, the photos, the videos, my ability to give and receive magic. She wasn't as shocked as I'd expected when I finished.

She leant back in her chair and nodded slowly. "Well, they are some incredible talents, and I see why you don't want anyone finding out, but can I be honest? It's what I would've expected from your mother's children. She was an incredibly strong and talented witch, and I imagine she, too, only let everyone in on a fraction of what she could do. She shouldn't have died."

Hmm, that wasn't exactly what I wanted to hear. Just when I was gaining confidence that I could out-magic Piranha, she had to throw that in there. My mother had so many talents and was powerful, yet it wasn't enough. Although, it was unlikely she'd been up against Piranha. She would've been too young, surely? Had Dana's dad killed her? Had a group of witches done it? Ah, crap. "Um, circles of witches. What's the likelihood of them coming after us with one of those?"

James and Fairweather looked at each other. Fairweather was the first to speak. "Your point is valid, Lily. We must consider forming one of our own."

James scratched his neck. His concerned expression didn't inspire any more confidence than Fairweather's assessment of my mother had. "It's dangerous. With that much power, anything could happen. And they'd need an extremely strong witch to pull that off. Unless their talent is like yours, Lily, they will burn out a lot quicker than you, and if they're strong enough… mass carnage is likely. Think World War III. Witches and non-witches could easily get caught up in the shockwave."

"Kind of like a firework display that got out of control?"

James nodded. "Yes, but not as pretty. Everyone would find

out. There would be eyes lost, fingers blown off hands, and much, much worse."

My brother really knew how to bring home a point. "Yeah, you're selling this so well. Problem is, if they do it, how can we not?"

"Lily's right, James. We can't hold back."

"So you're planning on helping us, on backing us up?" James seemed genuinely surprised.

She smiled. "Of course I am! I've waited a long time for this, to do what I should've done years ago. Your mother would've been very disappointed in me, I'm sure. I'm just glad I'm getting the opportunity now. Thank you."

James shook his head. "She would've understood. There's so much at play and much at stake. What could you have done by yourself?"

She pressed her lips together. "A hell of a lot more than what I did. Anyway, I don't want to put all this on you. At least I can step up this time. Hopefully, your mother, wherever she is, will forgive me." She tilted her head back and looked at the ceiling for a moment.

I gave her a sad smile. "We're happy to have you on board. Welcome to the team. Oh, and we call Regula Pythonissam RP for short. It's just quicker."

She chuckled. "Well, then, I shall call them RP too. So, you didn't just come here to spill. You came here to, I assume, see if you can find anything about the past in this office. Why don't you get started?"

I stood and pulled my phone out of my pocket. "I thought you'd never ask."

We spent two hours in Mum's old office. Every time I asked for information, up it came. One thing was for sure; Mum was very thorough, and she had enough on RP to bring them down. But some of that information made me want to be sick. If we didn't bring them down soon, the world would become a much darker place.

And the million-dollar question remained.

Why didn't anyone take on the case when she disappeared?

Hopefully, we'd soon find out.

CHAPTER 16

T hat night, we all met at James's again. This time, Agent Fairweather was in attendance, as was Cardinal. He took an oath of secrecy regarding everything we were doing and my secrets. Sheesh, the way we were going, everyone in Kent would soon know about my talents. They weren't so secret anymore. On the other hand, it was nice to have more people on our side. We needed everyone we could get. And because we might require a circle of thirteen, Sarah and Lavender had been invited. Millicent's dad, Robert, had also been recruited. Unfortunately, we were still two people short.

"I know someone we can trust, and that would leave us only one short."

James looked at Will. "Who?"

"Agent Roche. We interviewed that agent today, the one who placed that BS call about the results."

"And?" Apparently that agent wasn't a member of RP, so why had he done it?

"He was paid ten thousand Euros by someone who approached him on the street. He didn't see the harm in it, so he did it. Roche has fired him, and he's banned from entering their premises. Since he has a good record with the PIB and it was a misdemeanour crime, they've cautioned him. I think Roche wanted to go easy on him and not create an enemy. He has a man watching him, just to make sure, though. One wrong step and he'll be in jail."

Imani's brows rose. "Didn't see the harm? Pfft. And ten thousand Euros. That's one thing we can say about RP— they're not cheap."

"Apparently I'm worth it." I shrugged.

Will frowned. "Lily, you're worth millions. RP is totally cheap." Beren gave him a thumbs up.

"Aw, thanks." It was nice to be appreciated. Maybe I should add that to the list of things to destroy RP for: cheap-skates, don't value me enough.

James looked at Will. "Okay, well, contact Roche when we're done here, see if he's up for coming to our next meeting. We're at the pointy end of things, as you're about to find out. Lily's magic was very kind to us in finding out what Mum knew and what was destroyed by someone at headquarters. I'm worried we're going to have to deal with RP before we know who wanted everything covered up. Even though most of the files Mum created weren't destroyed until Dana started with the PIB, someone else made sure no one else continued with the investigation after Mum and Dad disappeared. Our chief suspect is Dana's dad, who worked at the PIB. He left before Dana started, but I don't know if he had enough sway with anyone to call off the investigation Mum had started. None of her documents mention Regula Pythonissam by name, but we've found records of the PIB buying weapons from Toussaint. There are bank statements and shipment details. So he definitely has ties to our organisation. There was another investigation into people trafficking that Mum had started a report on, but then she made notes saying the PIB had called her off that and said it wasn't important enough."

My eyes widened. "Not important enough? What the hell?"

James continued, "At the time, there were tensions with Russia and North Korea. I think a lot of their energy was going into that, and also into the usual witch crimes. It was a busy decade, apparently. In any case, we've found more information on Mont Saint-Michel, which confirms our parents were on the trail of stolen goods. They never actually found them, but they suspected they were there."

I looked at Will. "You'll be interested to know who RP stole that stuff from."

"Oh, who?"

"The people they enslaved. They didn't just enslave the people who worked for them, but their families too. There are thousands of families who do the bidding of RP—work for reduced wages or cover up crimes. Some of the victims are police, judges, doctors. RP's reach is wide, and they hold sway mainly over non-witches. Mum thought they were being coerced as well as threatened. Their network stretches across Europe, but the main players are Toussaint, Dana's dad, and that German woman, Katrin Brandt. That's how they make all their money—cheap labour, but it gets worse."

Beren leaned forward. "Worse? How can it get worse?"

James and I looked at each other. What was coming was shocking and reinforced the cruel nature of the witches we were up against. "I'll let you take this one, brother of mine." Yeah, there was no way I wanted to talk about it. My stomach curled in on itself, just thinking about it. I'd be lucky if I didn't cry when James communicated what we'd learned earlier today. And to think that my parents were the only ones who were truly fighting against this evil. They never stood a chance without the PIB's help.

James put on his poker face. Maybe he thought the less emotion he showed, the easier it would be to take. I didn't think anything could soften the blow of this. "All three of the RP leaders own large swathes of property in many European countries. They run hunting holidays on their properties for witches, but while they're there, they don't use magic to hunt. It's all about using non-witch technology… so guns and tracking by skill." Everyone stared at James, horror dawning. They knew what was coming. It was so quiet and difficult to breathe; it was as if there was no atmosphere left. "They hunt people—non-witches."

Liv slammed her hand on her mouth and gagged. Beren's mouth fell open, and Imani's face hardened, as if she were a statue. Will's teeth ground together, and his jaw muscles bulged, while Millicent just sat, dazed.

Robert's stoic expression gave the impression that he'd seen worse, and as a member of the armed forces, he likely had. "We suspected this, years ago. But we could never prove it, and the PIB didn't want to give the witches in the government forces much help. They didn't trust us. The PIB is an organisation unto itself at times. We had reason to believe there was a powerful group that were non-witch haters, for want of a better term. They believe witches are far superior and are working for a day when everything is out in the open and non-witches are our slaves. It seems we've found that group."

"Are you okay, Liv?" She did not look well.

She hugged her stomach and shook her head. "How close

are they to their objective?" No one answered. Everything had ramped up lately, and maybe it wasn't just because we were closing in on them. Maybe they were attaining a level of organisation and reach where they were close to acting in a big way. "Please don't let them win. Please."

Beren pulled her in for a hug. "I'll never let anything happen to you or your parents. All of us are going to work together to stop them. You have my promise on that."

"You have my promise too," said Imani.

"And mine," I chimed in.

Everyone else nodded or said, "Aye." And that was that.

Even though I'd been the one to discover the horrific news, James hadn't told me how he planned to deal with it. "How are we going to stop them?"

"This is where it gets tricky." My brother was the king of understatements. He had learned from the best though. And where was Angelica? I had a feeling we were going to need her when this all went down. "Even though we have proof because of Lily's talent, we can't use it in court or to get arrest warrants. If we do this, we're going rogue. All of us." He eyeballed each person at the table, one by one. "I can't guarantee we'll all survive, and that if we do, that we won't be arrested at the end of it. I need you to each reaffirm you're in this. If you're not, it's fine. We'll excuse you now—you'll still be bound by your oaths to protect our secrets, but you can walk away before it gets ugly."

Imani slowly stood and lifted her chin to gaze down at everyone with intensity. "I am here till the end. I've vowed to give my life to Lily and this cause if I have to, and I stand by that as much today as I did the day that I made that oath." I gave her a smile of thanks. I hoped she could see the love in my gaze. My friends were the best, the bravest.

One by one, everyone agreed they were in.

If I got any of them killed, I'd never forgive myself. But we had to get this done. I didn't bother hiding my relief when Cardinal, the last person to swear, sat after declaring his allegiance. I cleared my throat. "Um, I have one more thing to say… about the other reason this is urgent and we need to take this to them rather than wait. My mother had a list, something that was also destroyed. There was an address of a lodge in Germany where many rich and prominent witches hunted. She had a list of guest names. Among them were politicians, actors, even royalty. They might not all have hunted non-witches, but they are of the same mind—witches are superior, and our time ruling over the non-witches is coming. We need to stop this now, and even then, we may be too late to beat them."

"That is truly depressing," said Liv.

Will rubbed his chin. "This is truly huge. We're going to need other agents on hand to arrest some of these people. We can't have them running away or trying to keep the group going."

I gave him an "are you kidding" look. "Where are we supposed to get enough agents for that? People we trust who'll believe us?"

Will looked at James. "It's time to get serious. You and I need to get to the Paris agency. We'll weed out the dishonest ones or anyone with an affiliation to RP. No one can lie to you. Once we have our squad, they can help. We'll talk to Roche. He has closer ties to the Italian and German offices. We can figure out if we can use some of them too."

"All the while hiding it from Chad?" James raised a brow.

Will shrugged. "He was put there because he's incompetent. I don't think he's going to discover anything now."

Agent Fairweather put up her hand. "If I may speak?"

James smiled. "Of course."

"There are four agents I trust implicitly at headquarters. If I can get them to you for an interview, would you be willing?"

"If you can get them to agree to a silence spell regarding the interview and that you even took them to speak to us, yes."

She nodded. "I'm pretty sure I can make it happen. I'll have them ready for you for tomorrow morning."

James looked at Millicent. "It's your and Liv's job to make a list of addresses for these actors and politicians. Unfortunately, I don't think we can update that list of who's visited lately without surveillance of these properties. What we might want to do is check out their close associates for any suspicious activity. I know it's a long shot, but we need to scoop as many of them up as possible, send a strong message that this behaviour won't be tolerated."

"Where are we going to put them all when they're arrested?" asked Imani.

I cocked my head to the side. "Won't they just die anyway?"

"I have no idea," said James. "These are people in the upper echelons of the organisation, or at least respected members. Anyone else we've arrested were employees, for want of a better word. Maybe they all have to swear a death oath, and maybe they don't. I'm willing to take that chance, though. If they die, at least it will thin their ranks."

My brother was harder than I thought, but in this case, it made me proud rather than horrified. None of us were the same people we were a year ago—especially me. Unfortunately, by the time this was over, we'd all be even more changed, and maybe not for the better. But none of that mattered if we didn't survive it. So that was my priority—do whatever it took to survive and make sure those I loved did too.

I put up my hand. James gave a nod. "Yes, Lily?"

"I was just thinking. I know it's dangerous, but what isn't for us these days? Why don't we wear disguises and visit each of the hunting lodges we know about? I could take some photos of the past, and we can match those faces to ones in the PIB database or to online photos. Most people, especially rich or famous people, have some kind of social-media profile or make the news at some point. We can use facial-recognition software or magic to figure out who they are."

Imani nodded. Her face contorted into a "that's a great idea" expression. "I like it. Will and I can go with you. Some wigs and sunglasses should make us unrecognisable, even if we're caught on video."

Beren shook his head. "But some of those places are off the beaten track. Anyone going there to take photos is going to look suss."

This was our best chance to figure out who some of these people were—the fewer who got away, the better. We could tidy up the stragglers later, anyone we didn't get in the first round, but the more we got rid of in the first instance, the less likely the group was to return. Not to mention that many of them would probably go underground when they found out what was going on. "But if we're in and out quickly, what does it matter? They'll wonder what's going on, but they won't know, and if we strike in the next few days, they'll never figure it out. Who knows, they might even wonder enough that it becomes a distraction."

Beren wasn't giving up that easily. "Yes, but what if they tighten security and back off everything they're doing until things quieten down?"

Hmm, he had me there. "We can go at night, when it's dark. That would give Will a chance to tamper with any video cameras pointed at the outside. I don't need light to get my pictures. It's whatever was there in the past."

Agent Fairweather smiled. "That is such an incredible talent. Your parents would have been so proud of both of you. You've both become everything they could have wished for. Such wonderful humans."

Tears in my eyes and a smile on my face, I felt like a rainy day with a rainbow. "Thank you. That means a lot." I didn't often stop to wonder what my parents would think of James and me if they'd still been here. But, yes, I did think they would've been proud, and that gave me an expanding warmth in my chest.

James smiled, and his voice was gruff. "Thank you." He turned to me. "I think your idea is a good one. You, Will, and Imani get all the information you need from Millicent, and plan one night to get to all the places. Hopefully there aren't too many."

Imani turned to me and grinned. "We got this."

"We totally do." It felt good to be doing something, even if fear niggled in my stomach. I embraced it. It was good to be scared, to be wary. It would give us the edge we needed to get in and out safely. Fear wasn't a self-defence mechanism for nothing. Get cocky, and that's when it all came undone.

James turned to Cardinal. "We're looking for the optimal time to strike. Can you concentrate on the three heads of RP, find out when and where they're meeting next? That's when we'll hit them."

Cardinal nodded, determination in his gaze. "You got it. I'm taking leave from my job for the next few days so I'm free to work on this."

James smiled. "Thanks, mate. You're helping to save the world."

Cardinal grinned. "And what could be a nobler cause than that?"

Nothing. Absolutely nothing.

CHAPTER 17

The next day, I hung out at home, inflicted with all the nerves. I did my own HIIT workout to burn some of it off. After thirty minutes of push-ups, burpees, sit-ups, mountain climbers, and squats, I was ready to die.... Oops, not *die*, die, but, you know, I needed a shower and a rest. Funny how some jokes weren't as funny anymore. With a bit of luck, when this was all over, I could joke about dying after exercise. Goals.

Will and James were spending the day with Agent Roche. Hopefully they'd find enough agents we could trust. If they couldn't, well, we still had to go ahead and hope for the best. Which wasn't the most favourable plan, but we had no choice.

Not being able to watch TV or leave the house had me pacing and biting my fingernails. By the time Will got home at six forty-five, I had no nails left. I met him at the reception-room door because I happened to be pacing past. His face registered surprise. "Wow, that was quick. Were you waiting here for me?"

I laughed. "Almost. Waiting is the pits. I've been wandering around the house to pass the time. I watched the squirrels for a while. I asked Abby if she'd invite some in, but she didn't feel like it and went to have a nap." I rolled my eyes. "Cats can be so unreliable."

He laughed. "They are their own bosses. That's for sure." Ted's claws clicked on the timber floor as he trotted up to greet Will. Ted loved me, but Will was his favourite. I'd admit it hurt just a little bit, but I'd survive, and Abby did love me more, at least that's what I told myself.

My stomach grumbled.

"Well, hello there. It must be time for dinner. Does your stomach always know what time it is?"

"Hmm, I don't think so. It grumbles every couple of hours, just to make sure. Come on, I actually cooked the non-witch way in between pacing bouts. Can't you smell it?"

He sniffed. "Ooh, that smells good. What is it?"

"Traditional spaghetti and meatballs. It has lots of garlic, just in case we come across any vampires." I winked. "Anyway, let's eat, and you can tell me all about your day. You don't seem too depressed, so I'm assuming things went as well as can be expected?"

His smile said it all, well, even the fact he *was* smiling said everything. We sat at the kitchen table and dished up our own plates. As I savoured the first bite of rich Italian deliciousness, Will started. "Roche took another oath. He wants in."

"Yay!"

"Do you have to talk with your mouth full?"

"Yay isn't really talking, is it?"

He narrowed his eyes. "I'm pretty sure it is."

I shrugged, put more meatball in my mouth, and smiled. If

he wasn't careful, I'd chew it up and show him. Immature I knew, but if I were perfect, life would be boring.

"Right, so he's on board, and we interviewed 80 percent of his agents. We also got the German PIB in on the action. It was a ridiculously long day."

I swallowed the spaghetti I'd been chewing. I didn't want to upset petal. "How many have you signed up?"

He grinned. "Way more than we could've hoped for. Fifty-eight agents have taken an oath to shut RP down and obey orders given by James or myself."

My eyes widened. "Are you kidding?! That's massive! Roche was happy to turn over control?"

"More than happy once we showed him all the proof. He was quite overawed by your photography talent, by the way. I think he's going to have some work for you when this is all over. He has a few long-term unsolved murder cases he wants help with."

"Seriously? When this is over, I just want to go on holiday." I sighed. Meh, who was I kidding? Of course I'd help him. It was in my DNA. "Maybe when we've had a few weeks off, I'll go see him."

Will grinned. "That's my woman. I knew you would."

"Yeah, yeah." I swirled spaghetti onto my fork and stabbed a piece of meatball, then shoved it into my mouth. Yum.

"He also said that now things made more sense to him—about the enslavement of whole families. He's going to quietly investigate a few villages today. He has a feeling RP might have control of communities. Most of the families related to the people from the factory are from poorer areas. We also need to figure out how to release them from service so they can be safely questioned and not have to go back to that life."

"If they all have tattoos, I guess we could get Robert to

teach us how to unravel them? If he can work out one, surely they're all the same?"

"That makes sense. And now we have a bigger pool of agents who can help de-RP everyone." He gave me a measured look. "But we have to take down the top snakes first. You know it won't be easy."

"I know, but what's the point of believing we'll lose? If we don't believe in our ability to beat them, we're setting ourselves up for failure. Imagine what Angelica would say if she knew? She believes we can do it, I bet."

Fondness crept into his gaze. "She *would* believe in us." He smiled. "You're right. We got this."

"I'm always right. Didn't you know?" I smirked.

"I might hate it sometimes, but, yes, I'm starting to see." He winked. "Except when I'm right."

"As long as I'm right about the big stuff, I can concede the small things."

He laughed. "You're impossible."

I gave him a cheesy grin. "And that's why you love me."

"Maybe…. Or maybe it's because you never do what you're told? Or maybe it's because your jokes are so bad? Or maybe it's because y—"

My mouth dropped open. "Hey, hey, let's not get carried away here. Before you know it, you'll be breaking up with me. If you do, by the way, I'm keeping the ring. I'll hock it and take Imani and Liv on holidays."

He raised a brow. "Already planning on how to spend my money after you break up with me?"

I shrugged. "Beats being bored when I'm stuck at home by myself." I tried, but it was impossible to contain my giggle.

He grinned. "You're impossible, but I love you. And never change."

"I wasn't planning on it."

What I was planning on was killing Piranha. Did that make me evil? Would I even still like myself when this was all over? Who knew? What I did know was that I wanted to survive to find out.

The rest, well, I'd deal with it if I made it through.

Universe, if you care anything about fairness and love, you'll help us win, won't you? Silence greeted my question. *Universe?*

Another day, another level of danger. Some of us had spent the whole day at James's, prepping, with others going back and forth. His dining-room table had become the hub of operations, and he'd set up screens in the lounge room, like the ones set up for the factory operation. Tonight, Imani, Will, and I were wearing small video/audio devices, just in case anything happened and we needed to dissect it later. Millicent and James would be watching the live video feed to give us any warnings if we missed something. We each had a device on our chests and one on our backs—all the angles were covered… literally.

As I forced down dinner, Bagel and Cinnamon sat on the table near me, their own little plates in front of them. Millicent had been interpreting their chatter through dinner. They assured me everything would be fine and that it was going to be exciting rather than scary. I didn't want to argue with them because they were so cute, and how often did one receive advice from rodents? I was obviously living my best life.

I only ate enough that my stomach would keep quiet while we were out. This level of stress wasn't conducive to eating, even for me. We had a list of eleven places to visit—three in the UK, three in France, one in Russia, and four in Germany. It was going to be a loooooong night. Most of the places were at least a fifteen-minute car ride from the nearest landing point. Roche was doing his best to have agents ready to ferry us around. He was proving an exceptional team member. Again, I had to thank Chad for something. He'd basically introduced us and then annoyed the Frenchman enough that he was happy to go against him. I grinned. He thought he was making life harder for James, but he'd done the opposite. It was the little things. And it was funny how things worked out—not that they'd totally worked out yet, but what we saw as a near disaster with Will and James being stood down turned into a massive positive.

Millicent waved her hand in front of my plate. "Hey, what's so interesting in there?"

I started. "Oh, sorry. Just thinking."

She put her hand on mine. "Good luck out there tonight. We're getting close."

"I know." There was so much to say about how scared I was and what could go wrong, but I swallowed it. We didn't need more negative energy.

"Come D-Day, my cousin is mine. I want to cuff the bastard."

My mouth fell open. I'd never heard Millicent swear before. Ever. "He's all yours. I'm so sorry he did that to you. Family can be so disappointing sometimes."

"My father wants to kill him, too, but I managed to talk him into letting me arrest him. He'll probably drop dead anyway."

I laughed. "We've turned into a vicious lot, haven't we."

"Yes and no." If her fierce gaze wasn't enough to convince me we were doing the right thing, her words definitely were.

"We've been driven to this, Lily. Make no mistake, if we balk at the last minute, they will kill all of us, and the future for non-witches will be bleak. Steel yourself, lady. We're the last line of defence for what's good in this world. Never forget that."

I squeezed her hand. "Thank you, Mill. I needed to hear that. The last thing I want is for Annabelle to grow up an orphan in a world where witches call all the shots and non-witches are their slaves. I couldn't think of anything more disgusting. Besides, I guarantee it wouldn't be long before some witches became more important than others…."

"You've got that right. Let's stop it before it starts."

"Yes, please do." Liv sat on the other side of me. "How are you feeling?"

I smiled. "How do you think?"

"Well, for what it's worth, if you, Will, and Imani can't get this done, no one can."

"Aw, thanks. And for what it's worth, I won't give up, Liv. I'm in this till it's done." Bagel squeaked, and it sounded a lot like a cheer.

Liv's brittle smile lanced my heart. "I know. Thank you." She looked at the rat. "Did she just cheer?"

Millicent laughed. "Yes. She's pretty confident we're going to win."

I swallowed my comment again. This might be the happiest moment we had for a long time, and it was not in my nature to dash anyone's hopes. Nope. I held my hand out to Bagel. "High five." The little rodent tapped my palm. I grinned.

Imani wandered over. "I hate to break up the party, but it's time to get ready, Lily."

I sucked in a breath. So much for being ready for anything.

There was no banishing the dread that set anchor in the depths of my soul. It was wedged in tight and wasn't going anywhere. I did everything in my power to keep my voice steady. "Okay." I stood and magicked my all-black outfit of jeans, jumper, sneakers, and beanie-cum-balaclava. We didn't want to scare anyone in any of the villages we popped out in, but to avoid camera scrutiny, pulling down wool to protect our identities was for the best, even if it was just to stop the PIB identifying us later. There was no telling what was going to happen when this was over, and if I managed to survive, the last thing I wanted was to revisit the PIB cells.

I magicked my camera to myself and checked I had a full battery. "I'm all good to go."

Imani touched one side of her body, then her lower back. "Me too."

"Two guns tonight?"

She smiled. "I'll be ready for anything."

I gave my ladies a hug goodbye and gave the rats a little kiss on the head. "I'll see you guys later. Don't have too much fun without me."

Liv's smile was too bright. "We won't. We'll save all the fun for when you get home."

"That's what I like to hear. Okay, ladies. See you soon."

Imani and I walked into the living room, where Will was talking to Cardinal. Will turned to look at us. He donned his poker face. "Ready to go?"

I nodded, and Imani said, "Affirmative, boss."

Will turned back and shook Cardinal's hand. "Thanks again, mate. Good work." Our new recruit gave a nod and wished Imani and me luck, then strolled off to talk to James. Will looked at me. "Imani is going to ferry you back and forth. I'll take guard duty. I'll be the last to leave everywhere we visit.

Imani will be watching out for you, too, Lily. All I want you to do is get there and take as many photos in each place as you can. Once you're not getting any new pictures, let me know, and we're gone. If there's any problems, Imani will make the doorway and you both leave. If something happens and Imani can't do that, I want you to come straight back here. Understood?"

Oh, crap. Why did it always come down to having to agree to something I didn't want to agree to? Why did they even ask me anymore? It wasn't as if my track record with obeying orders was anything to crow about. But seeing as this was super important, I decided to just go with it. "Okay. If there's any trouble, I'll come straight back here." Will kept his bossy gaze on me. Argh, he was going to make me say it. "I promise. Happy now?"

"No. I won't be happy until this is done, and we're home and safe." He gave Imani a nod, and she made her doorway. I followed her through.

We'd started with the properties in the UK, and it had been rather uneventful, thank goodness, although I was still jumping at the smallest unusual sound. I'd taken quite a few photos, then, thanks to a handy little dongle thing I plugged into my camera, I texted them straight back to James so Liv and Millicent could get a start on identifying people. Agent Fairweather was also helping them out because we needed to process them as quickly as possible.

Our next destination was one I was super worried about because I had no idea what it was like, and from what was shown on TV in spy movies, Russian agents were the most horrible. I hoped we didn't get caught by any. If the movies were to be believed, most Russians at properties in the middle of nowhere carried machine guns 24/7, even to the toilet. Maybe I was being ridiculous, but it didn't feel like it when we stepped out of a public toilet into the freezing night to be greeted with a bomb of an old car driven by a guy who had a scarf up to his nose. All I could see were his dark eyes. He said something in a French accent. Phew, at least he was one of Agent Roche's guys. Will, skilled man that he was, recognised him. As he slid into the front passenger seat, he held out his hand. "Agent Remy. Thanks for picking us up."

He gave a nod. "My pleasure. We have about a twenty-minute drive. I will drop you two minutes from the property. You will 'ave to walk the last distance."

"We can manage that. Thanks."

The area just above my stomach pulsed the whole way as waves of nervousness broke against my chest again and again. I wouldn't be surprised if I looked ten years older tomorrow.

He let us out, and I checked my return to sender was up. As we walked along the road, the gravel crunching under our feet, Agent Remy did a U-turn and drove off. *Bye, bye. Wish I was going with you.* I gave a forlorn wave at the receding tail-lights. Will smirked and shook his head. "So far so good, Lily. There's nothing to be worried about."

I gave him my best "you've got to be kidding" look. I didn't want to encourage conversation for a change because what if someone heard us speaking English and decided to check it out.

When we were about ten metres from a driveway that was blocked by two tall timber gates attached to a stone wall, Will stopped. His magic was subtle and hopefully not detectable by anyone within a few metres. He disabled the video camera, then approached the gates by himself and opened them. This was way too bold for my liking, but we didn't have time for climbing over walls. And magicking ladders to every destination would be taxing on us since ladders were heavy and bulky. I would have preferred it to walking straight in, but what did I know?

We jogged down the long driveway, which wound its way through woods. Dogs howled in the distance. Shit. Had there been a sign about guard dogs? I didn't think to look, and since it was so dark, I could easily have missed it. The barking got louder. Will and Imani slowed, and I stopped. I pulled my camera out to see if I could get any shots before all hell broke loose. Hopefully whoever had visited in the past had at least wandered out here at some point. At the previous properties, we'd managed to get onto land at the backs of the homes, which is where people had drinks after hunting. I swallowed nausea that nudged its way up my throat.

The barking got closer. I lifted my camera. "Show me the witches who came here for hunting parties." Three people came into view, in mid-afternoon light. All men. I snapped the photos. I sensed Will next to me. "Leave, Lily. Forget the photos."

Snarling sounded close. Too close. Crap. I looked up to see Imani pointing her gun into the darkness. A snarling growl as a dog leapt, and yelling from further into the property. Crap. Imani fired her gun, then made her doorway. I had no time to see what Will was up to because I did as he asked and made a doorway in the fastest time ever. I jumped through into James's reception room. My panting was super loud in the enclosed space. Will and Imani arrived just after me, thank God.

Imani grinned. "Sheesh, that was close."

I stared at her. "You think it's funny?"

"No, love, but it was exciting. Don't tell me you didn't find it so?"

"Jesus, no. What the hell is wrong with you?" Will was grinning too. "Not you too." I looked up at the ceiling. "I'm with a couple of crazies. Who knew?"

"Are you right to go again?" Imani asked. "We won't worry about the Russian property anymore."

I raised my brows. "I should think not. You would've left your magic signature on the security system, Will."

"Well, that can't be helped. Hopefully they won't think to check it until tomorrow, and by then, it should've faded. I didn't use much power."

The reception room door opened, and I jumped. Millicent stood there. "What are you doing? It took a moment, but eventually, I realised what your cameras were showing. What happened?"

"Didn't you hear the dogs?" I asked.

"Yes. They didn't sound very friendly."

Imani frowned. "Not friendly at all. I had to kill one of them. I'm not happy about that. Those animals didn't ask to be caught up in this."

"Oh, no. What a shame." Millicent loved her dogs, and she looked genuinely sad. "Okay, kids, are you getting back to it?"

"Yep. We're off to France now. See you later." Will looked at Imani. "I'll go first. See you in a minute."

The next two properties were vacant for the moment, which made our job so much easier. No nasty surprises were more my speed. I took many photos. The same people were starting to show up. Seemed like they enjoyed hunting at different venues. Sickos.

The last property in France was in the mountains. Snow was scattered amongst the rocks, and the steep terrain was less than ideal. I couldn't imagine what it would be like to be hunted, stumbling up and down incline after incline. Were there cliffs to accidentally fall off? Was that preferable to being shot or tortured?

The lodge was a two-storey chalet affair sitting at the top of a hill. It would have had a glorious view during the day. Will had disabled the video cameras at the front, and then the ones protecting the yard around the house. We snuck past a triple garage and around the back of the building. We stayed low and next to the house so that if anyone was to look out the window, they wouldn't see us.

I crouched, leaning my back against the rear of the house. I raised my camera and whispered, "Show me who hunted non-witches here." What looked like a garden party was in full swing under pretty fairy lights. Only slightly more men than women. Everyone dressed for an afternoon of frivolity. Going on the garden's green foliage, and the guests' short sleeves and floaty dresses, it was summer. Drinks in hand, people laughed and chatted. Evil witches.

I snapped off shot after shot. It seemed they had had quite a few hunts here in summer. There were a couple of photos of witches in the snow, but it seemed that they preferred to hunt in more comfortable conditions. When I was done, we left.

When we reached our first German village, we exited the toilets and stood under a streetlight. Will's brow wrinkled. "Lily, are you crying?"

"A little."

Imani put her arm around me while gazing into the darkness around us. "It's okay, love. We'll put a stop to it soon."

A black Mercedes pulled up, and the driver waved at Will. Will gave him a nod and opened the back door for Imani and me to get in. Will sat in the front. The driver turned around and smiled at me. "Good evening. I'm Hans. Pleased to make your acquaintance."

I smiled back. "*Guten Abend*, Hans. I'm Lily. How do you do?" I never knew Germans were so formal, but I'd go with it. Hopefully, chucking in some high-school German would win me some brownie points. Not that I needed them. We weren't going to hang out and go have dinner with this guy. Would we ever see him again after this? It was funny how people touched upon your life, but then you never saw them again. What was it all for anyway? I shook my head at myself. I wasn't the first person to ask that question, and I wouldn't be the last. It wouldn't even be the last time *I* asked that question.

Roughly fifteen minutes in the car, and we turned off the autobahn and wound our way up. Maybe three minutes later, Hans pulled over to the side of the road. "This is where I leave you, I'm afraid. Good luck! Auf Wiedersehen."

"Ciao!"

Imani looked at me. "That's rubbish German, Lily."

"I know. It's Italian." I poked my tongue out, then quickly brought it back in again. "Man, it's cold. Surely we could've picked a better season for this?"

"Be thankful it's not the middle of winter," Will said. And he was right, but I wasn't going to tell him. I'd never hear the end of it. He smirked, maybe thinking my lack of answer meant I conceded that he was right. Doh! "Let's go."

An owl hooted. Yay, owl. I wondered what it was saying. If Millicent were here, I'd ask. Yes, Will could talk to animals, but only if they were making themselves clear. It wasn't his talent. Hmm, maybe we should've had a pet owl, one that could fly ahead and warn us of danger. I really needed an entourage of squirrels. They could scurry ahead, distract the enemy or throw nuts at them. Hmm, could they learn how to shoot? We could get them tiny little guns. I nodded slowly. Me and an army of squirrels. I wouldn't say no. Maybe something to work on when this was all over?

"Lily, what are you smiling about?" Imani kept her voice down, but she sounded amused, as if she knew she was going to get a ridiculous answer but was looking forward to it.

"Just future me and my army of squirrels."

She chuckled. "Of course. I can't believe I didn't guess."

"I know, right. You must be losing your touch." I smiled.

"It's inevitable when I hang out with you. It's all your bad jokes."

"Knock, knock."

"Who's there?"

"Lily."

"Lily who?"

"Lily, leader of the squirrel army."

"Oh, for goodness' sake, love. That was terrible. I just aged two whole years."

Will looked at me. "We should appoint you head of our torture chamber."

My eyes widened. "The PIB don't have a torture chamber. Do they?"

Imani and Will looked at each other. He was the one who answered. "Not officially, no."

"Oh my God. Who are you people? Seriously?"

Will's gaze was solemn. "I've never tortured anyone. Don't worry. It's not something they would do lightly."

I sighed. "It's fine. I'm just tired. I want this night to be over." Just to make a point, the toe of my boot caught on a small rock, and I tripped and flew forward. Thankfully, I managed to stay on my feet. "Crap."

Imani caught up to me and gently grabbed my arm. "Are you okay, love?"

"Yeah. Just tired. All the photo taking and walking." I gave her a tired smile. "I'll manage. We're almost done."

"Yeah, only four properties left, then bed." Will ran his finger down my cheek.

"Looking forward to it. I think I could sleep for a week."

Within the next couple of minutes, we came to our next property. This one was like all the others—high walls of over eight feet and timber gates that were impossible to see through. Hopefully, it would be unoccupied. Dreams were free.

Will's magic tingled my scalp, then stopped. He looked at Imani. "This one's a bit more complicated. They've woven magical alarms around the gate, so I could turn the camera off easily enough, but not the rest. It's going to take too long to unravel it."

Imani looked up and down the length of verge along the fence line. She tipped her chin in the direction from which we'd come. "What about that tree over there. We won't have to go anywhere near the cameras if we climb that and go over."

"Good idea."

Not a good idea. I wasn't a tree climber of note. In fact, when I was about seven, I climbed to the top of a pine tree and fell out, hitting every branch on the way down, which hurt but probably saved my life. Ever since then, I'd tried to avoid climbing if it was at all possible.

Will and Imani walked towards the tree. Will stopped after a few steps when he realised I hadn't budged. "Come on."

"I can't climb." The tree in question had no branches until about six-feet up. I could barely reach that to hold on, let alone pull myself up.

"I'll help you."

"Oh, like the time you 'helped' me over that wall?" Trying to catch Liv's old fiancé had resulted in super awkward wall climbing with less than stellar results—he'd basically thrown me over the wall. Yes, I'd managed to get over but not without some pain.

"You're still alive, aren't you? Come on. If anything happens, we'll go straight home after this one for Beren's healing before we go to the next."

I huffed. "You're not inspiring confidence, but fine." I hurried over and pulled down my balaclava. As much as I didn't want to climb things, I did want to get to the bottom of everything and finish this. No pain, no gain—no truer saying had ever existed, at least as far as my life was concerned. *Gah, stop with the pity party, Lily. Just get on with it.*

Imani was already in the tree. Of course she was. Will pulled his balaclava down, then looped his hands together to give me a leg up. I stared at it and raised a brow. "Do not catapult me over the branch. Just go easy."

"Noted."

I placed my foot in his hand and got ready to spring into the air. "On three. One, two, three." He launched me as I jumped, arms outstretched. I caught the branch and hung. Now what? Argh. I braced my stomach muscles and swung my legs back and forth till I managed to hook the branch with my ankles. I worked one leg up until my knee was gripping the branch. My awkwardness was unparalleled. I must've looked like a hippo trying to perform aerial silk acrobatics.

Biting pain scoured my palm and the underside of my wrist as I scraped them while manoeuvring into a sitting position. I bit my lip, gripped the branch overhead, and stood. As I carefully walked away from the trunk towards the wall, Will swung up where I'd been, as agile as a panther. What a capable poo head.

Imani disappeared over the wall, and I heard the muted thud of her landing. I wobbled the last little bit, adrenaline zinging through my body. Another owl hooted. My breath sounded ridiculously loud in the silence. Being hyperaware was no fun. I really could do without it right now.

My shoe touched the top of the wall. Once both feet were safely there, I reluctantly released my hold on the branch above my head and crouched carefully. My grip secured on the top of the wall, I lowered my body over the other side. I glanced down. Yikes. That was a long way down. I supposed I couldn't hang there all night. Time to drop.

I bent my knees on impact to cushion my fall. The shock-waves reverberated up my legs, but I seemed to have survived. Will dropped down next to me, silent, ninja-like. He grinned. I stared at him, one eyebrow raised. Show off.

He started up the slight incline with long strides. I went next, and Imani brought up the rear. Rather than wait until we saw the house, I lifted my camera and slowed. "Show me the witches hunting other humans." Anger simmered close to the surface. The two men in the photo were shown in fading light, but it was still bright enough that I knew who they were: Toussaint and Dana's father. *Click.* I asked the question again, but nothing happened. Imani had waited for me. "Thanks."

She gave me a nod, and we continued. This place was set far from the road. It was a while before a hulking shape of a building loomed in front of us. Will stayed back in the tree line, scanning for security cameras. While we waited, I lifted my camera again. "Show me the witches who hunted other people here." Daylight exploded through my lens, and I blinked. Argh, that was bright. Two black SUVs had parked at the front of the large, three-level hotel-style building. A group of men and women stood around chatting. Four held rifles. It looked as if they were about to go on a hunt or had just returned, and the rest had just arrived to partake in the "festivities." I clicked off a couple of shots, but they were still too far away to see everyone clearly. I recognised two of the men with guns—I didn't know who they were, just that they'd turned up in a couple of my other photos. A few of the hunters had their backs to me as well. I'd need to get closer. I also needed a different angle to capture the number plates.

Will pursed his lips. "They've got magic protecting these cameras. Again, I can disable them, but it will take a while, and they might feel my magic, this close to the place. We're going to have to take our chances and just move quickly, then leave."

Great. "I've already got a few photos. I need to get closer to the building to get better pics. And I really want to get around the back. Maybe we can range out to one side and I'll see if I can get more hunting photos before we go around to the back then come to the front and finish off?"

"What if there's cameras in the forest?" Imani made a good point.

"At least it's dark. Unless someone is manning the security, which they probably aren't, we should be fine. If we hear anything, just get back home. I would imagine cameras throughout the trees are to keep track of who they're hunting." He called them a choice word that almost made me blush, but I agreed with his assessment. There were no names or adjectives bad enough for these people.

"Okay, then. We'll do it that way," said Imani, "but now we have to move quickly. Will and I will follow you, Lily. We're here to protect you, so just concentrate on taking the photos. We'll let you know if you need to make a doorway."

"Okay." I hoped I was picking the right direction to find more evidence when I headed to our left. I walked as quickly as I could in the darkness, in unfamiliar territory. After a couple of minutes, I stopped and lifted my camera. "Show me the witch hunters." Two men stood near us, peering around a tree, guns aimed. My heart pounded, the blood pulsing past my eardrums. They were so close and so realistic, it was as if they were really there. I had to slow my breath before I fainted from hyperventilating.

My subconscious was whispering something to me, something that had the hairs on my arms standing at attention. I shivered. My forehead tensed. What was that in the distance? Crap. They were pointing their rifles at something… or someone. I hurried to get in front of the men, and I turned to take their pictures. Toussaint and Dana's father again. I growled.

"Are you all right," Will asked.

I grunted because I was not okay and voicing it wouldn't help anyone.

I turned back to face where their rifles pointed and made sure I took a shot that got them aiming at another person—we might need that later… if they managed to live through the arrests. A figure was running away. I hurried towards the person, which, as I got closer, looked to be a woman. She was wearing a ripped T-shirt and jeans, her shoulder-length hair loose and flowing behind her as she sprinted for her life.

Click.

My heart was beating fast, my breath loud and rasping in my ears, yet, I couldn't imagine how fast her heart rate had been, how panicked she was. This wasn't a game. She was going to die in the cruellest of ways.

I ignored the burn of tears as I approached the woman. I didn't want to see the fear in her eyes, the horror on her face, but it was my duty. I would record her plight, and I would help avenge it. It seemed like too little too late, but it was all I could offer.

The hairs on my neck stood on end. I looked away from my camera and around. Imani and Will were right next to me, keeping an eye out. Dread breathed down the back of my neck. Was someone out there about to strike? If so, I'd better get this done.

I put my eye back to the viewfinder and overtook the woman. Then I stopped, turned, and pointed the camera at her face.

As the world dropped out from under me, my knees slammed into the ground.

Not again. Not again.

I tried to breathe, but it was as though I was suffocating.

I tried not to think, just do. I pointed the camera back up at her face and clicked off a shot. The fear in her eyes was flecked with anger. Around my mother's neck was a silver collar. I would bet my life that it cut off her magic. She'd been helpless.

I scrambled to my feet, my cheeks drenched and cold despite the balaclava. Salty tristesse coated my tongue. I made sure I took a picture with those evil pigs pointing their guns at my mother, the look on her face as they did, the ring of death around her neck.

If I had to reveal my secret to the witch world to expose these sickos, I would.

Click. Click. Click.

When I was done, I lowered my camera and bent at the waist. I ripped my face covering off and made sure to keep my camera out of the way as I threw up, and threw up, and threw up.

"Oh my God, what's wrong?" Imani stood next to me and rubbed my back.

I stayed hunched over but lifted my camera up. She took it. "Oh, Jesus."

Yep, that was about the size of it. When I was sure I wasn't going to throw up again, I straightened and stared at the spot where my mother had stood years ago… well, not stood, more like passed through in terror. "I'm so sorry." Speaking was the wrong thing to do because the floodgates opened, and I sobbed. The violence of it was even worse than when we found my father. This time, I really didn't know if I could ever stop.

My mother.

Hunted like an animal.

Defenceless.

Petrified.

Like so many others.

I knew I'd really lost it when I screamed.

CHAPTER 18

The last little while had sliced by in a blur. As I sat on James's couch, the pain was akin to having been chopped into pieces. I clutched piles of damp tissues and wondered where they'd come from. A soft voice came from beside me. "Lily? Lily? Are you back with us yet?"

Liv.

I looked up and blinked, then turned to her. The tears that had seemed to have stopped when I wasn't really here threatened to return as I gazed into my friend's devastated eyes. I swallowed. I couldn't speak.

Across the room, Beren and Imani stared at me, concern radiating from them. This situation cared not for poker faces and outward projections of calm. No. This situation had torn the façade away and left us all reeling with its sickness, depravity, and senselessness.

I blew my nose again. "Has everyone seen?" She would know that I meant the photos. I couldn't seem to get it all out. The less talking I had to do, the better.

"Yes."

I shut my eyes for a moment, but the image of my terrified mother hijacked my brain. My eyes shot open. If it was going to be like that every time, I'd never sleep again.

Will wandered over. The love and sadness in his eyes tore into me all over again, and I bit my tongue to keep from weeping. The emotional hangover was going to be huge. If I could crawl into bed and stay there for a month, it wouldn't be enough.

"Do you want to go home? I'll stay with you."

I nodded, but then logic broke through my emotional hurricane. "We still have three places to photograph."

He shook his head. "No, we don't. We have over two hundred scumbags to identify. There's no way we have enough resources to arrest them all. We'll deal with it later. For now, you've done an outstanding job."

"But is it enough?" Until we found every last one of these disgusting excuses for witches, it would never be enough. "Where are James and Millicent?"

"Taking a moment."

I nodded. "I'd like to see him before we go." Seeing my brother's devastated face was going to be the hardest of all. Inside me, something broke, something that could never be fixed.

My transformation was complete.

God help Toussaint and Dana's dad because any shred of mercy I'd had was gone.

They would regret every last evil thing they'd done by the time I'd finished with them. They might have thought they'd escaped punishment for all the lives they'd taken, but I had news for them.

No one killed someone I loved and got away with it.

No one.

I awoke the next day with tears in my eyes and a wet pillow. I'd had nightmares of running endlessly, the howling of dogs and rustle of witches with guns never far behind. It was as if I'd sprinted a marathon. Even though my phone said it was after ten in the morning, I disputed whether I'd rested at all. Apparently sleep and rest weren't the same thing when your demons pursued you all night.

My head was heavy with grief and my sinuses blocked from all the crying. *Argh, mucus, you are not my friend.* I sat up slowly and swung my legs over the bed. I hung my head and shut my eyes as I waited for the dizziness to pass.

What would my parents say to me if they knew? What's done is done. Grieve for us but move on. Fix things. Use what you know to move ahead. Don't become mired in the morose quicksand of anger, loss, and hate. Use it to do what you must, but when you're done, leave it behind.

I wasn't ready to leave it behind yet, but the time would come. I would definitely use it to do what I must, and right now, I needed to wake up and get going. Depending on what Liv, Mill, and Agent Fairweather had managed to find out, we might be ready to move tonight. Damned if I was going to miss this because I was at home wallowing in bed.

I went to the bathroom and showered because I'd fallen in bed in a haze when Will brought me home. I dressed warmly and made my way downstairs. Not much could help me right now, but things would be worse if I didn't have a coffee soon. I did not need a migraine.

Abby met me at the bottom of the stairs, her long fluffy tail raised in the air. She meowed and walked between my legs. "Hey, gorgeous." I bent down and picked her up. I rubbed my face in her luxurious fur and gave her a kiss on the top of the head. "Are you hungry?"

She meowed, which I took for a yes. I carried her into the kitchen. Hmm, there were a couple of bites of food in her bowl. Maybe she was just saying good morning and asking after my health? "Can I ask a favour?"

"*Meow.*"

"Do you think you could invite the squirrels in for breakfast? I could do with a pick-me-up."

"*Meow.*" She jumped down and went to the back door. I opened it, and five minutes later, she returned, three squirrels in tow. I laughed. "Thank you!" Two of the squirrels shied at my excitement. I whispered, "Oops, sorry." The only squirrel who seemed comfortable was my friend from last time. I recognised the little scar on his left ear. "Hello, Grayson. Welcome back. Please come in." I stepped back and the little troupe entered, tails twitching.

I grabbed some nuts from the cupboard that I'd bought for these occasions. After Grayson visited last time, I was hoping he'd come back. And here he was with some friends. I held back the squee I wanted to release. If they ran everywhere and hid, it might be hard to get them out.

I sat at the table and put the nuts into a dish. "Thank you, Abby. You're the best."

"*Meow.*"

I magicked myself an extra-large cappuccino, and while I sipped it, Grayson climbed the chair on the far side of the table from me and haltingly made his way to the plate. How squirrels could move so quickly yet so slowly at the same time was a mystery. Their jerky little movements made them look like they were going to have a heart attack brought on from nerves at any moment.

I tried not to move too much so the other two would gather the courage. Eventually, they figured out I wasn't going to hurt them, or maybe they could smell the nuts and worried that Grayson would eat them all. Whatever it was, they climbed the chairs and made themselves at home at the plate.

We were all happily breakfasting when the reception-room door opened, and footsteps came down the hall. The squirrels stood and stared at the doorway. "It's okay, guys. It's probably just Will. Keep eating." One of them wasn't having a bar of it and turned to jump off the table, but Abby meowed, and it stopped. Its whiskers and nose twitched, and it stayed.

Will walked in, then stopped when he spied the party on the table. I gave him a cheesy grin. "Me and my posse are hanging out. Want to join us?"

He pushed his bottom lip out and nodded slowly. "Seems you're well on your way to building that squirrel army you were talking about."

"Just give me a couple of weeks, and me and my jittery sidekicks will be ready to conquer the world."

He laughed. "I can just see you all when there's a sudden noise."

I laughed too. That would be funny since I was just as jumpy as my furry pals. "So, what's happening?"

He sat carefully, and the squirrels went back to eating. "James is a bit better today, at least focussed enough to get this done. It looks like you are too." He stared at me. "Are you?"

I took a deep breath and sighed it out. "Yes. I'm ready to destroy them all."

He raised his brows. "Destroy? That's a bit… violent."

I raised one brow—sometimes less was more. "You got a problem with that?"

"Uh-uh, no. Definitely not. Destroy away."

"Thank you." A little tap on my arm that was resting on the table. I looked down. Grayson stared up at me with his orby little squirrel eyes. Sooooo cute! "What is it?" He looked over at the empty plate, then back at me. "Ah, hungry, hungry hippos." I smiled. "Here you go." I magicked more nuts into the plate, and one of the new squirrels turned and sprinted to the end of the table in fright before stopping to look back. When it saw the other two eating again, it hurried back over. "I think I'll call you Chicken Little."

Will chuckled and shook his head. "You're hilarious. How could I not love a woman who invites squirrels for breakfast?"

"I know, right?" I cradled my cup in both hands and brought it to my chest, the warmth comforting. "What's the plan for today? Please tell me we're going to go after them."

His gaze was measured and more poker-faced than not. I had no idea what he was thinking. "We're finalising everything now. The French agents have been a godsend. I don't know what we would've done if Agent Roche hadn't turned out to be an honest and principled witch."

"Do you think we'll be ready to confront them tonight?"

"I'm hoping. I've got a lot to organise. I'm liaising between James and Roche. We're going to use his men for the arrests and some of the German agents." He looked at the squirrels, one of whom was cleaning its ear. "Aw, look how cute that is."

I narrowed my eyes. "What aren't you telling me?"

"Me?"

I rolled my eyes. "Yes, Mr Obvious. You don't even like squirrels and now they're cute?"

His sheepish expression was bleatingly obvious. And, yes, I

WITCH WAR IN WESTERHAM

said bleatingly. "You can't blame me for not wanting to give you some not-great news."

"Spill. Whatever it is, we'll figure it out." After everything I'd seen in the last few days, it was as if nothing could possibly be that bad and I was immune to stressing about anything else. They'd put me through the worst, and no problem big or small was a worry.

"We can't locate Dana's father. We've had Cardinal monitoring the internet at both his residences, and they've been dead for the last couple of days." I finished my coffee and magicked it clean and away.

"You don't seem too worried. What gives?"

I shrugged. "Not much. I know how we can find him. In fact, I know how we can get him to come to us."

"Why do I get the distinct feeling I'm going to hate your suggestion?"

My grin was mirthless. "Because you are." I stood. "Let's go to my brother's. I prefer to only have this argument once."

"*Meow.*"

"Oh, sorry. I'd better let these little guys out. Thank you so much for coming to brunch. I enjoyed it." Grayson bounded over to me and looked up at me with the cutest little face. I imagined he was thanking me. "It was my pleasure. Please come back soon."

He chittered something to his friends, and they leapt off the table and ran to the door. Will opened it and let them out. By the time he shut it, I was standing in James's reception room. Wanting to get something over and done with was a wonderful motivator.

As Millicent opened the door and greeted me with a massive hug, Will arrived. "I need you to call everyone to a quick meeting, please."

She widened her eyes, then quickly reversed it with her eyebrows drawing down. "Okay. I'm scared to ask why."

"You'll know in a minute." I smiled, indicating I was in my right mind, and it was nothing like I was giving up.

She greeted Will, then turned and went through to the living room. Will and I went into the dining room instead. Liv and Agent Fairweather were at their laptops working. I sat next to Liv—I could always trust her to back me up. "Hey, ladies. How's it going?" They both looked at me warily as if deciding how to approach me. "It's fine. I'm upset, but I'm dealing with it. No need to tiptoe around me. I'm the same Lily I was yesterday with a small modification."

Liv raised a brow. "The *small modification* is what I'm worried about."

"It's nothing you need to worry about. Our enemies, definitely, but not my friends."

"That sounds serious," said my mother's old workmate.

Beren, Imani, James, Millicent, and Roche came into the room, saving me from having to answer. James met my gaze as he made his way to his chair at the head of the table. Curiosity warred with trepidation on his face. I wished he would just go back to having a poker face. That was an expression I could rely on. We'd lost Angelica's steady influence, and it was showing.

Once everyone was seated and staring at me, James asked, "I understand you wanted to talk about something."

I nodded. "I do." I had no patience and no finesse, so I figured I wouldn't even try. I was just going to drop it on them. "Will tells me that you can't find Dana's father."

"Yes, that's true."

"Well, I don't think we should muck around with this. After last night, they would know someone is closing in on them, and I'm sure they can connect the dots. I have the perfect solution, and before anyone shouts me down, I want you to think about how we don't have an alternative, and the longer we wait, the more prepared they'll be."

Beren eyeballed me. "You're not selling it at this point, Lily. The only thing I'm thinking is that none of us are going to like it."

I smiled. "You'd be right, B. But throughout this whole thing, nothing we've done is because we wanted to. We have to, and so it is with what I'm going to suggest. It's the most logical thing to deal with our issue. I, for one, don't want to be chasing Dana's father around the world for the rest of my life. I want this over and done within the next couple of days if we can manage it."

Agent Roche had a bemused smile on his face. "Miss Bianchi, you aren't the meek woman who visited my place the other day. Why haven't the PIB snatched you up yet?"

"They've tried. Ma'am keeps offering, but I have other things I want to do with my life. I was a photographer in a past life, a creative one. Anyway, enough of my dreams post RP." If we even get to that point. "I know how we can get Dana's father to come to us."

"Do tell," said James, his voice gruff and parental. It was the tone Dad used to use when he was waiting for a chance to interrupt and say no to something unreasonable we wanted.

"I just need to go out into the open somewhere and wait. Eventually, Dana will arrive because we all know she just can't help herself when it comes to me, and if we arrest her—surely if we have enough agents in hiding waiting, we can trap her— her father will come running. He wouldn't want his baby girl to die, surely."

Will's nostrils flared. "That's madness. What if someone

else turned up? Or what if they all turned up and overpowered us?"

"Apparently, her father wants me alive. She doesn't. She's more likely to do something rash, leave herself open." I stared at Will across the table. "I can do this. What if we have the thirteen waiting? We'll encircle her and trap her that way, and if we all have our return to senders up, no one will be able to touch her, or us."

James folded his arms. "Except if they arrive with thirteen of their own. You don't think they haven't been planning for this day for years?"

Roche nodded thoughtfully, and even though Imani wasn't shouting me down, she wasn't standing up for me either. I'd better come up with something else fast, or I was going to lose this round. "Send agents to arrest Toussaint and that German woman first." Okay, so I couldn't remember her name. I really was terrible at remembering things, but they knew who I meant. "Once everyone is in place, we strike, and I stand out in the open somewhere not too close to a lot of people, just in case it gets messy."

Beren pursed his lips. "Just in case it *gets messy*? Are you mad?"

I lifted my chin and took a calming breath. "Despite what happened last night and last week, no. I'm totally sane. But that can't be said for our enemies. The longer we wait, the deeper they'll burrow in, the more organised they'll be. We need to act now."

"No," said James, finality in his tone. "I can't agree to this, Lily. We still have time, even if it's a few days. I won't go rushing in before we've thought this through every which way. I appreciate you're willing to put yourself out there, but no." He looked at Will, then Beren. "I'm sure I have the full support of everyone here." If their nods were anything to go by, I was done.

Liv linked her arm through mine. "I think Lily's idea is a good one. She's strong enough to do this. You know it. We wouldn't even have gotten this far if it wasn't for her." She looked at me. "I believe in you." She smiled. "You can do anything."

I smiled back. "Thanks, Liv. This is why I love you. Such a supportive friend." I looked back at Will, Beren, then James. "That's fine. Well, actually, it's not really, but I'm right. You'll see. Give RP more time and we'll all regret it."

"Sorry, Lily. As strong as you are and as capable as all of us are, it's not the right solution. I think we can come up with better." James stood. "Back to work, everyone." Everyone stood—except for Agent Fairweather, Liv, and me—and slowly filed out.

I wanted to scream, but I didn't. Liv put her arm against me and rested her temple against mine. "They're just scared to lose you, Lily. James has been in a state all day. First your dad, then your mum. I don't think he can handle anything else. He even tried to tell Millicent she had to stay here when the time came."

I shook my head. "He can't protect all of us all the time. His wife is an agent, for squirrel's sake. That's something I'm going to do from now on, Liv, use the word squirrel more. I regret not using it more up to this point. No regrets if it all ends soon, right?"

She giggled. "You have your priorities straight. No one can say you didn't live your life to the full."

"Damn straight." My smile fell. "I know why he said no, but we can't make all our decisions based on fear. If we did, I'd be safe at home in bed. I'm scared to death, Liv, but I'm more scared of what will happen to everyone else but me if they're let loose. James is lying to himself if he thinks it's about being smart."

Someone put their hand on my shoulder, and I jumped. I jerked my head around. Imani. "Hey, love. For what it's worth, I know you're strong enough, but that plan is just too risky. Keep thinking. I know you'll come up with something else."

"Don't worry about it."

She squeezed my shoulder. "I just wanted you to know."

I smiled. "Thanks. Now get back to work."

"Yeah, yeah, and you hang in there." As she walked off, frustration frothed with more turbulence than a fizzy drink that'd just had ice cream dropped into it. Mmm, ice cream. Did James and Liv happen to have chocolate ice cream in the freezer? It was a good way to pass the time… eating ice cream. I stood. "I'll be back. Do you guys want a drink or something to eat?"

They both answered in the negative. More ice cream for me, then. I walked out of the dining room and into the kitchen, where Roche was on the phone, staring out of the back french doors, one hand on his hip. I would've laughed that he was drawn to the *French* doors—yes, lame joke, but that's me—but his pale face and slack jaw made me stop. Liquid dread, warm and sticky, flowed over me, raising goose-bumps from my scalp to my toes.

Crap.

When he hung up the phone, he noticed me standing there. He turned and stared at me. We stood there caught in the web of emotion between people who know the other has something horrific to tell them. It was that moment of angst, when it was bad but it could never be as bad as actually knowing. I hovered in that space until the weight of it brought me thudding to the ground. "What is it?" Maybe it wasn't my place to ask, but I couldn't leave him by himself, even in the time it took him to find James.

"R.P." His voice came out breathless but gathered strength even in its disbelief as he continued. "They set off a bomb at our Paris headquarters. Ten casualties, all of them men who'd sworn to serve our cause. Many more are injured. I'm of a mind to bring them here for Beren to heal. Would James agree to that?"

"Of course he would. Let's go." I didn't wait for him to agree; instead, I ran into the living room and told James. He barked orders and got everyone moving. Within thirty minutes, we had fourteen injured agents in makeshift beds throughout the house. Beren was going from person to person, healing them. He was going to be exhausted by the time he was done. One of the uninjured was an agent who had sworn to our cause and was also a healer. She worked side by side with Beren.

Once they were done, the agents stayed in their beds, sleeping. We needed them to get their strength back as soon as possible. Even if James didn't plan to go in hard tonight, it would have to happen soon, and healing really took it out of a person.

The feeling of dread hadn't left me. So many good souls dead, yet again. This was getting old. Anger festered in my stomach. Maybe it was lucky I hadn't made it to the ice cream. I needed fresh air, but leaving the house was dangerous, so I decided to wander, burn some energy. I made it as far as the hallway leading to the bedrooms when I came upon Will and James facing off with Roche and Imani. They all turned to stare at me.

I didn't want to anger James, but I was not going to say nothing. "Now do you see?"

He glared at me, then threw his angry gaze at the ceiling. "Dammit!"

I walked over to them. "There's no easy way to do this, James. Stuff it. So what if we die? If we don't do this now, so many more will die. We're not more special than anyone else. And if we can't beat them now with all our resources and support, it will never happen, especially with the PIB in disarray. I can't see anything improving over there. Mum and Dad wouldn't want us to stand here and do nothing."

The pain in his gaze when he looked at me again almost had me backing down, but I needed to stand strong. "You're right, Lily. I hate it, but you're right. I thought I could protect you and Mill, Annabelle, but I can't do shit. Hesitating was wrong. I'm sorry." He turned to Roche. "Please forgive my error in judgement."

"There is nothing to forgive, Agent Bianchi. I would have done the same. I would've been wrong, too, but the sign of a good leader is to learn from one's mistakes, no?"

James nodded. "Well, we're ten men down, and the other agents need to rest now. Have we got enough agents to arrest Toussaint and Brandt?"

"Yes. The Germans can cover us," Agent Roche answered.

"Okay, make the call." James looked at Will, regret on his face. "Can you call Sarah and Lavender now? This is way too heavy for them, but we don't have a choice. Our numbers are down, and they wanted to help."

Reluctance flashed in his eyes as he looked at me. I gave him a sad smile. "I don't want you to go either, Will, but here we are. We're all the world has. Risks must be taken and sacrifices must be made. My parents paid the ultimate price trying to stop them. We have to at least try."

His Adam's apple bobbed as he swallowed. "I know. I'll make the call."

And just like that, everyone was on board. I should've been happy I'd gotten my way, but I wasn't.

It was time to risk everything. Who knew? It might be time to die.

CHAPTER 19

W hen it came to arresting those leading RP, it was complicated. We weren't exactly going with my plan of luring Dana with the promise of killing me. Instead, German agents had confirmed Katrin Brandt was holed up in her German fortress of a home. It seemed almost too easy. There were a few things to do before we approached her because we didn't want her discovering we were onto her and then her travelling to who knew where. Even though RP was aware something was up, they had no reason to expect we knew she was one of the bigwigs. Our forays into their hunting properties didn't automatically mean we were after her, exactly, and we'd only made it to one of the four German properties.

Toussaint, on the other hand, was going to be a problem. He knew we'd been to his place and taken his key. Once he heard Brandt had been arrested, he would run for sure. But Agent Cardinal was more of a genius than I ever gave him credit for. He'd managed to hack into Toussaint's phone and had put a tracking spell on it. We only gained access because his number was known to the PIB. That's what you get for selling arms to the PIB—they end up with some of your information. Thankfully, he still had the same number, and Cardinal traced the phone via mobile-phone towers.

So, as it stood, we'd need to place spells over both houses to stop anyone travelling anywhere. Dana and her father might run, but since they wanted me so much, chances were, they'd eventually show up. If not tonight, then soon. And if not, we'd find them, eventually. If their network was broken, they wouldn't have nearly as much power either. That was our reasoning, anyway. We couldn't change anything, so we just had to go with it.

Toussaint, funnily enough, had holed up in his chateau in the country. Maybe he felt safer surrounded by a huge wall. Hopefully there wasn't a good reason he felt safer at his estate. Hmm…. Some of us were here, and some of us were at the German operation. Our thirteen were split up, but we had to, or there wouldn't be enough power to contain a witch in a huge house. While Imani, Will, Beren, and I held the spell over Toussaint's home, James and Roche were going in with some of our French agents to make the arrests. Everyone in the home would be arrested, and they'd sort out guilty and not-guilty parties later, assuming they didn't all die on us.

And assuming we survived to take them into the PIB.

Best not to think of that right now.

We'd all gathered about a hundred metres from the property behind some trees that bordered farmland. Will had built the threads of the spell at James's because it was something that took time. For the execution, though, we'd need a lot of power, so Imani, Beren, and I would link to him via my talent for the part where he threw it over the property and held it. Once that was done, Agent Roche and James would take the French agents and storm the property. Fingers crossed it went to plan.

As usual, we were doing this under cover of darkness. I didn't think I'd had so many late nights in a row as I had over the last week. Well, once this was over, I'd either be able to go to bed at a reasonable hour for the foreseeable future, or I'd be asleep forever. *Okay, don't go there, Lily. Not helpful. Squirrels. Think about squirrels.*

The day had been clear, but clouds had moved in, and it was sprinkling. None of us had an umbrella, and we weren't going to risk discovery by drawing power to magic one to us. Besides, what was a little rain when your life was at stake?

Will was distracted, since he was holding the spell threads together, waiting for the okay from James. All the agents had bulletproof vests on. They'd even given me one, not that I was supposed to enter the chateau, but who knew what was going to happen. I wasn't sorry I had it; that's for sure. It did feel a bit like I was in a movie. Terribly surreal.

As James went over the plan one last time with his agents, I bit my fingernails, Will stared in the direction of our target, and Imani and Beren chatted about whether spaghetti bolognese was better with or without garlic. For what it was worth, it had to have garlic as far as I was concerned. What kind of Italian dish didn't have garlic?

Gun in hand, James strode over to us. Oh, crap, it was go time. Will, Imani, and Beren gathered around us. My brother looked at each of us in turn. "We'll be right behind you. Cast the spell when you're near the front gates. We'll gain entry and go in ahead. Once we're on the property, come in so you can hold the spell more easily, but don't get too close to the house.

I'll leave two agents to guard you, but I can't afford any more. Sorry."

"Don't be sorry," Imani said. "We've got this. You just concentrate on what you're doing. We've all got our earpieces in, so let us know when you have him."

"Will do. We'll take him straight to the German PIB cells when we're done. The French ones aren't secure enough after that blast. Good luck, and I'll see you when we're done."

"Good luck, bro. We got this."

He smiled, and I gave him a thumbs up.

Will nodded, and our little group emerged from behind the protection of the trees, crossed the road, and jogged to Toussiant's. We stopped a few metres from the gates, and Beren and I held Will's and Imani's hands, forming a circle. Without waiting for Will to ask, I opened myself to the river of power, as did Beren and Imani. A hum vibrated around us as an incredible amount of energy poured through our portals to Will. We had to hurry because once we started, the drawing of magic would be so strong that witches within a one-mile radius would feel it.

Once Will had enough power, he squeezed my hand and Beren's. We, in turn, squeezed Imani's hands. It was the signal Will was going to release the spell. Which meant we all had to brace and hang on.

I shuffled my feet further apart and bent my knees slightly. I was ready.

He released it, and a kickback thudded into my stomach. It wasn't painful, just uncomfortable—certainly not as bad as I'd expected. But this was just the beginning. Holding this spell was going to be the trickiest part.

Will spoke for my brother's benefit, our communication

tech capable of two-way interaction. It was also being beamed live to the screens at James's and recorded. "It's done."

Within twenty seconds, James and the other agents stormed past. Magic I didn't recognise prickled my scalp, and the gate blew inwards with an ear-splitting *bang*. They rushed in. We gave them thirty seconds, then followed, staying just behind the two agents James had promised would help defend us while we were otherwise occupied. As we crossed into the property, gunfire rang out. I cringed at each volley.

"Keep your focus, Lily. We can't get distracted." Will spoke through gritted teeth.

"Sorry." I concentrated on the river of power and made sure I channelled everyone's power into Will. Despite the cool air, sweat drizzled down the sides of my face. Every now and then, it was as if someone pricked me in the stomach with a pin. "What's that?"

"They're trying to escape. But we're holding."

More gunfire peppered in the distance. Shouting. James gave directions for his men to take the chateau. An image of trebuchets and knights on horses came to mind. *Stay focussed, Lily. Damn you.*

As Imani and Beren fed their power through me, my blood increasingly warmed. I wasn't sure how long we could continue before I'd have to call time or burn from the inside out. My scalp itched, and I bit my lip hard to take my mind off it. How the hell were they managing this without someone like me to share their power? Will had explained it was a group-type spell, and whilst it was strong, it wasn't nearly as strong as ours would be with a single focal point. We would supposedly be less tired by the end of it too. That was yet to be proven though. I'd just be happy if we all managed to survive.

Knowing James was down there in the thick of it sent bile up my throat.

The heat intensified. I gritted my teeth and clasped Imani's and Will's hands tighter, the sweat pouring off me making the connection slippery. "Not long now, Lily." Imani sounded way fresher than I felt. "James should be done soon."

Or not

An explosion smashed us with a shockwave of deafening sound. A fiery cloud of iridescent orange illuminated the night sky as it billowed upwards. Thankfully, whatever had happened in the physical world hadn't destroyed our spell. But was James okay, were Agent Roche and all the other agents? I shared a panicked stare with Beren across our small circle. The two agents guarding us looked at each other, then at Will. "Go," he said. "Worse comes to worst, and we'll drop this thing and fight."

The two men gave him a nod, turned, and bolted.

I wanted to scream into my comms and ask James to check in—he'd been silent since the explosion; in fact, it sounded like the system wasn't working. "Will, can you hear me."

He furrowed his brow. "Yes, of course."

"No."

"No?"

"I can't hear you through the comms. We have no way to get in touch with James." I held in the scream that wanted to eject itself. I wasn't allowed to break ranks and run to find him either.

My breathing came faster as frustration and hysteria built. Will could probably sense it through our bond because he said, "We need to hold this spell, or all of this will be for nothing. We can't let them get away."

"But I haven't felt a prod for ages."

"That doesn't matter."

"Lily, hold fast." Gah, now Beren was in on it. I knew they were right; it was just so hard. So. Damned. Hard. If anything happened to James, Annabelle would be my only living relative, at least a close one. I had third and fourth cousins in Italy, but they were practically strangers, and as much as I loved Millicent, we weren't blood.

"Don't, die, damn you, James." I let the tears fall. No one could tell the difference with all the sweat pouring down my face and the rain.

"He's not going to die, love."

"How do you know?" Imani didn't answer, so then I felt horrible for shouting her down. "Sorry. I didn't mean to—"

"It's okay, love. We're all feeling it. Let's just concentrate on what we need to do, and we'll worry about the rest later."

More gunfire. I knew I wasn't being shot, but I didn't know how much more I could take. My skin was practically steaming. My throat and mouth screamed for water. "I don't mean to be negative, but I don't know how much longer I can hold this, Will. I'm shrivelling from the inside out."

He saw me then, really saw me. Even though he would've been struggling, he didn't have to channel power through himself. He would still be feeling the effects, but as the person who controlled the flow, I was copping most of the heat… literally. "Please, just a bit longer. I know you can do it."

I nodded. "Okay."

Another explosion, this time at the back of the house. God knew what was going on. This was crazy. The comms crackled, and I shut my eyes, waiting. *James, please.*

The voice was breaking up, and we only caught every second word, but it was James. It was bloody well James! My

scared tears turned into happy ones. "You— now. Drop—
okay— got them."

Will spoke. "Please repeat that, Agent Bianchi. You're
breaking up."

"We have them. You— drop the shield."

I opened my mouth and sucked in cool air as everyone
closed their portals, and the last of the magic dissipated. I
closed my portal and dropped everyone's hands, then I sat on
the ground and cried some more. I was such a weeper lately.
God, I needed some water. I stretched my legs out and lay on
my back. I didn't even care about the gravel digging into the
back of my head.

Imani peered down at me. "Ready for a nap, love?"

"Yes." That was all I could manage. One word.

"Well, you'd better hope Miss Evil Pants doesn't swoop
down right now."

"I can't see her getting in the midst of this. I'd take her for
someone who'd wait for a better time when I don't have so
much protection around me. Does anyone have some water?"
I lifted my head to stare towards the orange flames that
weren't as high as before but were still glowing in the darkness.
How many people had died?

Imani's magic prickled my scalp. "Here love." She handed
me a large bottle of water."

"Oh my God, you're the best! Thank you." I unscrewed
the lid and guzzled it down. There wasn't much left by the
time I stopped and realised maybe someone else was thirsty.
"Ah, sorry. There's a little bit left if anyone wants it."

"No thanks, love. We'll be going soon."

"Aren't you all thirsty?" Was I doing this magic thing all
wrong?

The lines in Will's forehead were more pronounced than

usual. "A bit, but you were bearing the brunt of the magic. Thank you. We all did a good job keeping things contained. I would've just been able to hold on by myself, but I might have broken down near the end. Thanks." He looked towards the house, too, then grabbed his phone out of his back pocket. He dialled someone. "Hey, James. What's the situation?" He listened for a couple of minutes. "Okay. Coming back now. Bye." He looked at Beren, then Imani, then me. "They arrested two housekeeping staff, who both died, four hench-men, who also died, Toussaint, another man, and a woman, and they all lived. Seems like we can work out the hierarchy from that."

"What about our agents?" Beren asked.

"He didn't get into that over the phone." Will made a doorway and offered me his hand. "Come on." I took it and let him pull me up. Stage one, at least here, was done. But how had they gone in Germany? Millicent and her dad were there, so were Sarah, and Lavender, for goodness' sake. Crap. Why had we said it was okay for them to help? I had a terrible feeling as I walked through Will's doorway, and it wasn't thirst.

I'd bet my favourite squirrel on the fact that the worst was yet to come.

And I didn't have long to wait.

Not long at all.

CHAPTER 20

W hile the team took stock at James's for a couple of hours, I went home and had a nap. I needed to recuperate, get some of my strength back. Will came with me, just to make sure he was well-rested, not to mention some of the activity had moved to German PIB head-quarters. Millicent had been injured, shot in the arm. Which was horrible, but Beren had healed her. They were both taking it easy for the next couple of hours. We just had to hope going after Piranha and her father could wait until tomorrow. We were definitely the walking wounded. Sadly, we'd lost five agents in France and three in Germany, including the man who was supposed to help us make up the thirteen.

We set our alarm to give us three hours' sleep. When we woke, it was just after three in the morning. What a ridiculous time to wake up. But criminals waited for no one. I supposed we'd check in with James and, if we weren't needed, go back to sleep.

I yawned and tapped Will on the pectoral muscle. Mmm, firm yet slightly squishy. Perfect. "Hey, call James."

"I'm on it." He grabbed his phone from the bedside table, turned the alarm off, and dialled my brother on speaker.

My brother sounded even more tired than I felt. "Hey, mate."

"Hey. Lily and I just wanted to check in, see if you needed us yet."

"Nah, I think we're good for now. I'm about to go to bed. We've got twelve of the more senior members in lock up. As well as Brandt and the three we caught at her place, we nabbed three others in separate German raids, and two in English raids. We're getting there. The ones we caught were from the photos. And Mill stuck her cousin in the slammer. You should've seen the lecture Robert gave him too. Looked like he was fairly senior because he's still alive, which Millicent isn't happy about." He stopped to take a breath, then continued. "We still need to work out how to find Dana and her father. We've begun interrogations, but it might take a while. I've sent everyone home to get some sleep. Rested staff are taking over while we prepare for the next phase. Be at mine at eight thirty tomorrow morning."

"Can do."

"Goodnight, James."

"Goodnight, Lily."

"Send Mill my love."

"Yeah, I will." His voice was gruff, and no wonder—he'd almost lost the love of his life tonight. "Bye." The phone went dead.

I kissed Will goodnight. As sexy as he was, sleep was more attractive right now. We had a huge day tomorrow. With a bit of luck, it would be the day Dana ceased to exist.

And I was ready. Bring. It. On.

In the distance, a phone rang. I pushed up through the fog of a bad dream, closer and closer to the sound. I opened my eyes and reached over Will, who grumbled, and grabbed my phone from the bedside table. What the hell? It was only 6:04 a.m. I blinked at the name on the screen. Robert. Millicent's father.

I flicked my thumb across the screen to answer it, but I didn't want to fully wake Will, who had rolled onto his stomach in a clear show of not wanting to deal with anything right now. I climbed over him and whispered into the phone. "Hello. Robert? It's a bit early, isn't it? Is everything okay?"

"That depends on who you ask, now, doesn't it?" I stopped in the middle of the room, icicles of dread stabbing every part of me. "And before you tell William who this is, think twice. If you don't come alone, Annabelle will die." Piranha couldn't have gotten to Annabelle. Surely? James's place was too well protected…. Only, my niece hadn't been there, had she? They'd given her to Millicent's mum to mind when we all went on our raids.

Crap.

I gagged and only just managed not to vomit. I flicked my gaze back to Will. Should I tell him?

"Don't be stupid, Lily. You know I don't muck around. And once I kill Annabelle, maybe I'll kill Millicent's parents too."

I hurried out the door and closed it softly behind me, then moved further down the hall. "I don't believe you."

"I'm switching to a video call, Lily. I hope you're decent."

I looked down at myself. Thankfully, I'd gone to bed in a

T-shirt and my fox pyjama pants. I held the phone away from my face so I could see the screen. My stomach dropped to the floor, and my body wanted to follow. My legs weren't up to their job of holding me up. They'd actually been doing quite a crap job lately.

Piranha was in a room I didn't recognise, sitting on a white sofa, holding my niece. Annabelle was fast asleep, oblivious to the danger she was in. Oh. My. God. I needed to call James.

Piranha grinned. "Sorry, but if you call anyone, she's dead, and it will only be the beginning. If you want her home safely, you need to hand yourself over. Once I have you at my mercy, I'll send this one home." She moved the camera up to her face so I could no longer see my gorgeous niece.

If I went without telling anyone and she didn't give Annabelle back, no one would ever know, and I would've failed doubly. But I believed her. She had nothing to lose and was crazy enough to kill an innocent baby. Imagine having to tell James I went against what she told me and his child was dead. Oh, God. I could hardly breathe. What the hell was I going to do?

"I'm sending you some coordinates, Lily. Get here within thirty seconds by yourself, or the baby gets it." The screen went black, and the call ended.

Stuff it. I magicked clothes on and memorised the numbers from the text that came through, but before I left, I opened the bedroom door. "Will, catch!" I threw him the phone, made my doorway, and left. I hadn't told anyone anything. I could honestly answer that if she asked, but as if I was going to just obey her without leaving evidence so someone could find me. I didn't trust that she'd send my niece back even if I did what she said. If I didn't come through for

Annabelle, we'd likely both be dead before breakfast time was over.

As I stepped through my doorway, I put up my return to sender. But what else would I need? How was I going to guarantee Annabelle's safety? Damn it! I was the least qualified person for this, and Piranha knew it. What would they have taught the agents to do in this situation? Never give in to the demands? Tell the police—well the PIB were police in their own right, but I should have contacted someone, surely? But then, if I did…. Argh, what a vicious circle. I didn't know that there was a right answer in this situation. Dana was unpredictable, well, not entirely. She was predictably murderous, and that's what I couldn't toy with. I had to assume she intended to carry out every threat. She held all the power in this situation. Annabelle's fate hung in the balance until she was safely back at home. I just had to make it happen.

I'd come through to a white room with a shaggy-style rug and orange sixties-style vinyl chair. The door opened before I could knock. The evil witch stood there, but Annabelle was nowhere to be seen. "Where is she?"

"Safe… for now." She laughed.

"How did you get to be such a b—"

"Now, now, you should be nice to me. I hold all the cards. Come in." The last was more an order than an enthusiastic welcome. I managed not to shudder as I walked past her, at least not externally. Who knew internals could shudder? It was a wholly unsettling experience, one I never wanted to repeat.

She pushed me in the back, and I stumbled forward. I wanted to fight back, but now wasn't the time. I needed to see that Annabelle was okay. "Where is she?"

"Not yet. I want you at my mercy before I reveal her whereabouts." We were walking down a hallway. Just as we reached a doorway at the end, the thug from the other day appeared, and he had an ugly friend. Both men were twice my size and glared at me.

Piranha gave me one more shove, and I flew into the chest of the thug I'd met before. He grabbed my arm and looked at Piranha. "What do you want me to do with her?"

"I haven't decided yet, but I want you to put the collar on her." She threw him a silver collar that looked like the one they'd put on my mother. If I waited any longer, I was never going to see Annabelle again. I just knew it. And I still had no guarantee that she'd make it safely home.

I narrowed my eyes and threw a hate-filled stare at the man holding me. "Try and put that on me, and you're dead." I jerked my arm out of his hold and turned to the evil one. "Where's my niece? I am not surrendering anything until she's back home and safe."

"Put the collar on, and I'll show you."

"Do you think I'm stupid?"

She grinned. "No. I know you are."

The thug gripped my wrist. I tugged at his hold. "Let go." He had a return to sender up, so I couldn't zap him. Unless…. Annabelle must be here somewhere. If I disobeyed, how was Piranha going to hurt her if she was busy dealing with me? They didn't know my special talents. If I timed this right, I could kill them all, grab Annabelle, and be out of here in five minutes. Was that really my inner voice talking so casually about killing people? And what if it went wrong and I managed to get myself killed? Would she kill Annabelle, or would it not matter? Maybe they were my options: try to escape, or, if I couldn't, make sure I died trying.

Now I had to hope Will didn't barge in too early and ruin everything. I guessed it was time to call action.

"Lily? Are you listening to me?" Piranha's face was twisted in anger. "You do realise I could kill you right now if I wanted." Her magic prickled my scalp, and a long-bladed knife appeared in her hand. The other thug grabbed my other wrist, and now I was seemingly helpless. They all had return to senders up, so they knew I couldn't use my magic against them. Surely I was helpless.

The men held me fast as Piranha slowly moved the knife-point towards my face. She prodded my cheek with it—not hard enough to draw blood but hard enough to make a lesser person pee their pants. I, thankfully, did not. I gave her my most deadpan look, as if I had not a care in the world. "It's nice to know you're scared of me." I smiled.

Her eyes widened, and she pressed the blade hard enough to prick my skin. I managed not to wince at the sting. "Not in a million years. These boys are just my guarantee that I can take my time without having to stop to knock you unconscious. I want you to feel everything I do to you. I want you to know, as you die, who is killing you."

"You've been watching too many movies. Seriously. Have you got any original material? Next, you'll be shooting at me, but no bullets will actually hit me." I laughed. "And, don't forget that we have to have the compulsory fistfight at the end."

She drew her arm back in a wide arc and slapped my face. My head snapped to the side. Ouch. That actually hurt. Why the hell was I waiting? It was her turn to laugh. "I'm enjoying this. But don't worry, I won't kill you… yet. My father wants to use you first." Her face twisted in revulsion. "He needs strong magic to put some plans into motion. He's waited a very long time, and even though your incompetent agent friends have put a dent in those plans, it's all going to be fine.

Once my father has your magic under his control, the world will be his."

Oh, this was interesting. So now maybe I couldn't kill them. I needed her to take me to her dad. Or maybe I could kill her and he'd come looking for me. Hmm, that was preferable. "Where's my niece?"

She laughed. "Oh, sorry, I forgot to mention that my father will be minding her until I've delivered you to him."

Crap.

I'd have to wait a little longer for my revenge.

She hovered the knife near my face again and flicked the tip of the blade across my cheek. I sucked in a breath, but I didn't cry out. I would not give her the pleasure. "Oops, I slipped."

"Yes, that's what happened to me when I killed your boyfriend. Oops."

Fire flared in her eyes, and she placed the knife blade at my throat. I held her stare and thought of my mother, of how she must have felt running from Dana's father and Toussaint. I let the hatred well up inside me, a scalding volcano of motivation to survive this and show no fear. I met her glare, second by second, any fear I'd felt earlier swallowed whole by images of my parents.

Revenge couldn't bring them back, but it would ensure I could sleep at night and that millions, even billions of future non-witches would be safe. Dana's forehead wrinkled, as if she wasn't sure about something. "Why are you smirking? Why aren't you scared?"

I smiled. "Because I know something you don't. Actually, lots of somethings. And when you find out what they are, it will be too late for you to do anything about it." At this point, I believed some of what I was saying, but it was pretty much cow manure. It was fun messing with her. Accepting that I might die was liberating. I'd already lost so much of what was dear to me; there was no way I was going to let them take my niece from her parents, and I knew I would do anything to stop that from happening.

At peace with my decision, nothing could hurt me.

Will burst through the reception-room door down the hall, James right behind him, both leading with their guns. I knew they'd find me eventually. But my message had no context, and James had no idea Annabelle's life hung on Dana's whim. Although they must have learned by now that she was missing, and they would know I only acted for important stuff. "Lily!" shouted Will. Our gazes met. His eyes were a tumult of worry, fear, and anger.

But that was all I saw before one of the men behind Piranha smashed me in the back of the head. Hmm, maybe I'd been too hasty in my previous assessment because that hurt like a....

And that's when I blacked out.

It was probably for the best, really.

My head ached, and there was pressure on my neck. Crap. I'd stuffed up, gotten too cocky, and I'd made my life harder. Of course I had. Without opening my eyes, I knew I was somewhere different, somewhere that Will and James would never find me.

Timing was everything. *Idiot, Lily!*

But then again, Annabelle was also everything, and without knowing where she was, we were in big trouble. I ignored the fear rumbling in my stomach. Maybe it was just hunger? If that was the truth, why didn't I open my eyes? *Let's just get this over with.* I was such a chicken sometimes, but not today. I wasn't going to let myself shirk my responsibilities.

I did it; I opened my eyes.

And it was just as I thought.

I was lying on another couch, and on an armchair nearby, Dana's father sat staring at me. He smiled. "Ah, Lily, so kind of you to join us."

I made a "you've got to be kidding" face. "Do all you criminals watch James Bond just for their one-liners? Or is that really how criminals talk, and the movie people researched it really well?"

"I see you haven't lost your sense of humour."

"Where's my niece?"

"Over there. Look, just as Dana promised—she's fine."

Dana sat in an armchair cradling Annabelle and cooing at her. It was about as comforting as watching a funnel-web spider coddle your baby. I just needed a giant thong to squash her with, and everything would be right with the world.

"She also promised that you'd send her home safely when you had me where you wanted me, and"—I reached up and touched the cold, metallic collar around my neck that definitely blocked my magic—"I'm pretty sure that's where I am right now. At your whim with no magic to protect myself. If you don't send her back now and I have proof she's safe, I will die rather than help you."

"Did you hear that, Anna, honey, your Auntie Lily is trying to make demands? She's so stupid. But we knew that, didn't we?" If Piranha thought she could build rapport with my niece, she was the stupid one. Annabelle had much better taste than that. Also, I wasn't going to bite. If that's what she wanted, it wasn't happening.

I looked back at Dana's father. "We both know I'm here because your daughter isn't magically powerful enough to help with what you want, so why don't you send her away, and we can talk business. But only after my niece is safe." Ha, I saw the glint of anger strike her face. If I managed to make her angry enough, maybe I could take advantage somehow. Was there a key for this contraption around my neck? If they wanted to use my magic, they would have to give me access to it eventually. Unless they were going to brainwash me like they did with Millicent. Gah! *Come on, Lily, you beat that vampire witch. They've got nothing on him.* My inner voice had a point. I really should listen to it more often, or was that what got me here in the first place?

Dana's father stood, and I struggled to sit up, but after impersonating a determined cockroach, I managed to. Damned if I was going to crane my neck looking up at him towering over me. He walked over to me and looked down. Damn. I was still looking up at him. "So, if I don't return your niece, you would rather die than help me? Are you sure?"

I stood and took great joy in the flinch he tried to hide. "Positive. Hurry this up. I always hoped I'd die suddenly, like without warning, because, really, we all die suddenly. Like, there is a point in time where it happens. It all just stops. I know with cancer, you might say someone died slowly, but at the moment of death, it happens all of a sudden."

"Oh for God's sake, shut up!" Dana yelled. Annabelle cried.

"Argh, now you've done it. You'd make a crap mother. And I wonder what Dana's mother would think of both of you using a baby to get me here? I have a suspicion she wasn't nearly as horrible as both of you. Imagine what she would say, knowing you've threatened the life of a baby."

Hmm, that got their attention. They both stared at me. Dana's eyes radiated anger, but what else was new? Her father, however, had that cold, controlled look of anger and pain, something that ran much deeper and could do infinitely more damage to another person when that was their motivation. Maybe I'd just thrown one insult too many.

Dana jumped up, the baby still in her arms, crying. "Stop talking about my mother. You don't know her. You don't know what she would or wouldn't think. You know nothing about her!"

I rolled my eyes. "If she was a half-decent person, then, yes, I do know what she'd think." I turned my gaze on Dana's father. "I also know my mother didn't kill her. Your father did." Okay, I didn't know it for sure, but he was there when she died, and my mother wasn't. I had to hope my assumption hit close enough to the truth to get a result.

"Enough!" my target shouted.

But since when had I listened to orders? "You killed her in your house, then burnt it down. I just can't work out why."

His face had paled—he obviously hadn't foreseen this turn of events. Dana hadn't missed his reaction, either. I smirked. "My mother didn't kill your mother. You've hated me for so long for nothing. Maybe hate your father since he was the one who did it."

"She's lying. How would she know how your mother died?"

"Admit it under magical oath, then." Ooh, now I was coming up with the good stuff.

Silence seized the room. Even Annabelle had quietened.

I stared at Dana's dad with a challenge in my gaze. He would never agree to that, even if he were innocent. As if a criminal about to use a victim for their own nefarious purposes would submit to a request from said victim. He would never lower himself. He hadn't kept that secret for over ten years just to let it all come undone now. As far as he was concerned, I was temporary, but he would have a lifetime with his daughter.

But it was too late.

Dana would always wonder. I had planted the seed, and I hope she choked on its fruit.

"Lies!" He slapped me. A jolt of pain cracked from my cheek to my neck. Bloody family of slappers. If I didn't already have a headache, I'd pull out my awesome headbutt and break his nose. But I needed to think.

"Take Annabelle home or I will die here. I've beaten a vampire witch. You think I'm going to succumb to you?" I spat in his face. Wow, that was so gross of me, but I liked it. *Nice work, Lily.*

He snarled and wiped his face. He grabbed me under the chin. "Do that again, and I'll cut your tongue off. You won't need that to draw magic."

I reached for my magic, but it wasn't there. Of course it wasn't. Grrr. Anger and fear entwined in my gut, and I wasn't sure which was getting the upper hand. Actually, as my knee rocketed upwards and smashed Dana's father in the balls, it was obvious that anger was winning. Yay, anger!

He grunted and doubled over. I pushed him out of the way and ran to my niece. They were obviously never going to send her back, so I had nothing to lose.

Nothing.

But Dana had magic, and I didn't.

She hit me with a wall of energy that flung me backwards. I slammed into the floor, the air rushing from my lungs. Dana screamed, "Clive!" Her two thugs came running, as well as two extras. One of them helped her father stand, and another put his boot on my stomach and pointed a gun at my chest.

Dammit! This was not how this was supposed to go. The bad guys were not supposed to win. I looked over at Annabelle, who'd started crying again. "I'm so sorry, baby girl. Auntie Lily loves you. I'll figure this out. I promise."

Piranha sauntered over and stood at my feet. Even though her thug had me in check, she kept just far enough away that I couldn't kick her. I smirked. "Still scared of me, even though I have no magic, and this moron has a gun pointed at my chest?"

Her lip curled up in a sneer. She held out my gorgeous niece. "I just wouldn't want you to do anything to hurt this one. Just imagine if she died, and you died, and your brother still hated you for all eternity. And he will hate you, you know." I did figure that might happen, but it was too late to cry about it now, and squirrel's bum I was going to give her the pleasure of seeing an iota of grief in my face.

"Scaredy-cat. I know squirrels braver than you." I grinned.

She flicked a finger at me, and it was as if acid ate through my wrist.

The tattoo! Crap. I'd forgotten all about it. So, it was still active, but maybe only when they were close to me. At least it wasn't going to do anything worse than cause me to grimace. And, yes, I was grimacing, which Piranha thought was amusing if her smile was anything to judge by. "Ah, good to see it's still working. Oh, look, little Annabelle has one just like Auntie Idiot's." She lifted Annabelle's sleeve to reveal a tiny tattoo, and my heart squeezed painfully. The tattoo's size made it look more like a lizard than a snake, but I wasn't going to joke about it.

The stakes just rose.

And it wasn't in my favour.

"Try a stunt like that again, and Annabelle will pay the price." Hatred bordering on insanity oozed from her gaze. A chill spread from my scalp to my toes. There was no doubt she'd make good on her threat. I'd just walked into this like the biggest idiot, but how could I not? Imagine if I hadn't come. Annabelle would probably already be dead.

There must be a way out of this.

Think, Lily. Damn you.

Unfortunately, Dana's father had recovered from our little incident. He stared down at me. "Insubordinate witch." He looked at the thug. "Bring her to the operations room. We're doing this now. It's about time those useless humans without magic felt our wrath." His crazed stare found me again. "Their time of dominance has come and gone. It's our time now. Those savages have held us hostage for too long. What a farce that we can't show our magic just so we don't make them feel bad. And if they think they can retaliate and kill us, as they tried hundreds of years ago, they have no idea what's coming. You, witch prodigy, are going to help me cast the biggest spell the world has ever seen. With it, we'll gain control over millions of people. And we're going to start with the army." His manic grin sent horror shuddering through me. What. The. Hell? "World domination must start somewhere, and it starts today."

Clive yanked me to my feet. He pulled me towards a staircase that went to a lower level. Just before we started down, Dana called out, "We burnt your mother out trying this, so good luck." She smiled and batted her eyelashes. How I wanted to rip them out and shove them down her throat.

I narrowed my eyes. I couldn't hold up the pretence that everything was fine when she brought my mother into it. Yes, I was giving her what she wanted, a reaction, but it couldn't be helped. "Was that before or after your dad and Toussaint hunted her down while she wore a collar?"

Dana's father grabbed my hair and yanked my head back. I grunted with the force of it. Damn. The more I showed weakness, the more they'd enjoy this. "How do you know this?"

He was staring at me from the side. I couldn't move my head—his grip was too strong—but I could give him massive side-eye. "I just know, like I know you killed your wife. You may think you have the upper hand right now, but you'd better watch your back. I'm way more than you bargained for." His eyes bored into mine, but he said nothing. All I got for my trouble was another jerk of my head. Man, that ached. I added it to the score I was going to settle as soon as I figured out how.

He released my hair, and I resisted the urge to turn and kick him in the shin. *Patience, Lily. You haven't worked out what you're doing yet. Don't make it harder.* Yes, that was something I had to learn—patience. Why was it so hard? Gah. One of these days I'd get it right.

The thug squeezed my arm as he forced me down the stairs. It ached, but I ignored it. I had more important things to think about… like whether I would poke Dana's dad's eyes out before I killed him.

The other three thugs followed us down. Right. Five witches to overcome, then upstairs to deal with witch face. I pretended it wasn't impossible. I had nothing to lose by believing I was going to turn this crap show around.

Something Dana's father said to me upstairs was niggling at me. *Insubordinate witch.* Yes! That was it.

We'd reached the bottom of the stairs, but it went down

another flight. Was this place on a hillside or had they dug out a basement?

Now, what had I been thinking of? That's right, insubordinate witch. I smiled. Someone else, a few months ago, had called me the same thing. It was something I was proud to be, and it was what had kept me alive back then. But it wasn't just what she called me; it was what I did after that… what I could do.

We stepped onto a concrete floor at the bottom of the second flight of stairs. The dark hallway was short and stopped at a stainless-steel door. Was this a bunker? Was he planning on blowing up the world? No, that was nuts, plus, his crazy daughter was upstairs. If calamity was happening, he would've brought her down here.

Dana's dad waved his hand near the door, and it slid to the side. Bloody collar. I couldn't feel when someone was casting magic. My time was coming, though. Patience. And that ring on his middle finger looked familiar—a thick gold band with a square-cut emerald in the middle. Where had I seen it before? Oh my God! It was one of the artefacts stolen from the PIB. I'd beaten the man wearing it, on the bridge in London. Angelica had been made to hand it over to Top-Hat director. How had Dana's father gotten hold of it?

The thug stopped my train of thought. He shoved me through the door and into a room lit with white fluorescent light, which showed concrete, concrete, and more concrete. At this end was a row of screens, computers as well. An empty space opened in the middle of the room, but at the far end was…. I sucked in a breath, and my heart raced. It took a moment to fully comprehend the horror. A row of twelve cages, seven-feet-high and about two metres by two metres each. Eleven of them were occupied by a single person and a mattress on the floor. It was too far away for me to see the people's faces clearly, not that they were all facing me anyway. Most of them lay on their mattress, backs to me. Two of them watched with blank faces. None of them had collars, so they must be non-witches.

Were these test subjects? People I was supposed to control?

Was that last cage for me?

Insubordinate.

Timing.

I slid my finger along the front of my collar and remembered my mother.

"Bring her here." Dana's father stood in front of the screens. Thug man dragged me over there. His three mates fanned out behind us. Maybe I needed to seem more helpless so they'd go away, or maybe he was going to remove my collar. If that happened, the plan I was formulating wouldn't have to happen, which was probably good because it was dangerous. I could kill myself trying what I had in mind.

He magicked something into his hand. It was déjà-vu city today. The two bracelets in his hand were also stolen from PIB with the ring, but they'd never been recovered. Apparently, they linked the wearers to amplify power. He tipped his chin, and thug man pushed me to him. Man, I was sick of being shoved from here to there. I turned my head and glared at the huge guy and considered whether I should knee him in the balls too.

My tattoo burned. I gripped my wrist and held it to my stomach. "Argh!"

Dana's father laughed. "Pay attention. See these?" He held up the bracelets, and once I focussed on him, the scalding subsided. "I'll wear one, and you'll wear one. I can draw all your power then, but I can also control you as I have the dominant bracelet." Of course there had to be a catch. At least they were going to have to remove my collar. "And, the beauty of these? I won't have to remove the collar. Unless I'm directing the flow of power, you won't be able to channel any. And while I'm drawing power, it is all mine to control." He stared at the bracelets, an affectionate smile on his face. Bloody weirdo, and also, crap. Looked like I was going to have to go through with my plan, but to do it now or when he had the bracelets on us? No, I needed to do it now. I could grab him and draw his power at any time. I didn't want him to have any advantage.

Looked like it was time to risk my life. I flicked my gaze to the empty cage. I was pretty much dead anyway. Being locked down here and used for the rest of my life was not an option.

I'd rather die.

"Hold out your hand." I did as asked while centring myself and finding my own power reserves. I'd broken through one magical bond months ago, and it was time to break through another.

Insubordinate.

I'll show you insubordinate.

Just as he was going to put the bracelet on, I made a fist and spun around, smashing thug guy in the face. Yikes that smarted! He dropped my arm—probably not because I'd hurt him that much, but getting hit in the face unexpectedly was bound to get a reaction. I sprinted to the far side of the room. Not to get away—that was impossible—but for them to drag me back would give me enough time to do what I needed to.

I reached the cages and my gaze met that of a skinny woman with auburn hair that had started greying at the temples. Her gaunt face looked unfamiliar, but her eyes. I knew those eyes.

"Lily?"

My breathing stopped.

That voice.

My heart raced.

They grabbed me from behind. I shut my eyes. I had to block everything out if I wanted to succeed. I'd deal with the shock later.

Someone kicked me in the side. I grunted, and sharp pain sliced through me, but I was somewhere else, deep inside. My reserves were there, and underneath them, that invisible life-line to the river of power that I could only access once I'd almost depleted my own power. Something that seemed to be unique to me. Angelica had meant to talk to me about it, but we'd never gotten around to it.

Now was the time I had to work it out, and fast.

Rather than draw all my power, I sucked in energy from the river through my lifeline, but it was only tiny bits of magic at a time. I fought as they dragged me across the floor. The longer I had to take power, the more I'd have to break this damned collar. And I had more reserves than the first time I'd done this. Experience and practice made a witch stronger, and I'd had plenty of that in the last year.

As we neared Dana's father, I gripped the collar and started feeding my magic into it. As I fed my own life force, I took in more from the river. I willed it into the collar and curled into a ball, using all my muscles so they couldn't unroll me and stick the bracelet on me. I drew power, fed it, and held my wrists into myself for dear life.

The tattoo scorched me, and sweat trickled down my face. I panted as my heart rate increased.

"Help me, dammit!" Dana's father.

Keep going, Lily. My stomach ached as I sucked from the river as hard as I could. It took excruciatingly more effort to do it this way compared to having an open portal. The collar heated, uncomfortably so. Was I getting closer?

A thug on each side, they tried to pry my arms out. "No!" I screamed.

One of my arms was stretched out.

Damn it!

I poured as much of my life force into the collar as possible. It singed my neck. So close. Someone grabbed my hand.

I forced as much power as I could in a last push.

The odour of burnt flesh filled my nostrils. A rushing noise filled the room, and the collar cracked. My portal opened, and the power poured in, the force of it flinging my body away from Dana's father. If I'd been standing, I would've been thrown to the floor. They probably thought I was possessed.

Ignoring my stinging neck and aching stomach, I scrambled to my feet and grinned. The five men stared at me, their surprised brains not sure how to deal with the situation. None of them had return to senders up. I mean, why would they? Was it wrong to feel joy?

Dana's father was the most dangerous, so I targeted him first.

Lightning shot from one hand and hit the bracelets, destroying them and severing his hand. He screamed. His thugs ran for me. I syphoned so much power, I thought I would self-combust. My body burned as if I had a fever.

I splayed my hands out and thought only of electricity, beautiful and deadly.

I cut down his thugs in front of him. My power shot through their hearts, leaving a smoking hole in each man. They fell to the floor almost in unison, a deadly ballet where I was the choreographer.

Dana's father drew magic while he gritted his teeth. I

laughed. "You picked the wrong witch, buddy. I'm going to enjoy this."

"No!" he screamed as he released his spell. What an idiot. In his panic, he hadn't noticed my return to sender. His spell forced me a step backwards, but that was it. His spell rebounded, and as his face contorted in horror, his magic hit. His body ignited. From his head to his toes, a conflagration of evil.

I didn't have time to deal with the caged people, who were all now standing, staring at the carnage. I magicked their doors open and called out, "You're free now. I'll be back."

I exploded the lock on the door—I didn't have time to figure out the code—and sprinted up the stairs.

It was time to save my niece.

Had Piranha felt all that magic? If she had, would it have mattered? She would've thought I was down there helping her father take over the world. I was pretty sure none of the screaming would've reached her either since the bunker was concrete.

The advantages were all mine.

But it wasn't over yet. That knot in my stomach was staying tied until I knew my gorgeous niece, Annabelle, was safe. There was nothing more dangerous than an angry mamma bear... except an angry auntie bear.

I raced from room to room, but she was nowhere. I bolted up another flight of stairs two at a time and slowed when I reached the hallway at the top. She'd better be here. I strode along the hallway and slammed open the first door. An empty room. I shut it and went to the next door. Maybe I shouldn't open it so violently. If Annabelle was with Piranha, I didn't want to scare her.

I opened the door like a normal person. Relief breezed

through me like the sigh of jasmine-scented evening air after a warm summer's day. Piranha sat on her queen-sized bed, my niece in a cot next to her. She was apparently reading from a kid's book. Creepy much? Playing happy families with a kidnapped baby? That was a new level of insanity I didn't need to see.

She jumped off the bed and slammed her hands on her hips. Her magic tingled my scalp. It was so nice to have no collar so I could tell when people were about to cast a spell. Her eyes bugged out. I grinned. She must have realised I didn't have a collar and that I had a return to sender up.

Before she could do anything, I drew magic and translocated Annabelle to the room I'd just seen. I didn't know if I had enough power to send her home, and it was risky, but having just been in the next-door bedroom, I knew exactly where to place her, but Piranha would have no idea where I'd sent her.

"How dare you! Where's my father?"

A bang sounded from downstairs, and the house shook slightly. What the hell was that?

"Ooh, you're in big trouble now. My father's coming."

Did I have the heart to tell her? Yeah, yeah, I did. "Your father's dead. I killed him."

"Liar!" Her magic tingled my scalp, but she didn't dare cast a spell at me. She was more sensible than her father.

"Well, to be honest, I didn't actually kill him. He killed himself because he didn't realise, as you have, that I had a return to sender up. You're smarter than him—I'll give you that much."

Shouting came from downstairs. Did they have backup? Damn. I'd better hurry this up.

She flew at me, a gun appearing in her hand. Crap. And

she had a return to sender up too. Footsteps thundered up the stairs. "You're a liar. My father's going to make you pay for your disobedience." She shoved the gun at my temple. "Get out into the hallway."

My mouth went dry—even though I had my magic, if she pulled the trigger, nothing would save me.

She followed me into the hallway as three men reached the landing. "Here, Father. I've got her."

Well, that wasn't Dana's father. She registered it the moment I did, but I didn't give her a chance. I ducked into a crouch and elbowed her in the stomach. The gun went off, and shards of brick exploded out of the wall. My ears were ringing, yet again. It was a wonder I didn't have tinnitus by now.

Before Dana could recover, I turned and punched her in the face. It felt as if my knuckles splintered. Such intense pain. "Argh!" But she screamed, too, and blood poured from her nose. She lifted the gun again, but I brought my fist down on her forearm, forcing her to point it at the ground, then grabbed her collar with both hands, yanked her body down as my knee went up. She cried out as my knee slammed into her stomach. As soon as she dropped the gun, Will pushed me out of the way and stood in front of her, his gun pointed at her head.

"You're under arrest."

She looked up at him and felt at the blood trickling from her nose. She glared at him. "No one's arresting me. No one puts me in jail." Her magic prickled my scalp as a doorway formed around her.

"No!" I drew my power without thinking of anything but stopping her. More lightning poured from my hand, spearing her through the middle. Her face registered shock, and she stared at me before the life fizzled from her eyes and she dropped to the ground, a great big hole in her middle. Will, Beren, and James stared at me. I bit my lip and shrugged. "Oops." If I said any more, I'd cry. I searched inside myself for guilt, for empathy, but I found none. Was my metamorphosis into cold-hearted killer finally complete?

I didn't have time to contemplate it. James grabbed my shoulder, panic in his eyes. "Where's Annabelle?"

"Oh, God, sorry." His eyes widened, and it looked as if something inside had just died. "Oh, no, um, she's fine. I mean, sorry I didn't say anything sooner, but I was busy." I nudged him out of the way and hurried to the first room near the stairs and opened the door. He was right behind me. "Look, there she is. Happy as."

Annabelle looked up at us and smiled. James choked out her name. "Annabelle!" He scooped her up and held her into his chest before holding her out again to look her over. Tears flowed from his eyes. "My baby. Oh my God." Tears pricked my eyes. But then James looked at me, although with all the emotions roving his face, I couldn't tell what he was thinking. "You've got some explaining to do, Lily."

Guilt swiftly took the bottom out of my stomach. "I'm sorry I didn't tell anyone. But she told me if I didn't come within 30 seconds, or if I told anyone, she'd kill Annabelle. I didn't know what to do, but I knew I couldn't just leave her to fate."

A war between anger and understanding played out in his eyes. "I need to get her home to her mother. We've both been going crazy."

I didn't think now was the time to tell him it wasn't my fault, that I was just doing what I thought was best. Maybe I had been wrong, and it was just lucky that it turned out how it did. It could've been so much worse. Will's hand landed on my shoulder. He whispered, "It's going to be okay." Relief was in his voice. James might not care that I was okay—he had more important things—but at least Will was happy I was alive. It hurt, but it was what it was.

"How did you find me?" After they brought me here, there was no way they could've found me.

Angelica appeared at the door. "Your ring, dear. I had a tracker put in it before Will gave it to you. I figured we might need it one day."

My mouth dropped open. "Angelica!" I knew hugging wasn't her thing, but I didn't care. I threw myself at her and gave her a huge hug.

She patted me awkwardly. "Yes, it's good to see you, too, dear. It seems you've been busy, as have your peers. There are a few stragglers to pick up, but we've finally destroyed RP. So, tell me, what else have you been up to?" She managed to extricate herself and looked at me.

"Um, Dana's dead father is in the basement. So are his henchmen, oh, and some prisoners. Oh, God." For the second time in five minutes, my stomach dropped out from where it was supposed to be. In the shock, action, and my switch into survival mode, I'd forgotten about the woman downstairs. But had it been my imagination? Sometimes we saw what we most wanted, even if it wasn't true. I pushed past Angelica, giving B a quick wave as I ran past and down the stairs. My legs had never moved so fast.

But was I running towards disappointment?

I was about to sprint down the second flight, but people were coming up, slowly. I stopped dead. The skinny woman with the auburn hair had just reached the top. She stared at me with familiar blue eyes, then smiled, tears glistening in her eyes. "Oh my, it is you. Lily Bianchi?" She placed a hand over her mouth as if it was a moment she never believed was possible. To be fair, I'd believed the same thing.

A wave of goosebumps flowed over my skin. How was this happening? "Mum?" Tears burned my eyes as we stepped towards each other. All the chattering around us, loud voices, it all fell away. We were in our own little bubble of awe. This must be a dream. Had I been knocked out and everything up till now was just me imagining how I'd wanted things to go?

I threw my arms around her. Her arms slid around my waist and she gripped fiercely. We pressed our cheeks together and cried, our tears mingling as if they, too, were overjoyed to have been reunited.

And then the chatter around us did stop. Someone gasped. Angelica's voice, as quiet and disbelieving as it sounded, still came through loud and clear. "Katerina, is that you?"

"Mum?"

I started sobbing, the emotion and shock in Angelica's and James's voices finally my undoing. I stepped back because she wasn't just mine. And I would bet a thousand lifetimes that she needed this, to be reunited with everyone, with the people who never stopped loving her, the thoughts of whom were probably the only thing to keep her going.

James and Angelica rushed to her, and they embraced in a big group hug, my niece in the middle of it all. "Oh my lord, who is this?" My mother sounded frailer than I remembered, and she was younger than Angelica. Being a prisoner had taken its toll. The thin woman was not the strong, athletic woman I remembered, but a few weeks out of this hellhole would fix it. I just hoped the mental scars were able to be healed, too, although that would take much longer.

James sucked in a shaky breath. "This is your first grand-child. Annabelle, meet your grandmother."

My mother shook her head, the pain of lost years in her eyes, the tears of joy and sorrow freely cascading down her face. She reached out, and James placed Annabelle in her arms.

It was a moment I would never forget.

Will placed his arm around me as I ugly cried.

When I'd imagined this day, my day of revenge, it had never ended like this. In fact, this wasn't an ending at all. It was a beginning. A big, beautiful, joyous beginning.

To be honest, it was about time.

There were so many questions I had for Angelica, but I guessed they could wait. There was only one question that really mattered. "So, Ma'am, are you and Mum coming home with us?"

Both women looked at each other and then at me. Their grins said it all. Funny how even in the house of an evil wannabe dictator and his mad-as-a-cut-snake daughter love could flourish and push away the gloom.

I smiled. "Well, then, let's go."

I took my mother's hand and led her through my doorway so we could start the rest of our lives… together. Our family could finally begin the real healing process. We'd been given a chance not many people got, and I knew we'd make the most of it.

I couldn't wait to start.

AFTERWORD

Well, if you've just finished this book, you've been on a long journey with Lily, her friends, and family. Thank you so much for coming along for the ride. I just wanted you all to know that Lily's story isn't over yet, and there will be more PIB books in 2021, just in case you were wondering. So if you're still enjoying the series, never fear! More books are coming—books 15 and 16 in the first half of 2021. For the latest news, you can follow my Facebook page, my Bookbub profile, or my Instagram.

Cheers

Dionne Lister

ACKNOWLEDGEMENTS

I would like to thank my readers, in particular the readers who have messaged me to chat about the story, tell me how much you're enjoying it, or just to say hello. It brings me so much joy to hear from you and to know my books are making a difference in your lives, even if it's just that they help you escape for a few hours when you most need it. I'd love to send a special shoutout to Susan W, LaDonna B, RaBea M, Terri S, Rashelle F, Bethsheba A, Pam K, Lesley M, Suzi T, Kara S, Mandi D, Lorna F, Theresa U, Sandra D, Becky N, Amy R, Victoria M, Valerie F, Robert R, Steffi H, Michelle W, Mel A, Valerie C, Niki S, Louise P, Alyssa D, Elizabeth N, Peggy M, Jackie D, Karen C, Rita C, Carol H, Linda M, Mary-Lou G, Raven A, Karen R, Marchido C, Katie DD, Margaret DL, Corin WF, Colin O, Beverley T, Maureen E, Tracy S, Ruth F, James K, Katrina W, Wynnie Reads, and last but not least to Shiela B, who messaged me at a most serendipitous moment, which helped me finish the book in the best way possible. Sorry if

I've missed anyone—I really do love you all, and I can't thank you enough for all your kind messages and support. I hope this book met your expectations. xx

ABOUT THE AUTHOR

USA Today bestselling author Dionne Lister is a Sydneysider with a degree in creative writing. Daydreaming has always been her passion, so writing was a natural progression from staring out the window in primary school, and being an author was a dream she held since childhood.

Unfortunately, writing was only a hobby while Dionne worked as a property valuer in Sydney, until her mid-thirties when she returned to study and completed her creative writing degree. Since then, she has indulged her passion for writing while raising two children with her husband. Her books have attracted praise from Apple Books and have reached #1 on Amazon and Apple Books charts worldwide, frequently occupying top 100 lists in fantasy and mystery. She's excited to add cozy mystery to the list of genres she writes. Magic and danger are always a heady combination.

If you're on social media, you can find Dionne on Facebook, Twitter, and Instagram.